DIE BEFORE YOUR TIME

by
Susan Polonus Mucha

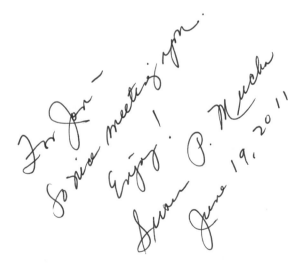

Mason Dixon House
Pennsylvania/Georgia

Mason Dixon House

Copyright ©2010 Susan Polonus Mucha

Case Bound/Hard Cover: ISBN 978-0-9802271-1-6
Perfect Bound/Soft Cover: ISBN 978-0-9802271-2-3

1. Medical thriller—Fiction. 2. Amateur sleuths—Fiction. 3. Bermuda—Fiction.
4. Kiawah Island, S.C.—Fiction. 5. Connecticut—Fiction. 6. Cape Cod—Fiction.
7. New York City—Fiction. 8. Lima, Perú—Fiction. I. Title.

Library of Congress Control Number: 2010913601

This book is a work of fiction.

Cover photo by Pablo Illescas
Jacket design by Dragon's Teeth Design

Mason Dixon House can arrange for speakers for your live event. Contact the
publisher at: publishing@masondixonhouse.com

Printed in the United States of America

Also by
Susan Polonus Mucha

Deadly Deception

For Edgardo ~ *still lighting up my world*

In memory of my father, Harold A. Polonus,
the writer in the family.

Thanks for the genes, Dad.

"…So sweet the air, so moderate the clime;
None sickly lives, or dies before his time."

– Edmond Waller 1645

Chapter 1
"Until death do you part."

They say your entire life passes before your eyes when you're about to die. Elia's life could have been written on a deck of cards and a Las Vegas dealer couldn't have flashed through the deck faster than she.

Not so for Luis. His vows two days earlier, "Until death do you part," did flash by, however. He sent a quick message to God—an order, really. "No! Not again." He grabbed for Elia who panicked and kicked against him flailing her arms. He held tight and helped her breathe. He began deflating his vest and slowly rose to the surface with his wife in his arms.

Two days earlier Dr. Luis Echevarria had gathered his new wife, Elia Christie, in his arms at the altar of the tiny seaside chapel in Bermuda, and buried his face in her mass of auburn curls. The words, "Until death do you part," shook him. His first wife had died suddenly in an automobile accident, and Elia had almost died a year earlier in Perú.

He shook his head as if to clear it. He kissed her, a sweet, gentle kiss, then turned to their witnesses, her grandparents. "*Señores*, I'll cherish your granddaughter until the day I die." He bent to kiss her grandmother.

Anna Maria Amauro reached up and laid her hand on Luis's cheek. She let her hand rest there for a moment. "She has said the same about you, *mi hijo*." Then she looked at the couple and was silent for a moment. "*Ustedes son muy bonitos.*"

They <u>were</u> beautiful. Elia had her American father's fair skin and her Peruvian mother's understated elegance. She wore a short silk dress in a soft coral color, which hugged her slim body like a slip. A creamy camellia was tucked behind one ear.

Luis, too, had the fair skin of his ancestors, who had arrived in Lima, Perú, from the Basque country of Spain. His black hair and onyx-colored eyes affirmed his Peruvian blood.

Señora Amauro sighed, then smiled at the young couple, reached for Luis's free hand and gave it a squeeze. Luis, at six-foot-two, towered over the señora who appeared fragile, which was misleading; her strength had carried her family through sad times.

Elia's grandmother, her mamama, looked like a classic Peruvian princess with her olive complexion and prominent cheekbones. Her black hair was pulled into an elegant twist complimenting the black silk suit she wore to her only granddaughter's wedding.

She looked from Luis to Elia, and then to Elia's brother, Father Rafael Christie, who had performed the ceremony. She tried to sweep all three into her arms. *"Bienvenido a nuestra familia, Luis."*

Luis's parents were no longer living, so he drank in the love of Elia's family. He turned to Elia's grandfather, Bernardino Amauro, and gave him a warm Latino hug. Señor Amauro's smile was warm, but the sparkle in his eyes had gone out when his daughter and son-in-law died in a plane crash.

"Luis, Welcome. Elia's parents would have been happy with her choice."

The only guest at the small family gathering was Vicente Pereda. "We're so happy to have you, Vicente," Elia said. "When we played together as children, would we have known you'd be here for my wedding?"

"I'm happy to be included." Vicente turned to Luis. "I need to talk to you, Luis."

"Sure." Luis looked closely at Vicente. "What is it? Do you feel all right?"

"Yes." He swiped his forehead with the palm of his hand. "Well, no. Maybe I'm just warm. It's something else. I need some advice. And some guidance. Maybe later? After dinner?"

"What is it?"

"I hate to bother you today. I think I have a problem." He paused, then added, "at work."

"We'll talk, Vicente, at dinner."

Elia had tuned them out and stood looking around the church. There were ten pews on each side of the aisle with room for four people in each pew. The wood was dark and smelled of lemon, but it couldn't mask a musty odor that might lessen only when the weather remained dry and the clear glass windows were thrown open for a week of sunshine. It was the view that stopped the parishioners from installing stained glass. Through the windows, the Atlantic met the sky in jeweled tones of sapphire and aquamarine and turquoise.

Elia's eyes scanned the tiny church. "Where's Raf? He was here a minute ago."

"Hanging up my vestments." Raf came from the sacristy behind the altar, wearing a black suit and a Roman collar. "I couldn't go to the restaurant dressed like St. Patrick." He pushed a shock of sandy hair off his forehead and put his arms around the newlyweds. "This is good." He genuflected in front of the altar and left the chapel with his family.

The small wedding party drifted to the street where a horse-drawn carriage awaited the bride and groom. Hundreds of feet below the glistening sea stretched out before them.

"We'll meet you at the restaurant," Elia said. "You'll get there before we do." She kissed each member of her family—the only family she had, and hugged Vicente. To her brother, she said a simple, "Thank you, Raf."

The carriage left the chapel, which overlooked Church Bay. The horses sauntered at a leisurely pace along the cliff road high above the sea. Elia and Luis had a slow-motion view of crystal-clear water. Dotting the Atlantic were countless sailboats tacking against the wind, their sails pregnant and white.

The road was narrow, a lane really. On the opposite side of the road, feathery tree branches reached the carriage and tickled it lightly. Steep banks were held back by weathered rocks. Lush ferns, flowering hibiscus and oleander grew in the crevices and flourished under the bright sky. Their sweet fragrance blended with the fresh scent of the sea.

Elia carried a silk wrap, the same coral color as her dress, but the afternoon was warm. She wouldn't have needed it anyway with her husband's arm around her. He pulled her close.

"You feel good," Elia said and snuggled closer to Luis.

When they arrived at the restaurant, Raf was standing in front wearing an anxious frown. He ran to the carriage before it came to a complete stop.

"Luis, we need you inside. They've called for an ambulance, but maybe you can do something."

Elia threw her hand to her heart. "Papá?"

"No, no, he's fine. It's Vicente."

"What happened?" Luis asked. He jumped out of the carriage and turned to help Elia.

"He collapsed at our table."

The three hurried into the restaurant where a group of diners and waiters stood in a huddle near the figure on the floor.

"This is a doctor, please let him through," Raf said quietly; the small group parted as smoothly as the Red Sea. The Amauros were kneeling on the floor beside their young friend. Raf helped them to their feet and Luis and Elia took their places.

Vicente's face was mottled and gray and perspiration soaked his white shirt. Luis felt for a pulse, which was thready and rapid.

Elia got to her feet and addressed the maître d', who stood nearby. "You called for an ambulance?"

"Yes, ma'am," he said. He spoke with a clipped British accent. "It should arrive soon."

"Would you please station someone out front to wait for it?" As Elia looked around the restaurant, people averted their eyes. She knelt beside her friend.

A look passed between Elia and Raf; he nodded and seated their grandparents at a table a few feet from the drama on the floor. "I'll see if I can help," he told them and left to join the tableau on the floor.

Luis took the cushions off several chairs. "Help me raise his lower body," he said to Raf. While Raf lifted Vicente's hips, Luis slid the pillows under him. Elia handed Luis some more, and he used them to raise their friend's legs. Luis put two fingers on the carotid artery at Vicente's neck. "Vicente, your blood pressure is low, but this position will help you. Take three deep breaths for me." He watched while Vicente complied.

The restaurant was small with only eight white linen-covered tables. Near the door, a few patrons waited in a cozy alcove with several chairs and a love seat.

"May we have that please?" Elia asked the maître d', pointing to a quilt that was draped over the loveseat. He handed it to her and she covered Vicente, whose black hair was damp and plastered across his forehead. She brushed it off his face with her hand.

"It's my belly. It's killing me." There was panic in Vicente's eyes.

"Have you ever had an ulcer?" Luis asked, as he palpated Vicente's abdomen; he hoped it was an ulcer and not an aneurysm.

Vicente grabbed his abdomen. He waited a moment before answering. "Six months ago. The symptoms disappeared with treatment. Was nothing like this."

"I think the ulcer's bleeding." Luis appeared calm. "Take a couple more deep breaths; an ambulance is on the way."

Vicente tried to push himself up on his elbows and grabbed the lapel of Luis's suit. "I can't go to the hospital." He emphasized each word. His respirations increased, and he became even more restless.

"You're a doctor. You know you have to get treatment." Luis took Vicente's hands off his jacket and held them in his own.

"Outpatient, then. I have a meeting tomorrow. I have to be there."

They heard the siren of the approaching ambulance.

"Vicente, maybe you'll only be in the hospital a few hours. We'll meet you there." Elia looked up at Luis as she spoke.

"Better yet, we'll ride with you," Luis said.

Luis met the attendants at the door and gave a quick history and preliminary diagnosis.

A paramedic took Vicente's vital signs. "Eighty-five over fifty," he said. He took it again. "No better." He began applying small patches with attached wires to strategic spots on Vicente's chest. A portable monitor came alive with the beat of Vicente's heart.

The Amauros left their table and came to stand behind their grandchildren, who still knelt beside their friend. Despite worried expressions, they both seemed calm.

The second paramedic started intravenous fluids. Then the two of them lifted Vicente onto the gurney and rolled him out to the ambulance. Luis and Elia followed.

"Elia, Luis, thank you for going with him," Señora Amauro said.

Luis nodded and helped Elia into the ambulance. An attendant entered after them. Raf got on for a moment to bless Vicente, then stepped off.

"We'll be right behind you," Raf said. He backed away from the ambulance, made the sign of the cross, and the ambulance pulled smoothly into the street.

Chapter 2

"Please," Vicente whispered, "please." He took hold of Luis's jacket and again tried to pull himself up.

"No, no. Lie down." Luis gently pushed him back. He adjusted the gurney so his friend's head would be lower than the rest of his body.

"No. Luis, I have to ask you something."

He tried to sit but the arm with the IV was strapped to a board and the other arm collapsed under his weight.

Luis put pressure on Vicente's shoulder. "You need to lie down."

Vicente looked at the attendant. Luis followed his gaze and frowned. "Take a deep breath for me." Luis's voice was calm, a sharp contrast to Vicente's. The paramedic moved over to Vicente and took his blood pressure. "One hundred ten over sixty."

"Good." Luis fingered Vicente's pulse and looked at the monitor. "Still fast. A hundred and thirty."

"Why? If his blood pressure is better, why is his pulse still rapid?" Elia asked.

"He's still bleeding. His pulse won't slow until his blood volume increases — until the bleeding is stopped."

Elia looked at Luis, her frown showing her fear. "Can we talk with him?"

Luis nodded.

"Do you mind if I move in here?" Elia asked. She had given her place to the medic.

7

"Yes, ma'am." He took one more look at his patient and moved to the foot of the stretcher.

"Vicente, tell us," Elia said.

"I can't go to the hospital." He tried again to sit up.

"No. You're going." Elia's voice was firm. She looked at Luis, who kept his fingers on Vicente's pulse. Vicente's eyes shot to the paramedic. The medic turned away and looked out the back window.

"I don't know how to handle this." Vicente looked at Luis. "Have you had patients die?"

"Of course, Vicente. I'm not God. Patients do die, but you're not dying."

Vicente shook his head. "Not me, Luis, not me."

Luis frowned, but before he could ask Vicente what he meant, the ambulance slowed. It came to an easy stop in front of the emergency entrance, and the paramedic swung open the doors and jumped out the back. "Doctor, we'll take it from here."

Vicente raised his head; his eyes sought Luis's. "We'll be right here," Luis said. "They're going to give you more fluids, maybe blood, and probably Zantac. It won't take long. We'll see you soon."

The paramedics pushed the gurney into the ER and past the open door of the waiting room. They stopped to speak to a nurse, who motioned them through a wide, brightly-lit hallway toward a treatment room.

Elia paused at the waiting room. There were about two dozen plain wooden chairs lined up against two walls. An admitting clerk sat behind an opened frosted window at the third wall. They hurried to catch up with Vicente and reached him as he was being wheeled into the treatment room.

"We'll see you when you…" The doors closed before Elia could finish the sentence.

Chapter 3

Elia and Luis had made their way through the hospital following exit signs. Luis pushed open a heavy door and hand-in-hand the two walked up a gravel path behind the hospital and sat together on a stone bench overlooking a bay. The sun was setting behind angry clouds, which appeared out of nowhere. The sky was pink and orange with slices of soft white peeking through a gray cover. The bay reflected the sky. The water was a slate of peach and blue marble.

"Is it serious?"

Luis put his arm around his bride and pulled her close. "He'll be fine."

"He's really anxious."

"That's common. He's lost blood and is confused. Everything's blown out of proportion. We'll see him when he's moved to his room." He traced her collarbone with his fingers. "Then, Mrs. Echevarria, we've got a wedding to celebrate."

"Vicente." Luis reached for Vicente's hand. "Vicente, it's okay. The doctors say you'll be fine." Elia and Luis had been waiting in Vicente's assigned room in the intensive care unit for half an hour when he was wheeled in from the ER. They stood aside as a nurse and an aide helped him get into bed. Vicente lay still, but his eyes followed the nurse's movements as she checked the heart monitor and recorded his vital signs. He looked up at the bag hanging on the IV pole; dripping blood slithered through tubing. He put his hand to his face and felt the naso-gastric tube that had been threaded through a nostril. A thin piece of adhesive tape secured the tube to the tip of his nose. He traced the tape on his nose with his index finger.

"Did you hear me? You're fine," Luis repeated, as the nurse and aide left the room. "That tube you're playing with will come out soon."

Vicente continued to run his hand up and down the tube; he pulled up the slack to stare at it. It was a clear tube and tiny clots of blood mixed with a clear solution ran through it.

"It emptied your stomach. You had quite a bit of blood in your belly." Luis put his hand under a section of the tubing. "This clear stuff is ice cold saline. It's flushing you out; you're almost clean as a whistle."

"My ulcer bled."

"We're waiting for the gastroenterologist, a Dr. Ramsey, to do an EGD. Then we'll know more."

Elia looked at Luis with questioning eyes.

"They're going to do an exam with a flexible tube so they can see the lining of the esophagus and stomach."

"I'm feeling better. Maybe we can forego the test." He spoke slowly sounding drugged.

"The only way to treat you is to determine the cause of your bleeding. The procedure can do that. You know all this, Vicente."

Luis turned to Elia and said, "This procedure will show any abnormalities, any tumors, or ulcers, or inflammatory disease." Luis turned back to Vicente and laid a hand on his arm. "You want to know, don't you?"

"I know you're right." He put a hand under the tubes and lifted them in a sign of surrender. "Medicine seems so different from this position, flat on my back."

"I talked with the doctor in the ER who treated you. He doesn't expect anything life threatening," Luis said. "In the future, watch your diet and alcohol consumption."

Vicente made a face. "Bland. Now that I remember. Baby food tastes better."

"Not necessarily," Luis said. "Listen to the dietitian when she gives you instructions. There are some clever ways to prepare food."

"I don't cook. Neither does my girlfriend."

"I'll call your doctor later this evening to see what the test showed. But I have no doubt you'll be fine."

It had begun to rain and sheets of water streaked the glass. Palm fronds blown by the wind slapped the window like the chamois strips in a car wash. Vicente's room, like all the others on the floor, was glass enclosed. Nurses could walk by and take quick peeks without opening a door. Tan draperies hung at the edges of the glass walls, ready to be drawn for privacy. A large picture window was off-center on the only solid wall. The view from the window served as art work by the Master: to the right the fourth floor room overlooked the town of Hamilton with its sherbet-colored buildings. Grooved whitewashed roofs topped every dwelling. The grooves guided the falling rain water into specially designed containers that saved it for daily use.

To the left and docked at the shore was a cruise ship, the only blot on the landscape. In the distance was the Atlantic blurred by the rain and dotted with a small armada of sailboats headed home.

"Tell us about your girlfriend," Elia said.

Vicente smiled. "Angel. Angel Carter. She's a physical therapist at the hospital." He looked at Luis. "I told her I was going to get your advice."

Elia was frowning. "Advice? So you knew you were sick?"

He shook his head. "No, it's not about me."

"Dr. Pereda?" A nurse pushed the door open. She carried a cloth-wrapped package, the size and shape of a dinner tray. "I'm Dr. Ramsey's nurse. He's on his way to do the EGD." She smiled at the patient and set the tray on a table.

"Can't it wait?" Vicente asked.

"As a matter of fact, it can for a few minutes, while he sees another patient. You have visitors; I'll send them in."

Raf stuck his head in the door. "I brought company, Vicente." Raf held the door open for his grandparents. "They're giving us five minutes. They said you're moving to a private room in a few hours, so we'll be able to stay longer tomorrow."

"We'll stop back later tonight," Elia said. She kissed Vicente on the forehead and hugged her brother and grandparents.

"Oh no you don't," Raf said. "Go. We'll take it from here."

"Listen to the priest," Luis said. He put his hand on Vicente's shoulder. "We'll see you tomorrow."

Vicente tried to sit up. "I have to present my paper. It's important." He collapsed onto the bed and caught his breath. He shook his head and reached for Luis. "Tomorrow, Luis? I need your advice."

"Tomorrow." Luis patted his shoulder. "Get some rest. We'll talk tomorrow."

Luis and Elia closed the door on Vicente and stood outside his room.

"What do you think?" Elia asked.

"I wonder what's on his mind." Luis sounded puzzled.

They peered through the glass and took one last look at Vicente Pereda.

Chapter 4

Elia slid off Luis. He reached out and pulled her closer, and cradled her in his arms while he caught his breath. The ringing of the telephone broke the spell.

Luis rolled away from Elia and focused on the bedside clock. "Seven-fifteen?

"Hello?" He said a quick, "Raf?" and swung his legs over the side of the bed sitting on the edge. He listened to his brother-in-law on the other end. "No." Luis turned to look at Elia, while he held the phone to his ear.

"Vicente?" Her eyes had opened wide in fear.

Luis nodded. He asked his brother-in-law some questions. "Thanks Raf; I'll call the doctor. I'll let you know."

Luis sat with the phone in his hand, staring into space.

Elia crawled across the bed and hugged her husband. "Tell me."

He laid the phone down, and turned to his wife.

"Vicente died early this morning."

Luis held her while she wept. "He was always so excited to see us when we spent our vacations in Perú. He lived down the street from my grandparents and we did everything together." She stopped to take a breath. "I think it was our friendship that brought the families together. You know how it is in Perú—everyone lives behind a gated wall, so it's not that easy to get to know your neighbors."

Elia smiled through her tears. "I used to think it was Raf he was happy to see, but—oh never mind." She looked at Luis and frowned. "But he wasn't that sick."

"No, he wasn't. Raf said he talked with the doctor last night after the EGD. The test showed erosive gastritis." He reached across the bed for Elia's robe. "Here, honey, put this on. I'll make us coffee."

Elia slipped into her robe, and Luis put on a pair of gym shorts. He threw some water on his face and brushed his teeth then rustled around in the kitchenette. He had the coffee dripping when Elia came out of the bedroom.

"What does that mean, erosive gastritis?" Elia had scrubbed her face to wash away the tears. She ran her tongue over just-brushed teeth.

"Vicente had a lot of diffused erosions in the mucosa of his stomach. That's not as serious as an ulcer. The bleeding was from the erosions, but the condition wasn't life threatening." He grabbed a cloth and wiped up spilled coffee grounds. "It's a self-limiting disease, meaning if it was caused from alcohol, for example, or too many aspirins, once those precipitating factors are out of the picture, the patient should improve."

"So why didn't he improve?" She sounded as though Luis should know the answer.

He shook his head. "I don't know. Something went terribly wrong. One thing I do know—he'll have an autopsy." He set Elia's cup of coffee on a table in front of the sofa, and began prowling around the small living area. "I don't think the doctor could have missed something after the EGD." Luis poured himself a cup of coffee, brought it to the sofa, and sat down beside Elia. "I wonder if he'd let me look at the chart."

Elia paused after taking a sip of coffee, placed her coffee cup on the table, and sat up straight. "We should have stayed with him."

Luis nodded. "Hospitals are dangerous places. I encourage all my patients to have a family member or friend stay with them."

"Dangerous?" Elia asked. "What can you expect a friend to do? Study medicine?"

"I tell my patients' families to think of themselves as advocates—and consumers. If they suspect something isn't right, they should speak up. Call the nurse, and make sure he gets there, pronto."

Luis cradled his coffee in his hands. "It's important to ask questions. When the nurse comes in with a medication, especially a new one, ask about it. Make sure the doctor ordered it for you and not the patient next door."

"Vicente was a doctor. And he was lucid. I would have thought he could have spoken for himself. Don't you think?" Elia asked, in that tone that begs agreement.

"I didn't think Vicente needed anyone. You're right, honey, he was lucid. It's not as though he had surgery and was drugged from anesthesia."

"But he was drugged. He sounded drugged when we were there." Elia had tucked her feet under her and was sitting sideways on the sofa facing him.

"But he didn't have anesthesia. Besides, I'm sure Raf would have stayed with him." He was silent a moment. "I could have asked him." Luis paused again. "I should have asked him."

"What do you think happened? A relapse?" Elia paused and said again in a sad tone, "We should have stayed."

Luis was silent. He had treated many patients with ulcers and erosive gastritis, the same as Vicente. Ulcer patients can hemorrhage and die. "Maybe. But there must have been an underlying problem."

"Heart? Maybe he had a heart attack?" Elia asked. "He seemed excitable."

"I had my eye on the monitor all the way to the hospital, and his heart waves were normal. I didn't see any changes. But I didn't see his electrocardiogram in the ER. That would have shown even an old myocardial infarction."

"A heart attack?"

Luis nodded. He got up and started prowling again then leaned against the kitchen counter and looked over at Elia. "I'll never get used to death; doesn't matter that I'm a doctor. I know I just met Vicente, but I see your sadness and I know what it feels…" He didn't finish the thought, but slowly shook his head.

There was a soft knock on the door. Luis opened it to Raf, who looked drained. "Come in, brother." Luis gave him a hug. "I'm so sorry about Vicente."

Elia stood and held her arms open to her brother. Tears welled up in her eyes. They said nothing for a few minutes, but just held each other.

"Sit down, Raf," Elia said. She poured her brother a cup of coffee.

"I won't stay long." They sat in silence sipping their coffee. Finally Raf spoke. "What could have happened, Luis? I wasn't given any details."

"Who called you? And how did they know to call you?" Elia asked.

"Dr. Ramsey called me about four because he knew you were on your honeymoon, but he didn't tell me anything. Just that Vicente had died."

"We'll go to the hospital and talk to him," Luis said. "In fact, I'll call him right now." Luis reached for the phone book and looked up the number of Queen Mother Hospital. He placed the call and was put on hold, then was told Dr. Ramsey would be at the hospital at noon.

Raf looked apologetic. "I hate that you have to do this, Luis." He looked at Elia. "And you, Elia."

She put her arms around her big brother. "Don't worry about us. It's Mamama and Papá." Her eyes glistened with tears. "Oh, Raf, how are we going to tell them?"

Raf grimaced. "I'll do that. I worry about Vicente's parents. I'll call them after I talk with *los abuelos*."

He stood. "Go to the hospital; find out what happened. I'll take care of things here." He paused for a slight second. "I know this puts a terrible damper on your important day, but there's nothing you can do for Vicente. Try to have a memorable honeymoon. I'm talking good memories. Not this one."

Luis rose and clasped Raf's hand in both of his. Raf hugged his sister, and Luis walked his brother-in-law down the path leading from the cottage.

Raf and Luis had become good friends when Elia introduced them in Perú. When one of Luis's friends and colleagues was mistakenly murdered instead of Luis, the intended victim, at Augusta National Golf Club during the Masters, he and Elia followed the killer's trail to Perú. Raf traveled to Lima from his mission in Colombia to visit with his sister and meet Luis. Before he returned to Colombia, he became involved in the intrigue, one in which his sister and Luis almost lost their lives.

"Thanks for coming, Raf; we'll see you when we get back from the hospital." Luis watched Raf walk toward his grand-parents' cottage, while Elia stood at their open door. As Luis turned to his wife, her chin began trembling. He reached for her, and she fell into his arms and cried.

"What do you think happened?"

"I don't know." Luis put his face in her hair. "I just don't know."

Chapter 5

"They are two strong people," Elia said after seeing her grandparents. The Amauros had talked with the Peredas, Vicente's parents, and told them they would bring their son home. "Thank goodness Raf's going with them. The Peredas will need him." Elia was silent for a moment. "Luis, I'm going to Lima for Vicente's funeral."

As she spoke, Luis stared at the sea from their private patio, his shoulders drooping. He took a breath, glanced at his watch, put a smile on his face and turned to his wife. "I guess you're right. And I'm not surprised. You go. I'll fly home." He kissed her lightly on the cheek. "Now, Mrs. Echevarria, We are going to see Bermuda. Ready to go into Hamilton?"

Elia put her arms around her husband. "Thanks for being so understanding. I love you."

"I'm not crazy about you returning to Perú after our last visit there. Talk about memories—bad ones." He hugged her tighter. "But you'll be a comfort to your grandparents and to Vicente's parents."

"I need to go for myself, Luis."

"I know that, too, *amor.*"

Elia stood on tip toes and kissed Luis on the cheek.

"I'm ready for Bermuda. Shall we call a taxi?"

"We'll probably miss out on the Bermuda experience if we don't rent motor scooters at least for one day, but you look too pretty to ride a bike. Let's at least take the ferry into Hamilton." He took Elia's hand. "Come here." He led her to the table where he had spread out a map of Bermuda. "Look, we walk up to the main road, catch a bus to Harbour Road and meet up with the ferry. What do you say? The ferry will take us into Hamilton and to the hospital."

"I'm really anxious to get there, Luis. Why don't we come home that way?"

"Ramsey won't be at the hospital for another three hours, and I doubt anyone else will give us any information. We can take our time getting to the hospital." He put Elia's hand to his lips and kissed her fingers. "Listen to your brother. He wants us to have some good memories."

He turned back to the table and opened his hands, palms down, and moved them across the map. "This is our honeymoon. We're going to do Bermuda."

Chapter 6

Luis and Elia climbed aboard a pink and blue public bus. The aisle was narrow and space was limited between rows. "A sports car has more room than this," Luis said. His head was bowed. "At least I can stand up. Sort of."

Elia looked at the confined area and spied two empty seats side-by-side. "Mind if I sit on the aisle?" she asked.

"Sure." After they were settled in their seats, Luis looked at her and said, "What's wrong?"

"I don't know. I looked at that tiny spot and I just couldn't go there."

"You're claustrophobic?"

"If I am, it's a new sensation. And not a nice one."

"You never felt it before?"

She wrinkled her nose and seemed to be looking into the past. "Yes. When I was down in the catacombs in Lima. Those narrow walkways. And low ceilings." She shivered. "Since then, I've been leery of tight places."

"Not to mention someone tried to murder you. Almost dying can get to you." His joke fell flat. In Perú she had been hit over the head, thrown into a bin full of ancient bones, shot at, and chased along a narrow cliff high above the Pacific Ocean.

He smiled at her, then looked away and studied the passing landscape out the window. He took a deep breath, turned back to his wife, and smiled at her again.

Now they were on a road high above the Atlantic. At each stop the bus filled rapidly. Camera-toting tourists outnumbered brown-skinned Bermudians. At one stop a short wiry fellow stepped onto the bus and took the seat directly across from Elia.

He wore a smile on his dark face and had a twinkle in his grandfatherly eyes.

"Good morning," he said to them. He carried a canvas bag full of books and set it on the floor at his feet.

Elia returned his smile, but before she could speak loud laughter erupted from the back of the bus. She glanced back at the noisemakers than turned her attention to her neighbor. "Is Bermuda your home?" she asked.

He nodded. "All my life, except for four years in New York for university."

"Don't tourists bother you?"

"Oh no, no, no, we love tourists."

She motioned to the back of the bus. "All tourists?"

"We Bermudians are taught to never be rude to a visitor." He shook his head emphatically. "Not allowed, no indeed, we are encouraged to be gracious." His accent was British, and it added refinement to the harsh racket coming from other riders.

He leaned across the aisle. "You're important. You're our main industry—tourism." His eyes twinkled again—a jolly elfin conspirator.

While Elia talked to her neighbor, Luis's mind was elsewhere. He conjured up one of his medical school professors talking about gastrointestinal bleeders.

"Careful, careful," he'd say, *"blood loss can be insidious. You won't lose a patient if you keep a close check on blood loss and replace it. But not too fast."* Then he'd say, *"Don't get complacent. The ulcer can erode the stomach and your patient can hemorrhage to death." Is that what happened, Vicente? You bled to death?*

"Luis, where are you? We get off soon." Elia was standing in the aisle.

Luis stood and was careful to keep his head from grazing the roof of the bus. When they got off the bus they were directed to the ferry. They walked down a flight of stone steps to the shore of a bay. Multi-colored blooms cascaded down the edge of the stairs. Pastel-colored white-roofed homes lined the hillside and ended at the edge of the barely moving dark green water. Five young teens clad in cut-offs disrupted the tranquil scene. They were jumping off the roof of the ferry station into the water. As the ferry lumbered to shore, they scurried up the bank, climbed a trellis of white, pink and purple morning glories to the roof and stood poised once again on the fringe of their perch.

Luis and Elia were the only passengers embarking, but they stood back as a tall, thin man left the ferry pushing a child in a stroller. Luis looked at his watch. Ten forty-five. Five minutes later, the ferry tooted three times and slowly moved away from shore. A loud thud rocked the boat. They turned to see the cause; one of the teens had jumped from the roof onto the moving ferry. He was dancing on deck like a young Muhammad Ali. Then he dove into the water and swam to his cheering friends.

Luis and Elia sat on a wooden bench as the ferry trolled down the middle of the bay. They passed pink, green, blue and peach-colored homes nestled in the hills. Tucked among leaf-filled trees and lush green plants, they looked like scoops of sherbet on layers of lettuce.

Luis reached for a ferry schedule from a rack near his seat and pulled his map out of his pocket. "We get off at the main ferry terminal in town and then walk a couple of blocks. Three more stops to go." He refolded his map and stuck it and the ferry schedule in his shirt pocket.

"This is picturesque and relaxing, but we'd get around faster if we rented a car," Elia said.

"We can't rent a car. No one can. Only way to get around is by taxi, bus, ferry, mopeds and scooters." He ticked off the list on his fingers. "And carriages."

"Why no car?"

"Probably because this is a small island and they don't want any more traffic. I read that homeowners are allowed only one car per household."

When they reached their stop, they strolled hand-in-hand in the direction of Queen Mother Hospital. They walked two blocks without saying a word. This was no Sunday morning sleepy village, but there were fewer cars on the roads than during the weekdays. Although most of the quayside shops were closed Sundays, tourists still flocked to the quaint town.

Buildings were painted soft rainbow colors and were as lovely looking as the pastel-colored homes. Shutters to protect windows and interiors during hurricanes bordered the windows. Streets were clean — not even a scrap of paper lying about.

"You're very quiet," Luis said.

"Just thinking."

He put his arm around her and pulled her close. "About Vicente."

She nodded and pointed up the street. "There it is."

Queen Mother Hospital was a four-story stucco building the color of a ripe mango. A portico covered the sidewalk and stopped two feet from the street seemingly reaching out in welcome. They walked through the main entrance into a refreshingly cool lobby. They approached the information desk and asked for Dr. Ramsey. The receptionist made a phone call and invited them to wait.

They sat on hard wooden chairs with their backs to a bay window. The window faced a courtyard on one side and the main street on the other. A potted palm stood behind one of the chairs.

"Sir? Ma'am?" The receptionist nodded toward a doorway. Elia and Luis stood when they saw Dr. Ramsey, his stethoscope draped around his shoulders, enter the lobby. He was accompanied by a man in his forties wearing a frown, a pink shirt, and an Argyle sweater vest. His tightly curling hair was cut short, and his determined blue eyes looked large behind thick glasses.

"Dr. Echevarria, Mrs. Echevarria." Dr. Ramsey reached out his hand to Luis. He extended his hand to Elia only after she first offered hers. "Dr. and Mrs. Echevarria, this is Dr. Jacob

Riser, a friend of Dr. Pereda's." His British accent rang sharp and clear.

"Dr. Riser," Elia said formally, "I'm sorry; we hadn't talked to Vicente about his friends with him in Bermuda."

Riser nodded. "We were here for the same meeting."

"Are you one of the speakers?" Luis asked.

"No, I just came to hear the latest research. I'm a physiatrist on the staff at Charleston Spinal Center.

"Physiatrist?" Elia asked.

"Rehabilitation medicine. That's how I know Vicente."

Elia cocked her head in question.

"Quadriplegics, paraplegics, stroke victims. We work with neurologists," he said.

"Vicente was anxious to get out of the hospital for the meeting," Luis said.

"He was a very responsible doctor."

Dr. Ramsey guided them to a sitting room off the main lobby. "Please excuse me, but I have a few more patients to see this morning. When Dr. Pereda's autopsy report is available, we'll talk."

"Dr. Ramsey, may I walk with you?" Luis asked.

Ramsey looked at Luis and hesitated before answering. "Certainly. Come along."

"I'll come too," Riser said.

Before Ramsey could answer, Elia spoke up. "Dr. Riser, could we talk? About Vicente? About some problem he had in Charleston?"

"I don't know if I can help you, but certainly we can talk." He sounded conciliatory.

"I'll meet you here," Luis said to his wife. "Dr. Riser," he said with a nod.

Ramsey gestured toward an open door. "Mrs. Echevarria, there's a small sitting room next door. You'll have privacy there."

Luis and Ramsey left the coolness of the lobby behind as they walked down a narrow hallway lined with offices.

Ramsey stopped in one and made a phone call. After a short conversation, he said, "Fax it." He replaced the phone and re-joined Luis in the hall. "Come with me. The pathology lab is faxing Dr. Pereda's autopsy report."

An alcove at the end of the hallway contained a fax machine and copier. When they got there, the report was threading through the machine. Ramsey picked up the sheet of paper and read it in the doorway. He stared at the words. He moved out to the hallway and the two doctors stood facing each other, their arms folded. "We have a problem, I'm afraid."

Chapter 7

Elia and Riser might have been characters in an eighteenth century play. Victorian chairs were arranged around a fluted three-legged table. A Tiffany lamp with a leaded glass shade provided soft light in this darkened room, a striking contrast to the light-filled lobby.

Elia sat forward in her chair, listening to Riser. If anyone had glanced into the room, they might have thought this was a mid-morning tea party—without the tea.

"Vicente was a last-minute addition to the program."

"How does someone get invited to speak at these meetings?" Elia asked.

"He was being considered to replace someone on the team."

"Team?" Elia asked.

"A group of doctors was researching a specific drug, and Vicente's chief was prescribing it quite a bit, meaning the patients Vicente was following were using it."

"And he was invited?"

"No. He asked to present a paper and some slides, and since he most probably would have soon been on the team, he was added to the program."

"What was he going to present?"

Riser looked away from Elia for a moment. "I don't really know, but most likely his information will be covered by another speaker. Some talks overlap."

"He didn't discuss his presentation with you?"

"As a matter of fact, we were going to go over his talk last evening."

"You mentioned his chief. Is he here for the meeting?"

"Frankly, I'm not sure. I haven't even signed in myself, so I can't say who is here."

"Who is his chief?"

"Paul Kittrick. Kitt. He's good."

"Chief of…?"

"Neurology. Vicente was in the neurology service."

Elia explained, "You see, we haven't talked in a long time. We just happened to be here at the same time, so we don't know too much about what he was doing. Did he seem nervous about the talk?"

"Probably no more than any speaker at his first major presentation."

Elia made a mental note to ask Luis if the anticipation of speaking in front of a large group of scientists would be enough to aggravate Vicente's gastritis. And a second mental note to talk to Paul Kittrick.

"You've been so kind to talk to me, Dr. Riser. Our family's understandably upset, and I know Vicente's parents will want to know as much as possible."

"Of course."

"When will you be returning to Charleston?" Elia, the journalist, looked in her purse for a notebook and pen, then stopped herself. She wasn't writing a story. She just wanted to make sense of Vicente's death. Something to tell his parents.

"I'm afraid I have to stay for the meeting. One of the bigwigs from the drug company is coming in from Connecticut. This couldn't have happened at a worse time."

Riser's last sentence felt like a whip across Elia's face.

He must have noticed her reaction. "I'm so sorry, I didn't mean that the way it sounded."

Elia leaned back in her chair and looked around the room. Sadness engulfed her, and she said nothing more. From where Elia sat, she could look out the door into the lobby. She saw Luis walking toward her.

"Elia, Dr. Riser." Luis addressed the pair as he entered the room. He was frowning.

"Luis, what's the matter?"

Luis pulled out a chair and sat down. "You'll want to hear this, too, Dr. Riser. I just saw Vicente's autopsy report."

Chapter 8

"**V**icente bled to death."

"But I thought they got the bleeding stopped. And what about the transfusion he got last night?" Elia asked.

"The night nurse checked on him every hour. Or so she told Dr. Ramsey. But there's a shortage of nurses here, just like at home, and Ramsey told me he wouldn't be surprised if she missed something. It was obvious he had hemorrhaged," Luis said. "Blood had oozed from every orifice. The medical examiner checked for fibrinogen in the heart."

"Fibrinogen?" Elia asked.

"Needed for coagulation. The M.E. inserts a long needle into the heart to determine clotting time of the blood. Vicente had no fibrinogen."

"So his doctor made a mistake?" Elia said. "The bleeding hadn't stopped after all?"

"No. No mistake."

"But how?" Elia began.

Before she could finish the question, Luis answered. "They found a massive amount of heparin, an anticoagulant, in his system."

Riser had been quiet through their exchange but sat up straighter in his chair at Luis's words.

"Meaning?" Elia asked.

"We give an anticoagulant, a blood thinner, to patients with heart attacks," Luis said.

Elia spoke slowly. "And Vicente did not have a heart attack."

Luis shook his head. "No, he did not."

"Can that substance be produced by the body?" Elia asked.

"Not in this form, no."

"He's got the nursing supervisor checking, but it's highly unlikely it was given by mistake." Again Luis shook his head. "No. There's a protocol to follow with this drug."

Luis looked at Riser, who was nodding in agreement.

"That's right. It's given by a doctor, and the patient is closely monitored to see if the clot has dissolved."

"According to Ramsey, who checked, the drug wasn't even in the ICU. It's kept in the pharmacy until the doctor orders it."

"I don't understand. How did Vicente get it?" Elia asked.

"That's the problem." Luis looked from Elia to Riser. "That's the problem."

Chapter 9

"We'll call you if we learn anything," Elia told Riser. "Where are you staying?" Riser pulled out his wallet and handed Elia his card. "Maybe we can get together after the conference and compare notes."

"We'll see. We're staying on the Old Cliff Road in the Waller Cottages." Elia gave him her card. "My cell's here. That's a good way to reach us."

After Riser left, Luis called Raf to tell him about the autopsy. Before he finished talking, he had a smile on his face. "Your brother said your grandparents are doing fine and they insist that you and I try to enjoy the rest of the day." He recited the lines as if rehearsed.

They made their way across the lobby and out the door. They stood on the sidewalk outside the hospital and looked up and down the street, as if trying to decide their next move. Hamilton Harbour was across the street.

"Got a coin?" Luis asked.

"We came from there." Elia pointed up the street.

"Settled." They started walking in the opposite direction. They walked in silence. "You're pensive," Luis said.

"Yes, I guess I am."

"Well?"

"Luis, you don't think the heparin was given on purpose, do you?"

"I can't see it."

"But if it was, by someone who knew Vicente's condition, and knew it would harm him, my question is, why?"

Luis frowned and took his time to answer. Finally he spoke. "I have no idea why."

"I wonder about Dr. Ramsey. Was he on the defensive about the autopsy report?"

"He was surprised that Vicente died. And definitely upset about the drug. But defensive? No."

They stopped at the end of the block and were about to cross when Elia pulled back. "Look right!"

"*Como?*" Luis looked to the right.

"British colony," Elia said. "They drive on the left."

"Ah, yes. I tried to drive in England and had such a hard time keeping to the correct side of the road, I had to give up; I got myself a Tube pass." He smiled at the memory. "Much easier. It's no wonder the British ride the subway — er —the Tube every day."

They watched automobiles, mopeds and scooters pass on the opposite side of the road. The traffic chugged at twenty miles per hour. Mopeds and scooters seemed to be the preferred mode of transportation. Men in neckties and long-sleeved starched white shirts, tailored Bermuda shorts, dark knee socks and dress shoes, and women with their skirts tucked around stockinged legs and hair mashed under helmets, shared the road with reckless tourists in bright-colored shorts, wrinkled T-shirts and dirty tennis shoes.

"That'll be us before we go home," Elia said.

They crossed the street, walked a few doors and paused in front of a restaurant. Luis looked at his watch. "It's way past lunch time; let's stop."

They were shown a table on a covered verandah on the second floor overlooking the street and harbor. They ordered wine and set their menus aside.

Luis took Elia's hand. "I love you, Elia. You're my life." He spoke quietly; his Spanish eyes were serious as he looked at his bride. Then he grinned. "And I pray we don't lose our lives when we get on mopeds."

"Is that the Bermuda experience you were talking about?"

"Yep. One of the doctors in the ER told me they see dozens of tourist accidents every week from mopeds and scooters. Vacationers are having fun, and bam!" Luis's fist hit his open hand.

They walked hand-in-hand past upscale shops and restaurants with British sounding names: Archie Brown & Son Ltd., The English Sports Shop, The Chancery Wine Bar and Restaurant.

"Luis, what's Dr. Ramsey doing about the medicine error?"

"They have a protocol to follow. After they run all the checks at the hospital, then they go further."

"Further?"

"He said they would have to contact the authorities. Police."

"Maybe we could talk to them."

"Honey, let Dr. Ramsey take care of it; they have to finish things at the hospital first."

They had stopped at a street corner and both hesitated. "Right, look right," Luis said under his breath. They dashed across the street. The traffic moved so slowly, the dash was wasted energy.

Once they were safe on the sidewalk, Elia said, "I want to call Vicente's parents."

"Want me to do that?"

"I'd like to talk with them. But, yes, it would be good if you could explain the medical part."

"I will. Let's go back to the cottage and call them. And then we'll find something to do indoors."

Chapter 10

The sun was setting when they retraced their steps to the ferry terminal. Luis pulled the schedule out of his pocket as they lined up to buy tickets.

"Ten minutes, if it's on time," Luis said.

"You can set your watch by it." A tall fellow in Bermuda shorts and sport coat stood behind them. "Sorry to pop in on your musings," he said, "but we pride ourselves on our timely ferries. If it says 6:47, it'll be here promptly at 6:47. And it'll be off as soon as all passengers present are on board."

Elia looked at the large clock on the side of the building. She watched its hands creep toward the scheduled time. "Sure enough. Exactly."

The waiting passengers filed on board—not hurriedly, but no one dawdled. The ferry pulled away and picked up speed as it headed toward the next stop.

"Elia, you're in another world." They stood at the railing and watched Hamilton grow smaller.

"Just thinking."

"And?"

"If it wasn't a mistake, then it was on purpose. So I want to know why someone had to do that. I want to know who."

Luis leaned against the railing, crossed his arms, and squinted at Elia. "I want the same, but it's up to the police. And we don't even know if Ramsey turned it over to the police."

"We might find something." Elia continued to stare at Hamilton.

"You're not writing a story, Elia. Let Ramsey and Bermuda police handle it."

"I want to be kept abreast." She turned to face him, as if to stare him down.

Luis took a deep breath. Then he held up his hands in a "stop" gesture and smiled a smile that reached his eyes. "Truce?"

"Are you backing down from this argument, or are you conceding?"

"Backing down." He gave her a quick kiss then consulted his schedule again. As their stop loomed near, he checked his watch and shook his head. "Amazing. To the minute." Elia and Luis were the only passengers disembarking. The tiny ferry station was deserted with one dim light bulb burning inside the station. It was cool as nightfall approached. A slight breeze was in the air. Elia shivered.

"Cold?" Luis asked.

"No. Just sad, I guess."

They climbed the stone steps in a comfortable silence.

Elia's grandparents were composed when she and Luis stopped to check on them.

"Raf talked with the authorities. We're taking Vicente home tomorrow," Señor Amauro said.

"I'm coming, too" Elia said.

"No, *hija*. Stay in Bermuda. This is your time."

"But we do have a favor to ask of you," Elia's grandmother said. She looked from Elia to Luis. "Vicente's father asked if you'd go to Charleston to arrange for someone to pack up his son's belongings." "I told him you would. Did I do right?"

Elia glanced at Luis before she answered. "Of course, Mamama, we'll go. I'll call Señor Pereda and tell him myself."

Her grandmother looked relieved. "I have his address, *hija*." She handed Elia a sheet of paper. "It's not Charleston. He lived near, though. On an island. Kiawah."

"We'll find it, Mamama." She took the paper and put her arm around her grandmother. "You take care of yourself. Promise me."

They said goodnight and then stopped to see Raf at his cottage and made plans to go to the airport with the family the next day.

At the airport, Elia made sure her brother had her international cell phone number, then she and Luis said goodbye to their family.

"I'm sorry about the sadness on your honeymoon, *hermanita.*" Raf said. "We'll take care of things in Perú." He paused as if he wanted to say something more.

"What is it, Raf?"

He shook his head. "*Nada.* Another time." He plastered a smile on his face.

Elia studied his face, then gave him a hug. She shooed him toward security. "Go, big brother. Call us from Lima." When he turned his back on them, Elia frowned. "What's on his mind?"

"Besides the obvious?" Luis shrugged. "Maybe it's just the obvious."

Elia was quiet and subdued.

"You're upset. It's only normal, Honey."

"Not only about Vicente. I'm always sad to say goodbye. And to send my entire family off on an airplane…" She trembled involuntarily. Her parents had been on their way to Perú for the Christmas holidays when their plane crashed over the Andes. Elia was a student at Notre Dame at the time and had planned to join them in Lima after her finals.

Luis put his arms around his wife. "I know."

She drew a deep breath and said, "Luis, thanks for being understanding about my going to Lima for the funeral."

Luis pulled her close. "You go. I'll go home and check on Blue. He'll be glad to see me. I'll arrange for the dog sitter to stay on."

"And Charleston?"

"You can fly into Charleston after the funeral; I'll drive from Augusta, pick you up at the airport, and we'll take care of Vicente's place." He kissed her on the top of her head. "Then we'll take some time for ourselves."

Elia nodded. "I can fly as far as Atlanta with you, then catch the plane to Lima. When Raf gets to Perú I'll let him know when I'll be there."

"This'll be your first time back since…" He stopped. He knew he didn't have to say anything about their near murders in Perú. "You'll be okay?

"I'll be okay." Elia suddenly shivered.

Chapter 11

Father Rafael Christie sat across the aisle from his grandparents as they journeyed to Perú with Vicente's body. He leaned back in his seat and closed his eyes. His fingers rubbed his neck under his Roman collar. He took a deep breath and exhaled through puffed cheeks and glanced over at his grandparents who talked quietly to each other.

I can't talk to them. They have enough on their minds. He felt a profound sadness. He needed his dad and mom. He needed guidance. *Jesus, help me. Give me wisdom.* He thought of the Wise Men who followed the Star on Christmas morning. *Jesus, send me my own wise man. Give me wisdom to recognize him.*

Raf had been a priest for eleven years. For most of that time, he had been in Colombia in his diocese's outreach program. Because of his Peruvian background and Spanish language skills, he was able to minister to the South American people as one of their own. Anyone not familiar with Catholics in that part of the world might have been shocked. But not Raf. He had spent his summers in Perú at his grandparents' home and had come to realize that Catholicism in South America was often more cultural than religious.

Funny, he saw some of that in his native Pennsylvania. You were Catholic because your parents were. But that's the way it should be: you learn from your parents. He thought of his sister in Georgia. He had visited her and observed. He got to know her pastor, another Pennsylvanian; he met many of the parishioners. The people in the South seemed grateful for their Catholic religion. Maybe because they had been discriminated against;

maybe because they still are. *Elia. Is she my wise man, Lord?* He thought of Elia's strength, of her grace, of her faith. He fell asleep with the thought of how quickly his prayer had been answered.

Chapter 12

Elia and Luis took a taxi from the airport to Hamilton, a thirty-minute ride. Both seemed lost in their own thoughts.

Elia broke the silence. "I want to stop at police headquarters while we're in Hamilton."

"Why am I not surprised?"

The taxi ride into Hamilton skirted the ocean. The Atlantic, its many shades of blue glistening in the late morning sun, spanned the island on the left side of the road. They reached Hamilton, and the town looked festive. From balconies and at each street corner, Bermuda's flag was flying beside Britain's Union Jack.

"What's going on? Why is England's flag flying everywhere?" Luis asked.

"The Queen is here. We're celebrating her visit, we are," their driver said in his British accent. "Prince Philip is with her."

Most shops were shuttered and had "Welcome, Your Majesty" signs in their windows. Citizens and tourists lined the street.

"We had heard she was visiting. That's why the people are out, to see her?" Elia asked. She turned in her seat to look out the rearview window.

"Oh, yes. Queen watching is a grand pastime for Bermudians and visitors. That's what the queue's for. They're lining up to catch a glimpse when she rides by on her way to the House of Assembly. There's a called meeting for her. And high tea, of course, this afternoon."

Elia took in the shuttered shops. "That's why stores are closed?" Elia asked.

"A holiday for the Queen's visit." The driver turned in his seat to smile at them. His jet black eyes, a shade darker than his skin, shone with pride.

The taxi took them up a steep hill two blocks off Front Street. The driver dropped them in front of a three-story stucco building. Its deep chocolate color gave it a look of permanence. With their backs to the front entrance, Elia and Luis could look over white roofs and see the ocean. They stepped away from the building and looked up to the top floor. As if on cue, they turned back as one and faced the water. Luis let out a slow whistle. "What a view."

They turned back to the building and Luis pushed open the door. They stepped into a large light and airy room. A woman officer dressed in long pants and short-sleeved white shirt stood talking with a similarly clad man. Both looked up and smiled when the door opened.

"May we speak to the person who is handling the investigation of Vicente Pereda's death?"

"Inspector Burnside," said the woman. She pointed to a wide staircase at one end of the room. "Second floor, directly at the top of the stairs. I'll ring him that you're coming. Your names, please?" The officer wrote down the information and reached for the phone as Elia and Luis ascended the steps.

On the second floor, a neat and dapper-looking man stood in the doorway of an office. He could have been Michael Jordan's clone, except for his five-foot-nine inch height. The sun's rays shone through the open windows behind him, polishing his bald pate to a high gloss. He wore a crisply starched white shirt, blue and white striped necktie, navy blue Bermuda shorts, black knee-high socks, and black oxfords.

"Come in. I'm Inspector Alex Burnside. Your interest in Dr. Pereda?" He raised his eyebrows with his question.

Luis extended his hand and introduced himself and Elia. "We're friends. We were with him shortly before he died." As Luis spoke, Burnside led them to chairs in front of his desk. "And we certainly didn't expect him to die."

Burnside nodded with his lips pressed tight. "Please, sit down." He stood behind his desk until they were seated. "Now, what exactly can I do for you?" His dark eyes looked from one to the other.

"It's about Dr. Pereda's autopsy. Would you tell us where you are?" Elia asked.

He sat back in his chair and made a steeple under his chin with his hands. He seemed to be studying Elia.

She could see it. Feel it. "Please forgive me," Elia said. "But we promised Vicente's parents we'd find out what we could about his death."

"I see." Burnside opened a folder on his desk and glanced at it. "You know about the hemorrhaging?"

"We do," Luis said. "I was with Dr. Ramsey when he got the report."

Again Burnside nodded. If his lips had been glued shut, they wouldn't have looked more sealed. He was silent for a few beats and looked from one to the other. Another nod, this one decisive. One more nod. "We don't know where the heparin came from, if that's what you're interested in. Every dose in the hospital pharmacy has been accounted for."

"Have you questioned the personnel in intensive care?" Elia asked.

A quick frown passed over his face, but he remained silent. He glanced at Luis then returned his attention to Elia. Finally he answered and sounded annoyed. "We have."

"She means we wonder if the drug had been ordered for another patient but it was given by mistake to Vicente."

"That would certainly make my job easier."

"You checked. So your job isn't easy," Luis said.

He nodded. "We checked."

Elia sat forward in her chair. "He was moved to a private room after we left," Elia said. "How about those people? And have any of the nurses been cited for medication errors? I suppose you checked backgrounds of all personnel?"

Luis turned in his chair to look at his wife. A slight shake of his head and an almost imperceptible smile followed. She sounded just as she had when he first met her when she was digging for facts to write the story about the murder at Augusta National.

"One thing at a time, Mrs. Echevarria." Now he looked annoyed.

"Look," Luis jumped in ahead of Elia, "this is a medication that could only have been given by mistake if it had been ordered for another patient and given to Vicente."

"Luis, they checked. Are you thinking it might have been a mistake, after all?" Elia said.

"Just the opposite." Luis looked at Burnside. "If every dose has been accounted for…"

Burnside pushed back from his desk and stood before Luis could finish his sentence. "If you'll excuse me, I have work to catch up on. Enjoy our island and let us handle this. I assure you we are quite capable."

"But you won't mind if we keep in touch?" Elia asked.

"I'll look forward to it." Burnside held the door.

Elia and Luis descended the stairs, and Burnside stood at the top watching them until they were out of the station.

"He certainly let us know that meeting was over," Luis said. They crossed the street and started down the hill. "You were kind of pushy in there, you know."

"You pushed a bit yourself. But he was too sensitive. All about turf." Elia dug in her purse for her phone and notebook. "Like who are we? And why don't we mind our own business." She rifled through the pages, then started dialing. "He has no idea."

"Who're you calling?" Luis asked.

Before Elia could answer, she was speaking into the phone. "Dr. Riser? This is Elia Christie. I'm glad I caught you; I was afraid you might still be in your meeting. I wanted to let you know that my brother and grandparents are taking Vicente home to Perú." She was silent while Riser asked her a question.

"Nothing. The police are investigating. It's about the medication he was given, but they're not telling us much."

As he spoke she gave the universal signal with her hand that he was saying something she didn't want to hear again. "I know, I know. Luis said the same thing. Too early." She stuck her tongue out at her husband.

She listened again to Riser on the other end of the line. She looked at Luis. "Let me check. Hold on."

Elia put her phone on mute. "He's invited us to go sailing and scuba diving this afternoon. What do you think?"

They had stopped walking and stood in front of one more closed-for-the-Queen shop.

"If you want to." His raised eyebrows, and hand gestures punctuated his words.

She nodded. "I'm fine with it."

They made plans to meet in two hours at the docks in Hamilton. They caught a taxi to their cottage, changed into bathing suits, shorts and tennis shoes and arrived back in Hamilton in time to stop in the dive shop.

Chapter 13

"There's Dr. Riser." Elia pointed to a sailboat as Riser jumped to the dock and walked toward them. The boat held Elia's attention. It was built of teakwood and polished to a rich luster and looked sleek and fast. Two men were rigging the sails and mast.

"Come on board," said Riser. His thick glasses had been replaced with equally thick tinted ones. "We're sailing with a fellow from Pavnor Pharmaceuticals and a friend of ours who sailed this boat over from Charleston. Nice, isn't she?"

A woman stood on deck watching them as they approached. "And this is my wife, Bonnie." Riser reached for his wife's hand. She was almost as tall as her husband. Her hair looked golden in the sunlight and her skin was tanned.

"I'm happy to meet you. Jake told me of your horrible loss. I'm so sorry." Her smile had turned to a concerned frown and her forehead crinkled into furrows deep as ruts.

"Thank you. Dr. Riser, how nice that your wife's here," Elia said.

"Please. Jake, Bonnie," Riser said.

"And we're Elia and Luis," Elia said gesturing to Luis. "Bonnie, it's nice you're here," she repeated.

"He couldn't keep me away from Bermuda."

"Bonnie's interested in our conference."

"Well, hardly. But I do try to keep abreast of things. Jake tells me you're from Augusta." She looked at Luis. "I know you're not. Your accent. From?"

"Perú. Lima."

"Oh, I see. Dr. Pereda." She turned to Elia. "And your accent isn't southern."

"Not yet. I haven't lived in Augusta long enough. I'm originally from Pittsburgh with a lot of time spent in Perú." She took a deep breath. "That's how I know—knew Vicente."

"Oh, yes." She didn't sound particularly interested and quickly changed the subject. "Pittsburgh. Know it well. I went to college close by. Near where the plane crashed on 9-11."

She took Elia's arm. "So, we have something in common. Come with me. Let's introduce you to our hosts."

"They were in the yacht race? I read about it," Luis said.

Riser laughed. "Hah! That's too much work for these fellows." He narrowed his eyes, as if in thought. "But they are very competitive."

"Frank Hanssen. And this is Aaron Scharff." Hanssen stuck his hand out. He was gangly, looked about forty, and had neatly trimmed sun-bleached hair. Scharff was a young fifty with dark hair and a mustache flecked with gray. His nose dominated his tanned face. He wore a golf shirt with the Pavnor logo embroidered on the left sleeve.

"I see you brought your own equipment." Hanssen nodded at the large nylon bag Luis carried on board.

"Just bought it. This is a treat. Haven't been diving for some time."

Elia smiled, but didn't say a word.

"Where are we going?" Luis asked.

"Shipwrecks. There're plenty to choose from," Hanssen said. "Are you certified?"

"I am," Luis said. "How deep will we be going?"

"We've got great visibility to 150 feet, but I don't like to go that deep. Nearby there's a shipwreck at about thirty. Does that sound good to you?" Hanssen talked and Scharff maneuvered the sailboat out of the harbor. "While we head out, take these beach towels to the foredeck and enjoy the sun. Go on, Jake and Bonnie, you too."

"We're fine here," Elia said. She spread the towel on a bench and she and Luis sat facing Hanssen and Scharff. "How's the meeting going?"

"Good," Hanssen said. He sat down across from them. Riser and his wife leaned on the rail.

"I hear it was your friend who died," Hanssen said. "I'm sorry."

"I guess you filled his speaking slot," Luis said.

"I'm not involved with the meeting. I'm just here for the sailing, but I'm sure the slot has been filled. You know how everyone wants more time to speak."

"Frank and Aaron are friends from Connecticut," Riser said. "But he's not in pharmaceuticals. What would you say your business is, Frank? Money?"

Hanssen laughed. "You might say that." He pulled out his wallet and handed Elia his card.

She took the card and dropped it in her bag.

"Do you know what Vicente was going to talk about?" Luis addressed the question to Riser.

Riser was busy slathering sunscreen on himself. He held the bottle out to Elia. "I don't. Not entirely. I told Elia that Vicente and I planned to get together Saturday evening."

"How about Aaron?" Luis asked Hanssen.

Hanssen inclined his head toward Aaron. "You'll have to ask him. I think your friend was using this meeting as his debut. You know, a chance to get his feet wet before becoming a formal member of the clinical trials team."

"We'll find out in Charleston, Luis," Elia said.

"Oh? You're going to Charleston?" Scharff looked over at the group.

"To empty Vicente's home," Elia said. "It's too much for his parents."

Scharff seemed to mull this over. The boat sluiced through the water. "We're almost to the dive site," he said. "Jake tells me you live in Georgia. You might be interested to hear about the dive site we're going to." He kept his eyes on the water in front of him. "The *Montana*. She was a Confederate blockade runner during the Civil War and carried a cargo of munitions and medical supplies from the British Isles to Wilmington, North Carolina. Bermuda brought her down."

"Bermuda?" Elia asked. "Didn't Bermuda support the Confederacy?"

"She did. She was a safe haven for it," Scharff said. "A stopping point for boats loaded with supplies. Vessels would carry goods from England, and Confederate blockade runners would pick up the goods and run them to Southern ports."

"But you said Bermuda brought the *Montana* down. How so?"

"Not like you think. Bermuda is surrounded by reefs. On the outside of the reefs the depth of the water is a thousand feet or more, but inside the reefs, the depth might be three feet, or thirty. The *Montana* hit a reef system and sank. Her crew and cargo were rescued, but the boat didn't make it. She lies in thirty feet of water surrounded by high coral reefs, not far from here just about eight miles from Hamilton."

"Coral reefs." Elia waved her hand to indicate a large expanse. "I imagine there are a lot shipwrecks out here."

"Hah. The reefs helped the Union side, that's for sure. There are several Confederate tramp steamers from the Civil War in these waters."

"Tramp steamers?" Elia asked.

"That's just a nickname for ships like the *Montana*. The sails would collect the coal ash from the vessels' furnaces." Scharff turned and pointed to their white sails. Picture the filthy sails. Get it? Tramp steamer."

"And today? Many shipwrecks?" Luis asked.

"Always have to be careful," Scharff said. "In 1997, a Chinese vessel was sent to the bottom by the Bermuda Government. The boat had been carrying illegal immigrants and was intercepted off Bermuda by the U.S. Coast Guard. It was towed to

Bermuda and, beyond repair, was scuttled. But there are wrecks out here dating back 500—600 years. Probably further back."

Hanssen joined the discussion. "Luis, I hear you're a physician. How about you, Elia? Are you a doctor, too?"

"No. I'm a writer."

"Oh? What do you write?"

"Feature stories. Who knows? I might write a story about this dive."

"Speaking of... You're certified to dive, aren't you?" Luis asked. "Or did I lie?"

The Risers and Hanssen looked in her direction. "I'm certified, but I think I better tell you something." She hesitated. "I'm really not comfortable scuba diving."

"Why didn't you say something? We don't have to be here," Luis said.

"We can just sail," Hanssen said.

"No. I want to do it. Slay my dragons—that sort of thing."

"I don't think diving is something you have to conquer to live a normal life," Luis said.

"Maybe. But it's one more thing."

"It's a shallow dive, you'll do fine," Bonnie said. "I conquered that dragon a long time ago."

"We'll be there in a couple of minutes," Scharff said. "Want to get ready?"

Hanssen stood and opened a closet. Four bright yellow tanks were lined up like soldiers. The regulators—breathing apparatuses—hung from hooks. Stacked neatly nearby were four BCs, the buoyancy compensators that, depending on how much air was released from them, would determine whether divers rise to the surface, fall deeper, or float at one level.

"You certainly keep everything orderly," Elia said as she stood inside the closet. She ran her hand lightly over the BCs. "Dry. This your first dive since you've been here?"

"We've been out. But not diving." Hanssen dragged a tank to Elia. "Here you go."

Elia opened her bag of new equipment and busied herself putting on booties, fins, and mask.

"Are you diving, Bonnie?" Hanssen asked.

"No. I may jump in to cool off, but I don't think I'll dive to-day."

"Okay. These are for you fellas," Hanssen said to Luis and Riser pointing with his foot to two tanks. "Aaron?"

"I'll be the designated driver."

Hanssen laid out BCs and regulators on a bench, along with two octopuses — the alternate air source for sharing air — if the need should arise.

"No belts?" Luis asked, looking around for a weight belt.

Hanssen held up a BC. "The weights are right here." He pulled up a flap on either side of the vest-like BC and slid out a nylon packet filled with weights. "Any trouble, just pull these rings and it'll slide right out of the vest." He demonstrated, and the weights thudded to the deck.

Luis hefted Elia's tank while she struggled into her BC, then lifted it onto her back and helped her secure it. Weighted down, she plopped backward onto the bench to wait for Luis.

Hanssen helped Riser and Luis into their equipment. When Luis was outfitted, he took Elia's arm and helped her stand. She squared her shoulders and stood straight.

They had reached the dive site. Two other boats were nearby.

"Looks like we'll have a lot of company," Luis said.

"This wreck's a popular site," Hanssen said. "It's not deep, so there're a lot of novices."

"Have you ever dived wrecks?"

"I have," Luis said.

"Same here," Riser said.

Elia shook her head. "No."

"Where did you dive?" Luis wore a questioning look.

"Augusta State's pool." She grimaced.

"The college?" Luis sounded confused.

"Classes. I took classes there." She held up her hands in a calm down signal. "I passed the course. I just haven't had the chance to go out on a—well—on a real dive."

The others on the boat were silent as they watched the exchange. Finally, Bonnie spoke up. "You'll do fine. Believe me, this will be a lot more fun than diving in a pool."

"And it's an easy dive," Hanssen said. You can see where you entered and where you can get out, by outside light. Good wreck for first-timers." He seemed to think of something. "One thing. Be careful going through the passageways; you don't want to snag onto anything."

"I'll be fine." Elia then looked at Luis. "Ready to go, Luis? Jake?"

"It's up to you, Elia," Luis said.

She hesitated, then said, "Let's go."

Luis, Elia and Riser sat on the edge of the boat, put their masks and mouthpieces in place, gave the thumbs-up sign, and fell backward into the crystal-clear water.

They deflated their BCs and floated toward the wreck. Immediately, they saw four other divers. They swam side-by-side down to the 236-foot tramp steamer. Near the wreck, fish swam in a kaleidoscope of colors: blue and green angelfish, rainbow parrotfish, blue chromis. Elia and Luis circled the boat three times, slowly, swimming with the sea creatures. Riser waved to them and swam over to the other divers. Just as Hanssen had said, when they poked their head into a hole of the wreck, they could look through and see light at the far end.

They pulled their heads out of the entrance as two divers swam past them and out through the passage. They caught a glimpse of another diver toward the back of the boat.

Elia signaled Luis to go inside. He swam into the *Montana*. She followed. Without doing much exploring, they swam out the opposite end toward a detached section of the boat. This was the stern, overgrown with coral with its fantail still distinguishable from the elliptical framework.

The silence deep beneath the surface overwhelmed Elia. For a second she lost sight of Luis and she felt utterly alone and found herself beginning to panic. She willed herself to be calm. When she spied Luis coming toward her, she relaxed and was able to breathe through the regulator the way she had been taught.

Luis pointed toward the way they had come, and she followed him back to the main section of the *Montana*. They passed through a ten-foot hole in the hull not too far from the surface, then went deeper. Here were two large paddlewheel frames, like small Ferris wheels.

Elia saw Luis swim down a passage and followed behind. But she stopped. She looked around at the crumbling walls, and felt them closing in on her. She backed up and felt herself bumping into something, but then she floated free. She looked behind her and saw another diver quickly swim away toward the entrance. The she looked forward to where Luis had gone.

Come back, Luis. I'm not behind you. She knew she should have stayed with him. She swam to the entrance and faced into the boat, watching for him. He returned and swam to Elia and signaled with his hands to ask what happened. She shook her head back and forth and pointed out. He nodded.

She took the lead and swam with the fish on the outside of the boat. She turned suddenly and faced Luis. She waved her hand rapidly across her throat, the no-air signal, her eyes wide open with panic. She grappled at her BC and grabbed for the weights and jerked them out of her vest and inflated her BC. She shot toward the surface.

Luis swam to her quickly. He barely caught the tip of her fin and pulled her down to him. She struggled frantically in his arms.

He pulled his octopus free, and with determined movements, put the regulator to Elia's mouth. She gulped a breath. Luis held up a hand, palm down. She understood and slowed her breathing. The hose was a yard long, but he held her arm to keep her close. He began deflating his vest and slowly rose to the surface with Elia.

Riser swam to the entrance of the *Montana* as Luis and Elia ascended. He followed slowly.

When Elia's head broke the surface, she ripped off her face mask, spit out the regulator and swam toward the boat. Luis was beside her.

Bonnie jumped in the water and swam over to Elia. "You okay?" she asked.

"Fine."

Hanssen stood on the ladder half into the water and gave Elia a hand up into the boat. He lifted her tank off her back, then helped Luis.

Bonnie swam to the boat and climbed up the ladder reaching for Hanssen's outstretched hand. "That was quick," she said to the couple. "I thought you'd be down a lot longer."

Before they could answer, Riser's head broke the surface. He swam to the boat and climbed out of the water. "Are you okay? I saw you buddy-breathing. What happened?"

"I lost my air." Elia wriggled out of her BC and dropped it on deck. "I panicked." She looked at Luis. "You thought I was going up too fast, didn't you? Worried about the bends."

"Bends? No. We weren't deep enough. But I did worry about an air embolism. You were holding your breath trying to reach the surface; that's when you get into trouble. You didn't get that far, so you're okay. You are okay, aren't you?" He looked at her closely. "Vision okay? No dizziness or chest pain? You don't seem disoriented."

"No, I'm fine. Mad at myself. I panicked." She pulled her fins and booties off then looked at her regulator and its attached hose. "It's slit."

Bonnie took the hose from her. "It sure is. Frank told you that's the problem with wreck diving."

Scharff had come up from below deck and took his place at the helm. "You must have bumped up against something. You fellows all right?"

While he was speaking, Elia picked up her BC to put it away. Inside the closet, she stepped in a puddle, and her feet went out from under her. She swung her arms out on either side of her body and slapped her hands down hard on the deck as she landed on her back. This move protected her when she hit the floor, a move she had learned years earlier in her Tae Kwan Do classes.

"I'm okay, I'm okay," she said to the men as they rushed to her side. "Just damaged my dignity."

Luis bent to help her. She got to her feet and looked at her damp hands. "I guess I slipped in this puddle."

Elia took the hose from Bonnie. "Let me see if I can get this repaired," she said. "Or I'll replace it." She looked closely at the neat gash and frowned.

Bonnie grabbed it back. "No need. We'll take care of it." She looked at Hanssen. "You will, right, Frank?" She threw the hose into the closet and shut the door, without waiting for an answer. "Let's head back, Aaron."

Aaron Scharff looked at Bonnie with puzzlement, then shrugged and maneuvered the boat around.

Elia and Luis pulled shorts and T-shirts over their wet bathing suits and looked at the sea while Scharff took them back to Hamilton.

"You're quiet." Luis had his arm around his wife. "Scared you, didn't it?"

Elia glanced at the closed closet then at the others on the boat. She shivered and leaned in closer to Luis.

The boat docked at sunset. Luis and Elia walked hand-in-hand through town. "I'm famished," Luis said, eyeing a couple of restaurants. "But we look like beach bums. No one will seat us."

"Pick a dive." Elia shook her head. "I can't believe I said that."

They chose a pub on the water. It was dark and smelled of spilled beer and stale cigarettes. Loud laughter came from a group of sinewy men seated around a battered oak table. Luis and Elia settled in a booth and ordered beers.

"I've been mulling something over in my head, Luis." She was pushing her cold bottle around in its puddle.

Luis reached across the table and took her hand. "I know, honey. I'll never ask you to dive again. In fact, I won't even go myself, if that's bothering you."

"No, that's not it." She paused. "How do you think a hose would look if it was cut during a dive at a shipwreck?"

"Jagged?"

"Well, it wasn't. It was a neat slice. How could that happen?"

"It happened. Is it important?" Menus were wedged against the wall with a Ketchup bottle serving as a bookend. He handed her one and kept one for himself. "It's not, because we won't dive again."

A waitress came and took orders for fish and chips. Elia continued pushing her bottle around in its little puddle. "Look at this."

"Your beer?"

"The puddle. Look, when I put my equipment away, the storeroom floor was wet. That's why I slipped. I hadn't expected a wet, slippery floor. It was dry as a bone when we dressed for the dive. I was the first person to put my wet equipment away. But why was the floor wet?"

Luis took a swig of his beer and set it in his own puddle. "It's a boat. Things get wet."

The pub was filling up and getting noisier. Elia picked at her French fries and nibbled at her fish. Luis cleaned his plate. "You going to eat that?" he said, with his eye on her sandwich.

"As a matter of fact, I am." She took a bite of her cod and looked across the table at Luis. "I'll split it." She gave him half and continued to pick.

"What else is on your mind?"

She waved a hand dismissively. "Let's go back to the cottage and give — I don't know — I guess Frank a call. I want that hose."

"Cottage, yes. Frank, no." Luis said. "At least not tonight, Señora Echevarria.

Chapter 14

Their cottage hugged a cliff; ten steps down, on a plateau, was a kidney-shaped pool surrounded by lush greenery. The foliage hid the pool from view from the cottages above. Luis and Elia had discovered the pool during an early-morning run, but in the dark they would have fallen in, except for patio lights shedding a soft glow over the water. If they descended another hundred feet, they would be at the edge of the ocean.

Before they reached their cottage, Elia said, "Let's take a swim." She led the way down the steps and shed her T-shirt, and stopped to step out of her shorts. Luis did the same. She looked toward the cottages and saw they were hidden from view.

She untied her bikini top and threw it over her shoulder at Luis. He was at her side by the time she shed her bikini bottom. He kicked off his trunks and picked her up. She wrapped her legs around his waist and they plunged into cool water.

Luis held on to Elia as they sank to the bottom, but he immediately pushed to the surface. "I promised you, no more diving." He swam to the shallow end with her legs still around him. They kissed and sank beneath the water. They were laughing when they surfaced.

"Yum." Luis said, licking the water from her face. They stopped moving suddenly at the same moment, and their heads turned toward the far end of the pool. Elia disentangled her legs, but kept her arms around Luis.

"Somebody's here," she whispered in his ear. "Can you see anything?"

Luis rotated so his body covered his wife. He looked over his shoulder in the direction of the noise.

A quiet moment, then they heard footfalls hitting the steps. "Were they in the water?" Elia whispered.

"I didn't hear anyone in the pool. No, I don't think so," he said into her ear.

"Damn." Elia swam to the ladder and climbed out of the pool. She grabbed her T-shirt, slipped it over her head, stepped into her shorts, and ran up the steps. She reached the top and crouched, and tried to see. She was still, and listened. A sound behind her made her turn suddenly, her hands out in front of her, a Karate Kid.

"It's me. Don't hit me." Luis had his shorts on and handed her their bathing suits.

She left them on the steps. When she started across the lawn, he grabbed her hand. "What are you doing?"

"Don't you want to know who was watching us in the pool?"

"Frankly, no. I don't even want to think about it. Some kid getting his jollies at our expense."

"Maybe. But let's look around before we go in. Where'd we drop our shoes?"

"Here." Luis swooped them up. They slipped them on and did a slow jog around the grounds.

Fifteen minutes later, they were back where they started. "You're probably right, Luis. Some kid." She was looking down the steps. "Did you bring my suit up?"

"Yes. And mine too. You dropped them on the steps." Luis ran down to the pool looking behind bushes. He stood on the bottom step and looked up at Elia. "They're not here."

Elia glanced over her shoulder.

They walked slowly to their cottage. "Crazy kids," Luis muttered. He pulled the house key out of a zipped pocket in his shorts and had it in his hand by the time they reached their door.

They stopped abruptly. On display on a low hedge beside their door, were Elia's bikini and Luis's trunks.

"Kids, huh? How do you suppose they knew where we were staying?"

"They followed us," Luis said.

She took the key from Luis, opened the door and walked through the cottage opening closets, looking under the bed and behind the sofa. Then she closed the front door and locked it.

"They followed us all right. But they didn't follow us from the cottage, because we didn't stop at the cottage. We came straight to the pool." She stomped around the living room. "I'm pissed. First, I almost drown in the ocean, then some peeping tom steals our bathing suits and tries to spook us by putting them at our front door."

Luis leaned against the closed door, his arms folded, a smile playing at his lips.

"And why are you laughing?"

"It's laugh or yell. You're doing enough for both of us."

She dropped onto the sofa. "I am, aren't I? I hope this was just a cheap prank." She looked up at Luis. "But I have a strange feeling."

"I hope you're wrong. But let's move out in the morning and check into a hotel. With security."

She nodded.

"You know, I don't think I've ever seen you so upset. Even when you got knocked on your head in Perú," Luis said.

"I am upset. With myself. Let's face it, I was vulnerable. We both were, without a stitch on."

"Don't get me started. I told you, I don't want to think about someone watching us in the pool. And I certainly don't want to think of someone seeing you nude." His frown turned to a grin. "Except me, of course."

"You'll get your chance, I'm taking a shower." She walked toward the bathroom, then turned in his direction. In slow motion she stepped out of her shorts and peeled off her T-shirt.

"It's ringing." Elia sat at the kitchen table in a fresh oversized T-shirt, her hair still wet from the shower. She had Frank Hanssen's business card in front of her and had just placed a call to his cell phone.

Luis padded to the refrigerator in bare feet and pulled out some lunchmeat.

"Hello? Frank? It's Elia Christie. Fine, thank you. We're both fine. I'm calling about the hose I ripped. I'd like to pick it up tomorrow. To replace it." Elia listened to Hanssen on the other end.

"Would it still be in the trash? Thanks, I'll wait."

Elia covered the phone with her hand. "He threw it away, but he's looking in the trash to see if it's still there."

"Is he on the boat?"

"Yes. He and Aaron are staying there." Elia stopped speaking as Hanssen spoke. She looked disappointed. "Thank you anyway, Frank. I'll buy you another one. Good night."

"Trash picked up?"

"Yes." She sighed, then took a bite of the sandwich Luis had made for her. "Any beer in there?" She nodded toward the refrigerator.

"Coming up, ma'am." He handed Elia a cold beer and opened one for himself, then sat at the table.

"Let's see Burnside tomorrow morning." She held Hanssen's card in her hand. "Did Frank say what he did for a living?"

"You've got his card. What's it say?"

"Wealth Management Consultant, whatever that means."

"Sounds impressive." Luis took a swig of his beer and reached for Hanssen's card.

Elia dug in her purse for her notebook and pen and began sketching her slashed hose. "Here." She turned the paper for Luis to see. "We'll show this to Burnside. He can think what he wants."

"And you'll let him worry about the investigation, right?"

"We have no choice. We're leaving soon."

His dark eyes seemed pensive as he looked across the table at Elia. He reached for her hand and stood and gently pulled her to her feet. "I'm ready to leave; it's getting a little spooky here." He wrapped his arms around her. "We'll see Burnside in the morning, then enough of this cloak and dagger business."

Chapter 15

"That's about it." Elia stood with her hands on her hips and looked around the bedroom. She knelt and looked under the bed. "There, we've got everything. I guess we're ready." The ringing phone brought her to her feet. Luis answered it.

"Raf? What is it?" Luis listened, then nodded reassuringly to Elia. "Of course," he said, "we'll take care of it this morning. Tell Vicente's parents Elia will bring them with her to Lima. She and I will meet in Charleston on her way home from Perú to arrange packing Vicente's house." Luis said goodbye with a simple, "We'll be in touch."

"What are we taking care of?" Elia asked.

"Vicente's bags. They're still at his hotel. Raf just talked with someone there; they packed them and stored them for pickup. We'll get them later."

"I hadn't given his things a thought. I'm glad Raf caught us. What about our suitcases?"

"Leave them here. We'll be back before we have to catch the plane. Right now, let's catch the ferry."

They turned the key in the lock and walked down the path that led out of their vacation complex and emerged into a narrow lane with stucco homes edging the curb. They turned at the first corner. A half-block walk and they veered onto a wider street lined by tiny shops, a straight shot to the ferry.

Luis looked at his watch. "Should pull up in about five minutes." They still had two blocks to cover to reach the ferry. It was a quiet morning; a roar of a moped startled them. When they turned to see the bike, it was racing straight at them. For a split second they stared at it, then Luis grabbed Elia's arm and yanked her into a doorway. The bike roared past, but came to a screeching halt a hundred and fifty feet away. The rider put his foot to the ground, swung the bike around, and shoved off toward Elia and Luis.

The two left their sanctuary and ran for a narrow alley, but not narrow enough to keep the bike out. As the biker turned into the alley, Luis and Elia ran around the corner. A shopkeeper had just stepped outside his back door. Luis and Elia raced past him into the shop. Elia flew through the door and Luis followed. He grabbed the man's arm and pulled him back inside as the moped roared past inches from the door.

"Which way's the ferry?" Luis shouted the question. They could hear the moped rev up.

The shopkeeper pointed to the front door. Luis and Elia ran out the door and down the hill toward the water. In the near distance, they heard a bike. They turned off the main street and ran down a side street toward the ferry.

Luis glanced at his watch. "Come on. It's time." He held tight to Elia's hand. They were above the ferry station and looked down on its roof as the moped flew over the crest of the hill toward them. They scrambled onto the roof as the ferry began to pull away from the dock.

"Let's do it," Elia yelled. Roll when you hit the deck."

They took running jumps and landed ten feet below. They both did as Elia said and rolled on the ferry's deck, which saved them from injury. They looked up to see the biker stare at them; he seemed to be rubbing his right elbow with his left hand. Then he turned and roared off.

They lay on the deck catching their breath and watched the shore as they drew away from land. Several passengers came forward to help them to their feet. They looked themselves up and down.

"One piece," Elia said.

An official-looking man approached wearing a starched white shirt with an insignia over a breast pocket.

"Sorry, sir," Elia said, "an old boyfriend was following us. Pay the man, honey."

Luis handed over a couple of dollars and waited until the man went up the stairs to the bridge. "Old boyfriend? Original."

"The real story is too bizarre." Elia was silent for a moment. "Maybe we should get off at the next stop and catch a taxi to Hamilton. I don't want to be on this ferry when it docks in town."

Chapter 16

Inspector Burnside listened to their story. When it was over, he rose slowly from his chair and left the room.

He returned five minutes later. "I'm sending people to the dock with your biker's description—what there is of it. That ferry's due into Hamilton soon. Let's see if he's waiting for you."

"Inspector, there's something else." Elia leaned toward Burnside's desk. "Yesterday we went scuba diving, and my hose ripped during a wreck dive. When I looked at the rip when we surfaced, it was a clean slice." Elia told Burnside about the dive, and finished up with the experience at the swimming pool.

Burnside took a deep breath and let it out slowly. "You haven't had an entirely pleasant stay on our island, have you? Maybe it's time to say goodbye to Bermuda."

"We're leaving today," Luis said. He looked at his watch. "In about four hours."

"I'll have a car drive you to the airport. Where are your bags?"

"At our cottage," Luis said. "We're packed and ready to go."

Burnside reached for his phone. "Someone will take you to pick them up then take you directly to the airport." He dialed a number and gave his directives to a subordinate.

"Anything else you have to share before you leave?" Burnside asked.

"Nothing, except, well—about the hose. There were only a few people on the boat." Elia shrugged and raised her eyebrows in question.

Burnside nodded. "I'll look into it." He strode to the door and held it open for them and beckoned to a uniformed policeman who hovered nearby. "Take good care of them."

"My brother left so suddenly, he didn't have time to pick up his bags. Would you swing by his hotel so we can get them for him?"

Luis glanced at his wife, but she wouldn't meet his gaze.

The driver stopped in front of the hotel and Luis jumped out. "I'll get them." He returned shortly with a small suitcase and a garment bag. The cop popped the trunk and Luis dropped the items inside.

The next stop was their cottage. "Can we have a few minutes to get cleaned up before the flight?" Elia asked.

She and Luis disappeared down the path to their cottage, while their driver sat in his car.

When they were out of earshot, Luis stopped and faced his wife. "Your brother's bags?"

"Burnside dropped the ball. He should have looked for them. I'm glad we're leaving before it dawns on him that Vicente's luggage might still be here."

"Maybe he thought Raf took the bags home to Perú."

"Maybe."

Inside the cottage, Elia dug in her suitcase for a sweater that she wrapped around her shoulders. She splashed cold water on her face, fingered curls through her hair, applied lipstick and a spray of perfume. "Ready."

They hurried to the patrol car and loaded their bags in the trunk.

Thirty minutes later they pulled up at the Civil Air Terminal. "Inspector Burnside expects me to see you through security, so bear with me while I park." The cop drove into a nearby lot and maneuvered into a small space. He and Luis carried the suitcases, while Elia took the garment bag.

Tight security and diligent immigration authorities ate up two hours. Finally, Luis and Elia said goodbye to their escort.

The flight to Atlanta took two hours. Luis walked with Elia to the international terminal.

"Goodbye, honey." Luis hugged Elia then watched as she boarded her flight to Lima. He started to walk away then stopped. He turned back and stood at the window until the flight took off. He frowned, took a deep breath, and walked slowly to his gate to catch the connection to Augusta.

Chapter 17

It was almost midnight when Elia landed in Lima. It didn't take long to get through immigration, collect her luggage, and maneuver to the lobby. She smiled when she saw her brother. But his face looked pinched, tired.

"It's always nice to come to Lima, but not for a funeral," she said, as she gave her brother a hug.

"It's nice of you to come, Elia, but no one expected you to cut short your honeymoon."

"Something made me come. I don't know. Maybe because—" she stopped, then said with a shrug, "I don't know."

"Don't know what?"

"Maybe we could have done something?"

"Don't start. It'll never end." Raf hailed a taxi and carted the bags to the car. "Come on, the grandparents are waiting up for you. The funeral's tomorrow and then we'll get you back home where you belong."

The next morning Elia was dressed and ready to leave the house when Raf came through the front door.

"Where were you?" Elia asked as she hugged her brother.

"I'm a priest. Where do you think?"

Elia stepped back and looked quizzically at her brother. "Is that an attitude I'm getting?"

He ignored her question and headed for the kitchen with Elia following.

"What are you up to?"

"I'm seeing Vicente's parents this morning." She picked up Vicente's suitcase and garment bag to take to the Peredas.

"Hold it. I'll carry that for you." Raf took the luggage and walked with his sister. The Peredas lived three houses down from Elia and Raf's grandparents. The street was quiet, with gated courtyards of eight-foot wrought-iron fences bordering the walks.

"Here you go, Sis." Raf put the suitcase at the door and handed Elia the garment bag.

"You're not coming in?"

"No, I've seen them already, and I'm saying the funeral Mass. You go and have your cry with them."

Elia nodded. Raf kissed his sister on the cheek and left before the maid answered the door.

Elia sipped coffee with Vicente's parents. His mother, dressed in black, was the same age as Elia's mother would have been, if she had lived. Just that thought saddened her. She couldn't help comparing the two of them. Señora Pereda's eyes were red and swollen. She held a tangled mass of wrinkled tissues that she switched from hand to hand as they talked.

Elia remembered her grandmother telling her that Señora Pereda was one of those mothers who couldn't bear to be present when her children got their childhood shots. But her own mother never let on if she was suffering when her children were hurting. As she thought about it now, Elia realized her mother must have been quite the actress. How many times had her mother taken her or Raf to the emergency room for stitches. She always seemed calm. Of course, her mother never had to endure the death of a child, as Señora Pereda was doing now.

And maybe her mother had to be tough living so far from her family. Elia's dad was an American from Pittsburgh, and he took his bride there to live. A promise he made to his wife, and a promise kept, was to spend vacations in Lima.

Her dad was gentle and kind and always seemed able to handle any crisis that occurred; Raf was his clone. But Elia learned that it was her mother who had exhibited serenity at the time of her and her husband's deaths in a plane crash. A young college student had been sitting beside her mother when the plane began experiencing trouble.

Her mother took the young man's hand and said a prayer, a one word prayer — "Jesus." She said it with quiet dignity and seemingly without fear. Her parents perished, but this young man was one of four survivors, and he shared her mother's last minutes. He said she gave him strength and courage with her short prayer.

Elia felt a warmth, a peace, a comfort when she had heard the story. She knew her mother so well, and knew her mother felt safe with Jesus in those last moments.

Señora Pereda sat weeping as they talked of Vicente. Her husband was quiet at first, appearing lost in his own thoughts before he spoke. "Elia, I can't figure it out. My son was a doctor. Why would someone want him dead?"

"I don't know." Elia shook her head. "I just don't know." She glanced at Vicente's luggage. "Could we open his suitcase? Maybe there's something there to help us."

Without answering, Señor Pereda pulled the suitcase toward him and tried to open it. "It's locked. Didn't you have to open this in security?"

"No. I went through with no problem."

Señor Pereda left the room and returned with a screwdriver and hammer. He pried the bag open and looked at the contents. His face crumpled. Vicente's mother reached over and touched her son's clothes and wept some more.

Elia stroked her arm. "I'm sorry. I know this is hard. May I look?"

Señora Pereda nodded and Elia carefully looked through the bag. Under the clothes she found a manila folder. "Do you mind if I open this?" This time both Peredas nodded.

Elia scanned the papers, then looked at the parents. "I'd like to take this home with me to show Luis. These are some kind of medical reports. Vicente was anxious to talk with Luis about a problem at the hospital, but never got a chance. This might have something to do with that problem."

"If this will help us understand why our son died, please, take it," Señor Pereda said.

"As soon as I get home, Luis and I'll go to Kiawah and take care of Vicente's house. My grandmother gave me the address, but how can we get in?"

"We have a key." Señora Pereda stood and walked over to a clock hanging on a wall. She looked sheepish. "We've always put items in the banjo clock. We don't lose them that way." She opened the front of the clock and pulled an envelope from a stack of papers. "Here it is. He wanted us to have a key in case we…" She stopped speaking, took a breath.

"We'll take care of everything." Elia stood to leave. "I'm so sorry." She gave the bereaved parents hugs and left them to their grief.

She walked home with Vicente's key clutched in one hand and the manila folder in the other. One more job. The funeral.

Chapter 18

Elia stood on the periphery of the group surrounded by centuries-old tombstones. Some were chipped and stained, others, just as old, showed evidence of loving care. Most were over five feet in height.

Her grandparents were nearby; Raf was saying final prayers over the casket. Elia detected movement to her right and saw a cemetery worker in white coveralls hovering nearby. She turned her attention back to the service. She frowned and turned to look at the worker. He was staring at her with hatred in his eyes. She immediately looked away. Then she gasped. "Oh, my god!" she said under her breath. She turned back. But he was gone.

"Raf, you'll think I'm crazy, but I saw someone at the cemetery who looked — I don't know — familiar — frightening." They were riding in a taxi to the airport. Elia was booked on the 12:20 a.m. flight to Atlanta, and then on to Charleston. She told her brother about her experience in the cemetery.

"What'd you mean?"

"I saw hate in his eyes."

"You shouldn't have come. Perú is dredging up memories."

"You think I'm crazy." It wasn't a question.

"No. I just don't think a cemetery worker would even know you, let alone give you threatening looks."

"Threatening. Good word. He looked like he wanted to kill me." She crossed her arms over her chest in a defensive mode. "Do you think it's him?"

He shook his head and put his arm around her. "No. But I'm glad you're leaving. Do you want me to call Mario and Carlos?" They were the police officers on the case of the person responsible for murdering three men and attempting to murder Luis and Elia in Lima the year before. He was never found.

"They'll think I'm crazy for sure." She put her head in her hands, then looked over at her brother. "Maybe I am crazy."

"You're not crazy. This place just brings up a lot of sad memories." He was silent a moment. "For me, too."

She punched his arm. "Don't talk like that. You're a priest. I can't have you sad. You have to buck me up."

He opened his mouth, then pressed his lips together.

"Raf? You wanted to say something?"

He shook his head. He reached over and squeezed her shoulder. "You help out the Peredas at Vicente's, then go home to Augusta and start your new life. You deserve it."

Elia looked at her brother, at his drawn face. "What is it, Raf? You look so…" She waved her hands in a circle as she tried to come up with words. "Distressed. Sad." She touched his face. "Not peaceful."

The taxi stopped at the entrance to the airport. "Let's get you checked in, then we'll talk."

Thirty minutes later they sat at a small table and sipped strong coffee. "I'm coming to the States."

"For a visit?"

"Longer."

"But what about your work in Colombia? Who's going to take care of your people?"

"That's just it, Elia. I'm tired. I'm tired of taking care of people." He held up his fingers and put quotation marks around "taking care of."

"I'm tired of being the calm reassuring one when bad things happen to people."

Elia reached across the table and took her brother's hands. She had tears in her eyes. "Oh, Raf. I'm partly to blame. I lean on you."

"It's not you. I'm your brother. We lean on each other." He squeezed her hand. "I wasn't going to say anything, but I need you."

"What can I do? Anything."

"Pray for me. Pray that I work this out."

"Work this out?"

"My vocation. I've been talking with my spiritual director the last few months and I'm going to see my bishop when I get home." He shook his head. "I don't know if I can live as a priest anymore, Elia. I'm tired. So tired."

"Is there something else?"

"What do you mean?"

"Well, you see how happy I am with Luis."

"If you're asking me if there's a woman involved, the answer is no. This is about me. About if I'm doing what God wants me to do." He looked down at his hands encased in Elia's. "And if it is, I pray He helps me."

"Are you lonely, Raf?"

"What priest isn't lonely? We have no family, no home." He nodded.

"You've been in Colombia a long time."

"It's not Colombia. That's just the way it is. Priests are alone." He held up his hands. "Wait. You have to understand. We make our family with brother priests. It's a special bond we have. Like ours, Elia. We really consider each other brothers."

"Tell me, what's going on?"

He looked around the coffee shop. "I don't know." He paused. "I had so many expectations when I was ordained." He pointed to himself. "Expectations of me. But of others too."

"Disappointed?"

"In myself."

"You're a good priest, Raf. Don't think you're not." Before he could answer, she trudged on. "Everyone expects you to be the strong one. The one people go to with their troubles. You're a mediator, a counselor." She again reached for his hands. "You have to comfort them when they have deaths in their families. It was you I leaned on when Mom and Dad died. And now you're taking care of everyone with Vicente." She gave his hands a squeeze. "You're always the rock."

"I've been thinking a lot, Elia. It's not only that. It's the scandals in the priesthood, it's the negativity. It's the war between the liberals in the church and the conservatives. Sometimes there's just no peace." He shook his head slowly. "Just no peace."

"Raf, you talk about expectations. I've known young, newly ordained priests. Some of them are haughty; they think they are so important." She waved in the air as if to erase her statement. "They are important, but they aren't humble, and priests should be humble. But that's the point. Priests are human. They aren't perfect. They have their idiosyncrasies, their histories."

She took his chin in her hand so that he had to look in her eyes. "You're not God, and don't think you are. You aren't perfect, so everything can't be perfect."

She leaned back in her chair and crossed her arms in front of her. "Humility. Be humble enough to realize that the problems in the church aren't yours to fix. And pray for wisdom. Wisdom to show you how you can meet this challenge." She sat up straight to emphasize her points. "We all have challenges. Be humble, Raf. You're human." She sat back, nodded, and said, "Pray for humility and wisdom."

Raf smiled. "That I am praying for, and in my wisdom I confided in my little sister. I miss Mom and Dad, Elia. I want to talk with them." He paused, then said, "But you know what? You have a lot of both them in you."

He looked at his watch and sighed. "You have to get through security."

She gathered up her belongings. "I'm sad for you. For your unhappiness."

"I'm all right."

"She hugged him. You know what would Mom say?"

He smiled. "Give it to Jesus."

She put her hands on his shoulders and smiled back. "And?"

"And don't take it back. Let Jesus take care of it."

"Pretty smart Mom we had. Heed her advice."

They hugged one last time. "I'll call you when I'm in the States, Sis."

"Not just call. You come to us." She turned and walked through security.

As soon as she was out of sight, Raf dropped his bravado. He whipped off his Roman collar and stuffed it in his pocket and wiped the perspiration from his forehead and neck.

Elia arrived at her gate at the first boarding call. She whispered a prayer for Father Rafael as tears flowed down her cheeks.

Chapter 19

Luis pulled into the Charleston airport as Elia's flight landed.

He parked and reached the waiting area before passengers deplaned. Elia was one of the first off the plane and she rushed into Luis's arms, bursting into tears.

Luis held her, then stepped back and looked at her. "What is it? Why the tears?"

She shook her head. "I don't know. I'm just glad to see you." She paused. "I had a talk with Raf."

Luis held her at arms' length and looked at her. "And?"

"He has some questions."

"Questions?"

"His vocation."

"What's the problem?"

"I'm not sure. I don't think he knows. But he's working on it. He's coming home to see his spiritual director and his bishop."

"It's a hard life. But rewarding, I'd think."

"Just keep him in your prayers."

"Will do." Luis gave her a hug. "Come on. I've got a surprise for you."

When they drove out of the airport, instead of heading to Charleston, they went in the opposite direction.

"We're not staying in Charleston?" Elia asked.

"No, Mrs. Echevarria. Vicente's place is on Kiawah Island, so I thought, why not; that's where we'll stay. Have you ever been there?"

"No. I've never even been to Charleston. I'd say this is a treat for me but that's too heartless." She grimaced.

"You can't keep thinking that way. So—be a little heartless." He took his eyes off the road and grinned at her. "For me?"

Elia nodded. "You're right. From now on, it's all about us."

They crossed over Highway 17 onto Main Road, crossed the Intracoastal Waterway, and soon were traveling on Bohicket Road beneath a canopy of majestic oaks decorated with Spanish moss.

It was high tide when they crossed over one more bridge—this one separating Kiawah and Seabrook Island.

"Look." Elia pointed to three dolphins frolicking in water brought in by the tide. "I've never seen a dolphin out of the ocean."

"This is ocean. The sea is filling the marsh." He slowed down. "What a sight."

They neared the security gate with three cars in front of them. To their right, a car went through a separate gate for property owners only.

They pulled up to the window. "Echevarria," Luis said.

The guard checked the computer. "Don't see you. Another name, maybe?"

"We have reservations at The Sanctuary."

"Oh, no problem." The guard handed Luis a day pass and a map of the island. "Put this in your windshield. When you check in, you'll get a pass from the hotel." He pointed to a dot on the map. "The Sanctuary's down this road two miles on your right. You'll see the sign."

As they drove off, Elia looked behind her. Several cars were waiting to go through the gate. "They seem to be very careful about who gets on the island."

"They are. You have to have a purpose to come on the island. Homeowners have to call in passes for friends who visit, if even for an hour or two."

They drove down the road toward The Sanctuary. Sea grass, native to the island, lined the road and swayed in the soft breeze like pink feathers on two-foot stalks.

They turned onto a tree-lined driveway speckled with oleander. At the end of the drive stood the yellow stucco and red brick resort, its five-star rating elegantly evident from afar. They parked in front of the hotel and relinquished their car and bags to the valet.

They rode the elevator to their floor and ten minutes later Luis had Elia in his arms and carried her over the threshold into their suite. Wall-to-wall windows overlooked a grassy courtyard and the Atlantic Ocean beyond.

Elia slept the afternoon away. When she awoke, Luis was in the sitting room reading the papers Elia had found in Vicente's suitcase. He was frowning.

"What is it?" Elia sat beside her husband.

"I'm trying to remember something from several years ago. When I was doing my residency in New Orleans — something's familiar here."

"Is that Vicente's speech?"

"His notes. And he was about to open a can of worms."

Chapter 20

By midmorning the following day Luis and Elia had hopped on bicycles and were following directions from the concierge at The Sanctuary to Vicente's home. They followed the bicycle path that cut through thick vegetation. If they used their imaginations, they might have thought they were on a deserted island. They passed lagoons and spied alligators sunning on banks. A small fox ran across their path into the woods, and an owl hooted nearby. Before they turned onto Vicente's street, they passed another lagoon that in the evening would be home to a couple dozen snowy white egrets that would fly there to sleep in the trees.

Vicente's home was on a cul-de-sac. Many homeowners on Kiawah rented out their homes, but not on this street. With few exceptions, most of these owners lived here full-time, or came to the island on weekends. Vicente was the only renter on the street.

It was quiet. They rode into the driveway, parked their bikes, and looked at the house, then at each other.

"Let's go." Luis took his wife's hand. In her other hand, she held the key given to her by Señora Pereda.

They climbed the steps to the front door and Elia put the key in the lock. But before she turned the key the door drifted open.

Luis flung open the door. "What the…"

Elia gasped. They stood anchored to the floor. The place had been trashed.

Chapter 21

"What the hell were they looking for?" Luis stepped over lamps and sofa cushions strewn on the floor. "And who the hell are they?"

Elia walked into the living room and slowly surveyed the clutter. "Maybe they didn't find it."

She stepped gingerly over Vicente's possessions then stood still and shook her head, as if in slow motion. "How sad. All his earthly belongings—violated."

The entire back wall of the house was glass. From the dining room, sliding glass doors opened onto an open deck. Elia walked out onto the deck and stood there looking out on the marsh. The tide was coming in and small whitecaps danced over the water. She smiled. And then remembered where she was—and why.

She returned to the house and stood in the middle of the living room and scanned the mess. It looked to her as though whoever did it was haphazard in his search. Lamps and pillows were on the floor, some pictures and accessories, but as sloppy as the place looked, she had a strange feeling. "They didn't find it."

"It being what?" Luis had stooped and was looking through papers strewn on the floor. "And what makes you think they didn't find whatever 'it' is?"

"I don't know. Maybe because it's time for things to go our way. For Vicente."

She pulled out her notebook and a handkerchief from her bag and poked around. "Ah, here it is." She retrieved the phone from the floor and picked it up with her handkerchief. She tapped in 911 and gave the dispatcher the information. "They're on their way. And they're calling Kiawah security."

A Charleston County police officer arrived on the tail of a Kiawah security guard. They stepped through the door and almost at the same time let out soft whistles.

Luis told the officers who they were and why they were there. He explained about Vicente's death, presumed to be murder.

"Notice anything missing?" Charleston had a notebook and pen in his hand.

"We've never been here before." Elia shrugged her shoulders. "How would we know? And Dr. Pereda rented this house furnished; we wouldn't know what was missing."

While they were speaking the Kiawah guard made a phone call and ordered the front gate closed to exiting traffic. He directed his attention to Elia and Luis. "We don't know when this happened, but maybe they're still on the island."

"Don't you have a record of who comes and goes?" Elia asked. "I noticed the scrutiny at the front gate when we drove in."

"We'll check our records, but it could be anyone."

"Oh, so it's not difficult to get admitted to the island after all? Elia asked.

"I didn't say that. But we can't know everyone who's in a car."

Luis had been sitting on a barstool seemingly oblivious to the exchange between the two. "Wait a minute. I got in just by saying I had a reservation at the hotel."

The guard nodded.

"So all anyone has to say is that they have a reservation," Elia said. "So anyone could come in." Before she got an answer she said, "What about someone coming to a private home? Or a renter?"

"The homeowner calls in a pass," the security guard answered, sounding defensive.

Luis watched the exchange and was silent as he rocked back and forth on the stool. "Doesn't make sense. Who would call in a pass for a burglar?" He held up a hand. "Let me put it another way. Who would want his name on a pass—if he knew he was going to rob someone."

Elia and Luis were ushered outside. They sat on the front porch while the police were inside. An officer came out to speak to them. "You can leave. We got in touch with the owner, and he'll fly down day after tomorrow to look the place over. He'll be able to tell us what's missing."

"Good. We'll meet him here," Elia said. "We have to know what not to pack."

"We'll let you know when we're finished here." He looked in his notebook. "Got your contact information." He stood there looking at them, as though he were willing them to leave.

Elia sat looking out across the street into the wooded area that served as home for local bobcats. She was frowning.

Chapter 22

"You're quiet." Luis glanced over at Elia. They rode side-by-side on the bike path on their way back to The Sanctuary. Neither seemed to admire the scenery.

"I think we should take Vicente's girlfriend with us when we meet the owner."

"He wouldn't claim something of Vicente's."

"No. But she might notice something missing."

Luis nodded. They rode in silence.

Elia broke the silence. "Motive. There's always a motive." They had parked their bikes in racks and had sauntered down the boardwalk to the ocean and were sitting on the top step that led to the beach. "Always."

"What are you talking about?" Luis kept his eyes on a shrimp boat far out in the ocean.

"When I was writing the story on violent crime investigators in Augusta that's what I heard from the police. Motive. Find the motive and it'll lead to the criminal."

"I guess that's what I've been trying to figure out; why?" He stood up. "Let's go back. I want to get to my computer. There's something I want to look up."

Thirty minutes later Luis and Elia sat on their balcony eating lunch ordered from room service. Luis bit into a crab cake sandwich, took a swallow of milk, and stared at his laptop.

"I knew I had heard about this. Listen." He set his milk down and sat on the edge of his chair. "This is an article written in 1968. It documents medical cases of paraplegic and quadriplegic soldiers in VA hospitals during the Vietnam War. They had all been given the same drug for spasticity related to paralysis, and some, no not some, many, developed a life-threatening liver disease."

Elia moved her chair so she could look at the computer screen with Luis. "What does it mean?"

"Wait a second." He scrolled down the page. He didn't take his eyes off the screen.

He turned and picked up Vicente's report and flipped through the pages. Slowly the blood drained from his face.

Luis pushed out of his chair and paced like a cat around the small balcony. "I read every word of Vicente's notes for the Bermuda conference. Every word." He turned to look at Elia. "He was doing a rotation at the spinal center here on the neurology service. According to his notes, he treated a lot of wounded soldiers. Saw a lot of paraplegics and quads."

"And?"

"And he saw a lot of hepatitis."

"Liver disease?"

"A life threatening liver disease."

"Coincidence?" Elia held a forkful of salad suspended in the air as she waited for Luis to continue.

"Elia, it looks like the same drug. It has a different name. But what doesn't have a different name is the drug company. Pavnor."

Elia put her fork on the plate and turned to look out at the sea. She turned to Luis. "The same drug company... I knew it. My scuba diving accident was no accident." She shivered. "I wonder where Aaron Scharff is now."

"These notes. I think there's more." Luis was out of his chair pacing around the small balcony.

"What?"

"Vicente had something to say to me."

"But you have his report; that's good, isn't it?" Elia set her salad aside and turned back and forth in her chair to follow Luis as he paced. "Doesn't that tell you?"

"Why would he be murdered? Why would his place be ransacked? Over a drug?" He shook his head. "Pharmaceuticals are big business, but there has to be more."

"Maybe if we knew what those people were looking for, we'd know what Vicente wanted to talk to you about." She swiveled to keep her eyes on him. "Isn't that what you mean by 'has to be more'"?

He stopped prowling. Maybe so. But how would we ever know." He slammed his hand down on the railing. "Damn! Why didn't I let him talk when he wanted to."

"Oh no, you don't." She stood and put her hand over his. "Don't even think it. He was sick and shouldn't have been talking." She stepped back. "Please let's not go there."

He nodded. "We'll let Burnside know about the break-in. And the police are out at Vicente's right now." He patted his pockets and pulled out a card. "Here it is. One of the cops handed this to me."

"And what would you tell him? That your wife thinks someone sabotaged her scuba gear in Bermuda? That'll go over big." She shook her head in dismissal and sat down to pick at her salad.

"Got another idea?" Luis sat down opposite his wife and looked at her with raised eyebrows.

"No. I guess you'd better make those calls."

Chapter 23

"W should talk to Angel. Vicente said she knew about his problem."

"And we have to offer our condolences. Besides, she really should come with us to the house when the owner's there." Elia leafed through the phone book. "I'll try her at work." She found what she was looking for, wrote the number in her notebook, and dialed the number to Charleston Spinal Center.

When she asked for Angel Carter, Elia's call was transferred to the Physical Therapy Department. A few minutes later, Elia carried on a short conversation.

Luis looked at her, as she replaced the receiver. "Well?"

"She's there, but was busy with a patient. She gets off work at seven. I left a message that we would be there by seven, and that we'd like to meet her." Elia looked questioningly at Luis. "Maybe we can take her to dinner? And since we're going to the hospital, we could see Riser before we see Angel. Good plan?"

"Good plan."

"I'll try to reach him." She placed the call and set up a six-thirty meeting at the hospital.

It wasn't difficult to find the spinal center; in fact, they had passed it on the way from the airport. It sat back from the road almost hidden by a thick stand of trees. The color of old putty, it blended in with the landscaping.

They entered the hospital through the front door. Inside, soft colors added a calming effect to the lobby.

They followed the receptionist's directions and walked down a carpeted hallway to Dr. Riser's office. Passing them as they approached an open door was a slim blonde woman. She glanced at Luis and seemed to gasp. But she kept walking.

Dr. Riser was standing behind his desk when they knocked at the open door. He seemed startled to see them.

"We're not early, are we?" Luis asked from the door.

"No, no. Come in." Riser cleared his throat. He reached out and shook their hands. "Luis, Elia. Welcome to Charleston. I'll let Bonnie know you're in town. We'll have to get together." He motioned to the door. "That was Angel Carter, Vicente's girl."

"Oh, that was Angel?" Elia stepped back through the door and looked down the hall. She was gone. "How is she? We'll be seeing her later this evening."

"Distraught." He settled in the chair behind his desk and motioned for them to sit down. He looked at Luis. "What can I do for you?"

"After we saw you in Bermuda, Elia and I ran into some trouble."

"Trouble? Such as?" Riser leaned forward in his chair; a frown creased his brow.

"We were chased by some lunatic on a motorcycle, some-one broke into our cottage, and—"

Elia jumped in. "And someone ransacked Vicente's house on Kiawah."

Riser seemed to lose some color. He took off his glasses and slowly ran his hand over his face. He shook his head. "Do you know why?" His voice was raspy.

Elia put her hand on Luis's knee and answered quickly. "We thought you could tell us." She watched him closely. "Vicente was having a problem at work, wasn't he? Do you know what it was?" She tried not to sound confrontational.

"I'm not sure." Riser took a deep breath and replaced his glasses. "He talked to me about a medical problem, yes, but I don't see how that would cause all of this trouble."

"What kind of medical problem? His performance?"

"No, no. He did fine at work. In fact, Paul Kittrick seemed to think highly of him." He looked as though he wanted to say more.

"Yes? Paul Kittrick?" Elia asked.

"I had heard Dr. Kittrick — Kitt — was going to tap Vicente for chief resident."

"But?" from Luis, who was now leaning forward in his chair.

"But he didn't." He held up his hands, palms out. "Don't know why."

"No idea?" Elia asked.

"No idea."

Luis pursued another avenue. "The medical problem he talked to you about. What was that about?"

"He wasn't well. Had an ulcer."

"That's it? How about a different kind of medical problem?" Luis asked.

Riser sat very still. "What do you mean?"

"The conference. I read his notes for his paper — the one he was going to present in Bermuda."

"And?"

"You read the finished paper?"

"I did."

"I'm curious." Elia jumped into the exchange. "Who presented his findings? I understand someone was going to read his paper."

Riser looked away from the couple. He took another deep breath, then said in a voice barely audible, "No one."

"What?" Luis jumped up from his chair. "Why? Cyptolis is killing people." Anyone walking in the hall would have heard his outburst.

Elia reached up for his hand and tugged him back into his chair. Now it was his turn to take a deep breath. He shook his head, as though he couldn't believe what he had just heard.

Riser had gotten up and closed the door during Luis's outburst and returned to his place behind his desk. "I wasn't in charge of that meeting. I had no say about the speakers."

"But didn't you give any credence to his findings?" Luis whipped out the report from his jacket pocket. He flipped a couple of pages, and began reading about side effects.

"Look. I did want him to present the paper. I'm just saying I didn't push it after he died."

"I don't get it. Vicente was dead. At least don't you think you could have read the paper out of respect for him and the work he put into his research?" Luis willed himself to speak calmly.

Riser shook his head. "Maybe you're right. But I think he should have done more research before he put the treatment of so many of our soldiers on the line. And I'm not the only one who shares that opinion."

"Paul Kittrick wasn't particularly happy with his paper." He hesitated. "You asked why Vicente wasn't appointed chief resident. I think it had to do with the fact that your friend wasn't afraid to speak up when he thought something wasn't right. He didn't mind rocking the boat. Kittrick doesn't like rocky boats."

"But his findings — " Luis began.

Riser interrupted. "My god, man, these young people were over in Iraq and Afghanistan fighting for us. We should give them anything we can to make them more comfortable. Dr. Pereda jumped the gun."

"Wait a minute." Elia held up a hand to stop Riser. "Just exactly what does Cyptolis do? And why do you single out soldiers?"

"We don't just give it to soldiers, but the majority of our patients in the spinal cord unit are just back from the wars. I'm sure if you checked with other doctors in civilian hospitals, they use Cyptolis for their spinal cord patients."

He looked at Elia. "It successfully treats stroke, multiple sclerosis and cerebral palsy patients as well. You want to know what Cyptolis does? First you have to understand what these men and women are going through.

"Let's talk about spinal cord injuries, because that's what Vicente saw a lot of at this hospital." He leaned across his desk. "A big percentage of spinal cord patients experience spasticity, and due to this spasticity about half of them experience pain and limitation of activities. Just the word spasticity suggests the other illnesses I mentioned; do you see?" He addressed his question to Elia.

She nodded, but said nothing.

"I know Luis is familiar with this, but one component of spasticity is these patients have exaggerated tendon jerks. This is an upper neuron syndrome.

"To further answer your question, this is considered to be the only motor neuron symptom to respond to therapy." Riser again directed his attention to Elia, not even glancing at Luis.

"There has been more research, of course, and more conclusions, but just this one idea is enough to help doctors seek a readily available treatment for spasticity." Now he looked at Luis. "And one of those treatments is Cyptolis."

"Are you aware about a thirty-year-old study about this exact same drug?" Luis asked Riser.

Riser frowned. "What are you talking about? I've read the literature. This drug has only been out a short time. The trials have just been completed. We expect full FDA approval any time now."

"I don't understand how it can be given to patients if it's not fully approved," Elia said.

"Nothing new, Elia. Jake knows this. It wasn't until the early 1960s that the FDA began tightening its review of drugs. Congress ordered the FDA to review all new medications. Drugs before then are now supposed to be evaluated, but some companies insist they're grandfathered in. So drugs that go back decades are still on the market.

"Jake, remember the vitamin E injectible from back in the 80s?" Luis turned to Elia. "One of those grandfathered drugs, E-Ferol, a high potency Vitamin E injection, was routinely given to premature babies. But when about a hundred had serious reactions from the drug, and forty died, it woke up the FDA. It began to scientifically test the grandfathered drugs."

Riser added, "The FDA says it's trying to expel them from the market."

"Well that's a good thing," she said.

"Not good enough," Luis said. "Plenty are still being used and we are paying for them."

"Excuse me?" she said.

Luis glanced at Riser, who was nodding in agreement. "Medicaid pays for them."

"He's right, Elia. I've seen data that reported that within a recent three year period Medicaid paid nearly $198 million for more than 100 unapproved drugs."

"And most of them were for common conditions—colds, pain." Luis had picked up the tutorial. "The FDA admits there might be thousands of unapproved drugs on the market.

"What makes it worse," Elia said, "is that Medicaid patients are poor. It's like they're not important."

"That's not it. Private insurance plans cover them, too." Luis looked disgusted. "Some medications don't help, and some make people sicker."

"And some kill," Elia said

Luis still had the papers in his hand. "What are the contraindications for Cyptolis?"

"It's safe. Common side effects. Drowsiness, dizziness, weakness. But they're usually transient."

"But what are the contraindications?" Luis pressed.

"The usual. Watch for hepatic involvement. We always look for that with returning soldiers. It's hard to know what is endemic to a region. Seems as if a strain of hepatitis might be in the Middle East."

"Why do you say that?" Elia asked.

"Because many of our soldiers have developed the disease, that's why."

"Did anyone besides Vicente think the hepatic involvement might be from Cyptolis?" Luis asked.

"I haven't heard." Riser stood, a preamble to the end of the meeting. "I really have to get back to work. Again, I'm sorry about Vicente's death. He was a good doctor." He walked to the door, opened it.

"I'd like to read the completed paper," Luis said at the door.

"If you read his notes, you know everything that was in his paper." Riser paused.

Luis didn't move, just stared at Riser.

"I'll try to get you a copy."

They were out the door when Elia stopped and turned back to Riser. "Dr. Kittrick. Did he ever sign in for the meeting?"

"I didn't see him, maybe." He stood at the door until Elia and Luis were halfway down the hall. Then he closed the door, turned off the lights, and sat in the dark behind his desk.

Chapter 24

Angel Carter stood in the doorway of the nearly empty lobby and looked over the room. She wore scrubs and had dark circles under her tired-looking eyes. But even so, she looked like a model—a young Christie Brinkley. Elia and Luis stood when they saw her; Elia walked over to her.

"Angel?" Elia held her arms out and wrapped them around the woman who had been so important to Vicente. Angel crumpled against Elia and cried.

She sobbed to the sounds of soft music playing in the background. Elia took her hand and led her to a chair in the corner of the lobby and introduced her to Luis.

Angel was quiet for a few moments. She dried her eyes, and smiled at Luis and Elia. "I thought it was you when I passed you earlier in the hall. Vicente told me he was going to your wedding." She turned her attention to Luis. "And when I saw you in the hall, I knew you were Peruvian. You remind me of Vicente." She took a deep breath. "He was looking forward to meeting you. Even though he didn't know you, he was sure he could trust you."

"Trust me?"

"He was so sure about you. He told me that if Elia Christie chose you, you were all right." She smiled, then fell silent.

"Did you know what he wanted to talk to me about?" Luis's tone was gentle.

"Yes." Her voice was soft. As she spoke, she played with the ID tag hanging around her neck. "We talked about it. He tried to get some help, but hospitals are small towns, and doctors belong to the same fraternity." She clenched her jaw. "His next step was the FDA." She paused. "What's the use." It wasn't a question.

Elia reached over and laid her hand across Angel's. "Angel, are you aware that the police in Bermuda think that Vicente may have been murdered?" Angel gasped audibly and jerked her hand to her mouth. She shook her head back and forth. "No," she whispered.

"They'll find who did this to him, Angel. But if they knew what Vicente was concerned about—what he wanted to talk to Luis about—maybe that'll help. Maybe it's related."

Angel bit her lip. "It is. I know it. I know it." She moved to the edge of her chair. Before she could say anything further, a woman in scrubs entered the lobby and motioned to Angel.

"Excuse me a second, please." She took a deep breath before walking away.

She returned moments later. "I'm so sorry. It seems I have a patient waiting for a treatment. Thank you so much for coming." She took another deep breath and turned to leave.

"Wait, Angel," Elia said. "We have to talk. I thought you got off duty at seven."

"I do. I did. I mean I'm on second call, and a patient was ordered a stat treatment a short time ago. The attending asked for me to do it." She shrugged. "I'm off tomorrow. Could we meet then?"

Elia pulled out her notebook. "What's your home phone number and address?" She scribbled down the information. "We'll call you in the morning." Elia gave Angel a hug. "I want you to know that we promised Vicente's father we'd look into things here. We'll pack up his house; maybe you'd want to help?"

Angel nodded. "Can we talk about it tomorrow? I don't know if I can do that." Another deep breath. "I'll try."

Elia gave her another hug. "I know how hard this is, but we have no idea what's Vicente's, and what's not. The police want to know what might be missing. But we'll talk about this tomorrow."

Angel nodded and turned to leave.

They watched Angel leave the lobby. Elia called after her. Angel turned as Elia went to meet her. "Who ordered the stat treatment tonight?"

"Dr. Riser." She gave a stiff wave and hurried out of the lobby.

"Well, that didn't get us very far." Luis and Elia were at Heges Restaurant. They were nursing Margaritas at a table in the bar. The entrance to Kiawah was right down the road.

"We tried, Elia. We know Vicente was concerned—upset about Cyptolis." Luis frowned, as if he had more to say.

"Luis? What?"

"We don't know why he was so secretive. He was going to present his paper, so that's not secret. What was he so frightened about?"

"His job? Could he lose his job?"

"I wouldn't think so. When I was in training, our professors gave high marks to anyone who presented a paper—whether it was in support of acceptable common practice, or not."

"But it sounds like he lost out on the chief resident position for being outspoken."

He took a swallow of his drink. "Sounds like it; that was a low blow."

"Frightened." She looked around the centerpiece at him, then finally pushed it out of the way. "Was he frightened? I mean, I know he was sick and scared about that, but was he frightened about work?"

"What do you mean?"

"Maybe he wanted to talk to you about the outspoken business. Like should he be."

Luis looked around the bar. "Thought so." He nodded in the direction of a corner table. "Thought I smelled cigarette smoke. It's banned in Georgia."

"Luis, Vicente."

He leaned in and said in a whisper. "He was murdered. I'd say he had reason to be frightened."

"But you haven't read the paper he was going to present—just his notes. Do you think there was something in the finished product? Something to be secretive about? Scared?"

"Riser promised me a copy."

"Well, not quite. He said he'd try to get you a copy." Elia licked the salt from the rim of her glass. "Angel might be able to tell us. Vicente was scared. I thought he was panicky because of his sickness, but I'll agree with you. Maybe his paper had something to do with his fear."

"If my hunch is right, it had everything to do with it." Luis motioned for the check. "I've got some research to do."

Chapter 25

"It's from Bonnie Riser." The concierge had handed Elia a message when they returned to the hotel. "She wants us to call her." She tucked the message into her purse. As soon as they got to their rooms, she returned the call. "Just a second, let me check with Luis."

Elia pressed the mute button. "She says Aaron Scharff's company is here for a meeting and the CEO is having a party in his suite tomorrow evening. We're invited. Want to go?"

Luis nodded. He was already seated in front of his computer.

"Yes, Bonnie, we'll be there." She jotted down the information. "Thanks. See you tomorrow."

Luis leaned back in his chair. "Another meeting? No wonder drugs cost so much."

"What are you working on?" Elia sat on a loveseat with her feet tucked under her.

"I want to know what other new drugs Pavnor Pharmaceuticals has come up with."

"And?"

"And maybe this has happened before. Maybe they've taken drugs off the market because of reported problems, and then put them back on under a new name."

"Luis, you can't mean this was blatantly intentional. Surely this is sloppy research. Or maybe it's lax reporting? What kind of people would intentionally put something on the market that would hurt patients?"

"It's been done. Sometimes drugs with serious side effects serve a greater purpose, and the drugs are left on the market.

But there's a black box around the name in the PDR to give doctors the information about the problems."

"PDR?"

"Physicians' Desk Reference. Lists every medication. With pictures, uses, doses, side effects, contraindications — everything about a drug. And a black box is placed around a drug with problems." Luis looked up from the computer.

"But that's not all. There's something called an adverse event." He interrupted himself to explain the term. "That's any adverse change in health or any side effect that shows up in a patient from the treatment in a clinical trial. Or even shows up within a pre-determined period after the treatment is completed. And these events have to be reported to regulatory authorities."

"Everything?"

"Everything." He paused. "Serious problems — if the patient requires hospitalization, or develops a life-threatening condition, or hell, dies — serious problems have to be reported immediately. Minor problems just have to be documented in an annual summary."

"And Cyptolis?"

"*Nada.* Nothing. No black box, no documentation of an adverse event."

"Why not? Luis, why would someone hold that back?"

He shook his head.

"And why try to kill us?"

"We weren't killed. Just frightened. Maybe to scare us off." He shrugged.

"Why?"

"And why murder Vicente?"

"To cover up." She sounded sad.

"That. And what's the root of all evil?"

"Money."

Chapter 26

Elia and Luis were up early the next morning. After coffee, Elia looked at her watch. "Not too early." She dialed Angel's number. "Angel? It's Elia. We're going to Vicente's this morning. Would you like to meet us there?"

She frowned as she listened to Angel's response. "I know this is a bad time for you, and we hate to rush you, but the home-owner is coming in tomorrow and we want to get Vicente's personal items out of there." Elia looked over at Luis and shrugged. "Angel, we have to talk. Please come." She replaced the receiver a moment later.

"Well?"

"She's coming. I hate that I'm pushing her. I know when my parents died, it was terrible to go into their house and pack up. Raf and I cried the whole time we were working."

"It's tough." He lapsed into silence. He, too, had to pack up after a death. He stood at the door of the balcony looking out at the sea. Elia came up and slipped her hand into his. "Let's hop on our bikes and blow off this melancholy."

"What time do you think Angel will get here?" They were riding beside the water on hard-packed sand.

"She said an hour, or so."

"That'll give us time to ride to the end of the island and back before she gets here." Luis checked his watch. "Let's shoot for ten at Vicente's."

They rode in silence. The tide was out; the beach was vast. "What are you thinking? Elia looked over at her husband. "You're lost in thought; I can tell."

"I'm thinking I'd like to get my hands on that paper Vicente was going to present."

"You have his notes. That's not enough?"

"I just can't see it."

She put on her brakes and stopped suddenly. Luis was twenty feet ahead of her when he looked over and saw she wasn't following.

"What is it?" He rode back to where she had stopped.

"Motive. What's the motive? Cover up? Money? Maybe it doesn't have anything to do with the drug."

"Well then, what's Vicente have to do with it?"

"Luis, you said yourself that you couldn't find anything in the notes. Maybe it's something else."

Luis shook his head. "What are we doing? This isn't our job. Let's clear out Vicente's things and let the police sort it out." He turned his bike around. "Let's go back and get started."

They pushed their bikes up the ramp to the boardwalk that crossed over dunes. In Kiawah, the dunes are fiercely protected. No one sets foot on them. Homes are built far from the ocean, back behind two dunes.

They walked their bikes down the path toward the street. It was cool under the canopy of trees. The mass of vegetation bordering the path was thick and jungle-like.

They walked single file until they were on the road. The streets were almost empty; tourists would soon start coming to the island, but it would still be quiet—even the beaches. A wide expanse of sand at low tide gives everyone plenty of room.

When they reached Vicente's street, their pedaling slowed. "I know how Angel feels. I don't want to go in, either," Elia said as they parked their bikes in the driveway. "Does it bother you?"

Luis put his hands on Elia's shoulders and looked her in the eye. "You knew him. You have memories. I have none. Of course you are affected." He pulled her close and gave her a hug. "Honey, I'm so sorry." Then he released her and took her hand. "Come on; let's get started."

They opened the door and stepped into the mess they had seen earlier. "What were they looking for? Did they find it?" Elia turned in a circle. "I hope not."

She dug through her purse and pulled out her notebook. She picked up Vicente's phone, and studying her notebook, began punching in numbers.

Chapter 27

"Who are you calling?"

"Vicente's father. Maybe he…Wait, it's ringing." When Señor Pereda came to the phone, Elia spoke quietly to him. She explained the scene in his son's home.

"I have no idea what people are looking for, or whether they found it. I know we talked about this, but have you thought about anything that might help?"

Elia shook her head to let Luis know what Pereda's answer was. "Señor, we met the woman Vicente was seeing. She's going to help us pack up his belongings."

Elia paused and then said almost to herself, "I wonder where Vicente would hide something." She was jolted out of her reverie and held the phone tighter to her ear. She seemed to pay close attention to whatever Pereda was saying.

"Banjo?" Elia said. "Of course!"

"Banjo?" Luis mouthed.

"*Gracias, señor*, we'll call you later. *Salud a tu esposa.*" Elia put the phone down. "Banjo clock. The Peredas have a banjo clock hanging on the wall in their parlor in Lima." Elia held up the house key she still clutched in her hand. "Vicente's mother kept this key in the clock." She spun around looking at the walls. "Vicente has one, too."

"There it is." Luis pointed to a clock hanging on a far wall. It did look like a banjo. It was about twenty-six inches in height and ten inches in width at its widest part. A gold eagle finial rested atop the mahogany case.

Luis stood in front of the clock and studied its face. He had been collecting antiques for several years, and had several old clocks. "Sessions. Nice."

"Don't touch it." Elia dug in her purse for a tissue. "Here, use this."

"What are we looking for with this clock?"

"Whatever someone else was looking for."

"Documents, let's hope." At the bottom of the clock, beneath the hanging pendulum, was a glass door the size of a greeting card. The glass was covered with an aged painting. It was a tranquil scene of a man and boy fishing from the entrance of a covered bridge. In the painting, a small boat sailed in the distance.

Luis opened the glass door. "Like father like son. Well, like mother…" He held up a key, studied it and handed it to Elia. "I was hoping for something more."

"Well, it's a start." She slipped it into a pocket.

Chapter 28

Angel arrived on schedule. She parked her car beside the bikes, turned off the engine and sat in the car looking straight ahead, her hands still on the steering wheel. She laid her head on her hands. Prominently displayed through the windshield was a long-term visitor's pass

Elia looked out the window. "Angel's here." She squinted. "What's she doing? Just sitting there?" Elia was about to open the door when Luis stopped her.

"Wait. She'll come in when she's ready." He poked around in the kitchen and found a tea kettle. "We'll give her something hot and soothing when she comes in."

Elia sat on a stool at the bar and watched her husband prepare the tea. "You know, the first time I met you, I sat at your kitchen counter." Elia had gone to Luis's home to interview him for the story she was working on for *Augusta Magazine* about violent crime investigators. As a feature writer, she had never written about crime, violent or otherwise. But that story changed her life. And Luis's.

He stopped what he was doing and looked at her.

"What is it, Luis?"

"You came into my life like an angel." He leaned across the bar and kissed her gently on the lips. "Okay. Back to work."

He opened the freezer and found a box of Thin Mints Girl Scout Cookies. "Ah. Vicente and I had a lot in common." They stopped their bantering when the front door opened and Angel gasped.

Elia met her at the door with a hug and led her into the kitchen. "This looks like the only spot they didn't tear apart."

Luis gave Angel a hug and motioned for her to sit. He cut up a slightly withered-looking lemon, poured the tea, and dropped a slice in each cup. "Drink this, Angel. It'll warm you." He put his hand on hers and gave it a squeeze.

He set out the cookies. When Angel saw them she smiled. "Vicente bought four boxes. Girl Scouts were selling them outside the grocery store." She took a sip of her tea. "We stopped on the way to the island, and there were Girl Scouts sitting in front of the door selling box after box." Her smile disappeared. "He told them he'd be back next year."

The three of them were silent.

Elia cleared her throat. "Angel, we have to talk."

"I know. I want to."

"We think Vicente's death had to do with the paper he was going to present."

"But maybe not, Elia," Luis said. "I didn't see anything in his notes to suggest that he was going to talk about something that would cause his..." he hesitated and glanced at Angel, "his murder."

"The drug shouldn't have been on the market; wasn't that what he was going to talk about?" Elia said. "Simple as that."

"Vicente is," she stopped. "Was very ethical." Angel was about to continue when the doorbell rang.

Luis went to the door. They heard, "Oh my god," in a woman's voice. Luis led the woman to the kitchen.

"Bonnie?"

"Elia." Bonnie Riser came and gave Elia a hug. "And you must be Angel. I am so sorry for your loss. Vicente was such a nice man, and according my husband, a good doctor."

"Angel, this is Bonnie Riser, Dr. Riser's wife."

Bonnie held out her hand to Angel.

"How did you know we were here?" Elia asked.

"Jake told me you were going to be packing up." She looked across the bar into the living room. "What happened here?"

"A break-in." Elia said.

"On Kiawah? That doesn't happen very often." Bonnie walked into the living room and looked around. She shook her head. "What'd they take?"

"We don't know. We don't know what was here. Angel's going to help us."

"I know you have a lot to do, but I wanted to invite you to our spa here on the island. You come, too, Angel. You both could use some pampering after all you've been through." She looked around the room again. "And what you still have to go through. Would tomorrow suit you?

"Angel? Can you?" Elia asked.

She nodded. "Thanks, Mrs. Riser. I'm free."

"Wonderful. And call me Bonnie. Let's meet at the spa at two." She gave directions. "Give my name at the desk if you get there first." Bonnie turned to leave, then stopped and addressed Angel. "Shall I call in a pass for you?"

"No, that's okay. I have one through Vicente." She sighed. "I guess it's still good."

"Good. I'll see you both tomorrow."

Elia looked out the window as Bonnie got in her car. "Angel, how could she call in a pass for you? And how did she get on the island?"

Angel joined Elia at the window. "See that sticker on her window? That gets her in. The Risers have a home here."

"They live here?" Elia looked astonished.

"Not really. Weekends, I guess."

Chapter 29

They stepped out of the elevator and walked half the length of the hall and stopped in front of elaborately paneled double doors. One knock and the doors swung open. They were welcomed by a middle-aged man dressed in black pants, white shirt, and black bow tie. Behind him were similarly dressed people serving drinks and hors d'ouevres.

They found themselves in a room-sized foyer. As they walked through the foyer to the living room, Elia's heels clicked on the marble floor.

The balcony doors in the living room were opened to the ocean breeze. The sun had not yet set, so the view was the focal point for the guests already assembled. Soft music played over speakers.

Luis! Elia! Welcome. Frank Hanssen broke away from the couple he was talking with and strode to the new arrivals. "I am so happy to see you again. I had hoped Bonnie would invite you. Come with me. I'll get you a drink." He motioned to one of the waiters, who approached with a tray of wines, bourbon and scotch.

"Now I'll introduce you to our host." Hanssen took Elia's elbow and guided her and Luis down the hall to a dark-paneled study. The man behind the walnut desk had just set the phone down. He had a pad of paper in front of him and circled the name Jack Alexander, a reporter at *The New York Times*. He stood when Hanssen tapped on the open door.

Harry Millen was tall, thin, and balding. What hair he had was gray. His white shirt was heavily starched and seemed to sit back from his neck, as if it held the man in high regard and would not touch him.

"Bermuda? Sailors?" he said when Hanssen introduced them as friends from Bermuda.

Luis smiled and shook his head. "Hardly. As a matter of fact, we were there for our wedding."

"And a friend of ours was there for a conference," Elia said. "He was going to present a paper on one of your drugs, but he died before he got the chance.

Millen looked at Hanssen and frowned. "I heard. I'm sorry. I hope his paper gets published posthumously." Millen walked toward the door and ushered his guests ahead of him.

Bonnie and Jacob Riser had arrived by the time Luis and Elia returned to the party. Bonnie glanced at them, but her gaze rested elsewhere. Elia turned to see who or what held her interest. It was Frank Hanssen.

Before Elia could react, Bonnie came forward. "I'm glad you're here. I saw you coming from the study with Harry. Good. You met our host."

Millen welcomed the Risers, then went off to greet more guests. Bonnie turned her attention to Hanssen, and Riser spoke with Luis. Elia sipped her drink and watched Bonnie and Hanssen. Bonnie's blonde hair fell over her left eye, and she slowly pushed it back.

Hanssen had his back to Elia, but she saw him shift his weight and take a deep breath. When Bonnie left him, he turned and looked after her. Then he looked in Elia's direction. She was staring.

Chapter 30

"I knew I didn't like him." Luis and Elia had made their way to the dining room and the buffet that awaited. If this had been a sit-down dinner, twenty guests could have been seated comfortably at the table. A butler's pantry separated the kitchen from the dining room. Staff from The Sanctuary were working in the non-descript kitchen, obviously there only for caterers' use.

"Frank." Elia showed her contempt.

"Frank? Why single him out? What about Bonnie? From what you said, she was the one doing the flirting."

"Men. You're all alike." Elia turned to leave, and Luis reached for her hand.

"What is it? Why are you taking this out on me?"

"You're right. Bad memories, I guess. That cheating creep I used to date popped into my head."

"And the girl? She had a lot to do with it, too." Luis smiled. "You emptied your apartment when he was out of town, dumped his things on the street, and moved to Georgia. Perfect." He squeezed her hand. "And I for one am glad you had a cheating boyfriend."

"What!"

He held onto her hand. "Admit it. Aren't you?"

Elia took a deep breath and nodded. "I am now, but back then I hadn't met you."

"Seriously, it's none of our business. Forget it."

"Forget what?" Hanssen had ambled up as they were talking.

"I don't know. I forgot it already." Elia pierced a shrimp with a toothpick and dipped it in the seafood sauce.

"Frank, we're surprised to see you here. We didn't know you were in town." Luis moved along the table as he spoke, sampling local fish.

"I have friends at Pavnor, so I was included tonight." He looked around the room. "Big party." He lowered his voice. "Have a meeting at a fancy resort, and not many people pass it up. Especially if the spouses are involved."

"Pavnor has a lot of meetings. You were just in Bermuda a few days ago."

"That wasn't a Pavnor meeting, Elia. That was a scientific meeting. A few Pavnor people were there along with reps from dozens of companies."

The suite began filling with more guests. "Speaking of spouses, Aaron Scharff's wife is here. Come with me, I'll introduce you. As they made their way to the living room, Hanssen stopped midway and was about to speak to a man who was engrossed in conversation. He caught the man's eye, nodded, and said, "Kitt."

"I'll introduce you to Kitt later when he's not so busy." Hanssen took Elia's elbow and guided her through the room.

Even though the night was mild, a fire burned in the fireplace, which was flanked by bookshelves overflowing with hard back copies of classics and popular fiction as though someone lived there permanently.

Frank inclined his head to a woman standing beside the fireplace. Dot Scharff looked at her watch, then glanced at the door.

Frank held out his arms to Scharff's wife as he crossed the room to greet her. Her face was almost hidden behind oversized glasses. She gave Hanssen a half-hearted smile and glanced again at the door as she absently brushed a few curls off her forehead. Hanssen made introductions.

"Where's Aaron?"

She frowned. "He had an errand to run." Again a glance toward the door. "He should be here any time."

"Are you staying here?" Elia asked.

The question erased Dot's frown. "Yes. But not in something as grand as this." She made a sweeping motion with her arm.

"It is lovely. I wonder how many suites the hotel has."

Elia turned to Hanssen. "Do you have any idea, Frank?"

"Don't know, but I understand this one is the best—the presidential suite. In fact, President Clinton stayed right here recuperating after surgery."

"I can imagine that. It's roomy enough for several presidents."

"Thirty-five hundred square feet of roomy comfort." Frank said.

As they talked in the living room, the doorbell sounded.

While Elia and Hanssen carried on their conversation, Luis noticed Millen going to the door and talking to two uniformed police officers. He saw the color drain from his host's face. Then Millen walked slowly toward them. He whispered something to Dot Scharff and escorted her and the officers to the study.

Hanssen and Elia continued to carry on a conversation after Dot excused herself from the group.

Luis looked down the hall toward the study, and when Millen came out a few minutes later, his skin was chalk white. Luis approached him. "Harry? What's the matter? You don't look well."

Millen shook his head. "It's Aaron Scharff. He's had an accident."

"Bad?"

"He's dead."

Chapter 31

"What kind of accident? Elia and Luis had retreated to their room. "Auto?" Elia sat on the edge of the bed and waited for the answer.

Luis nodded. "On Main Road. Apparently he was on his way to the party. He had a woman with him. She's critical."

"Where was he coming from? Wasn't he staying here?"

"He was. And that's what Harry Millen says has him confused. They played a round of golf today with Hanssen and another fellow and talked about the party. He told Harry he was going to the spa and then take a nap."

"What was so important to take him off the island? That's a thirty-minute trip down a long narrow road."

"Harry didn't know. He was surprised he didn't arrive with Dot.

"But the woman. Who is she?"

Luis shook his head. "When we met Scharff in Bermuda, didn't he tell us he lived in Connecticut?"

"So?"

"So how does he even know anyone in Charleston?"

"His wife said he had an errand. Maybe he was picking up someone for the party."

Luis shrugged.

"Think the police will tell us anything?"

"You're kidding. Why would they?"

Elia jumped up from the bed. "Because Vicente was involved with Pavnor and he's dead, that's why. And now someone else involved with Pavnor is dead."

Luis was silent.

"Luis, you were there, do you think Millen was surprised to hear of Aaron's accident, or was he acting?"

"If he was acting he did a great job. I don't know many actors who can turn pale on demand. He was upset. Very upset."

"We have a busy day tomorrow," Elia said.

"Oh?"

"First we'll do some packing at Vicente's, then we'll drive to the accident scene, and then I relax at the spa. I am really looking forward to that.

Chapter 32

By 8:30, Luis and Elia headed out of the parking lot on their bikes. It took them ten minutes to reach Vicente's house. Elia pulled two keys out of her jacket pocket. She studied one, slipped it back in her pocket, and used the other to open the door.

"I always know when you've got something going on in your head." They had been working for two hours, packing contents of drawers and closets. Luis taped up a box and waited for a reply.

She held up a stack of cards and papers. "I feel like a voyeur."

"A voyeur?" He lined his box up beside four others and sat down on it. "That's what you're thinking about? Being a voyeur?"

She shook her head. "No. Where's Angel? She was supposed to help. We have no idea what might be hers, or what she might want. I don't know what to do with half this stuff." She picked up a handful of utensils from a kitchen drawer and dropped them on the counter."

Luis held up his hands in a stop gesture. "Did you stop to think this might be hard for her?" He reached for her hand and pulled her toward him. "This isn't like you."

Elia burst into tears. "We shouldn't be looking through his personal belongings. Look." She handed Luis a tattered valentine from a box. It was a handmade card. A paper lace doily and red and pink construction paper were cut into hearts in three different sizes and pasted one on top of the other. The pink heart had writing in red ink.

Across the miles, I send my smiles
And say, be mine, my Valentine
*And I answer **your** plea*
I'm yours, with glee
   Love,
Elia

Elia took the card from Luis. "I had such a crush on him. I was in fifth or sixth grade." She held up the card. "Why did he keep this? After all these years?"

"He loved you."

Elia sat back down on the bed and let the tears fall. "Angel should be here."

Luis took her hand and steered her toward the kitchen. "Hot tea. You're tired and you have a lot of work to do. Don't take it out on Angel."

"I know this would be hard for her, Luis. It's hard for me, too. I had to do it for my parents."

"She's young, Elia. And she's all alone. You had Raf to help you. You told me so yourself."

"She has us. We're here to help."

"We're strangers, honey. She's devastated."

She got up and put her arms around Luis. "You're a wise man." She kissed him on the cheek. "And I'm a brat."

"You're human. And because you're human, you need a cup of tea." He winked at her and brewed the tea.

They sat at the kitchen counter, drank tea, and finished off the Thin Mints.

"She could have called."

Chapter 33

"Why are we doing this?" Luis was behind the wheel as they drove down the narrow two-lane Main Road toward Charleston. Huge ancient oaks bordered either side, their giant umbrella-like branches sheltering the road. The sun seemed to flash on and off, as it peeked through the leaves.

Before Elia could answer, Luis slammed on his brakes as the car in front of them stopped suddenly to make a left turn. Brakes squealed behind them as a small car, unable to stop, shot to the left of Luis's car and stopped in time to avoid hitting the turning car. It was over in a matter of seconds. The small car returned to its lane and continued on its way—this time in front of Luis.

"*Mierda*! Why are we doing this, Elia? This could be a sign."

Elia had her hand over her heart. She took a breath. "You led me to believe the police wouldn't tell us anything; I thought we'd look around on our own." She patted her chest. "And keep your eyes on the road."

"Where was the accident?"

"I asked at the security gate if they'd heard anything. The guard told me fifteen minutes from Kiawah. After that scare we just had, I'm surprised there aren't more accidents."

There was no shoulder, and in between the grand oaks were thin pine trees. No place to go if a car left the road. And pine could be as lethal as oak.

"Luis. There. That's it." On the opposite side of the road, the brush was flattened and two pine trees were marred with gouges. On closer inspection, glass littered the road. Luis pulled into a driveway ten feet from the scene. A man and woman sat on the porch of a faded green cinderblock house. The man was almost as skinny as the pine trees; the woman sturdy looking as an oak. Their ancestors had lived on the little piece of land since they were freed from slavery one hundred forty years earlier. Some of their longtime neighbors had given up their homes to deep-pocketed horse breeders. But this couple had no plans to sell out.

The man practically jumped off the porch; the woman ambled down the three steps, her worn shoes flopping on her feet.

Luis and Elia walked over to meet them.

"We noticed the trees. Looks like something hit them. What happened?" Elia asked.

"Terrible accident." He turned. "Where's my woman?"

"I'm right here. And it were no accident. I seen the whole thing; you didn't." The woman was short of breath after her walk from the porch. "I seen it. I sat right here and seen it."

Luis spoke in a calming voice. "Let's take a minute. We'd like to hear."

The woman's breathing slowed. "They didn't have nowhere to go."

"What do you mean? Were they trying to pass?" Elia asked.

"No ma'am. A car come onto them from the other way. The way you just come from."

"The other car was passing someone?"

"No ma'am. It just come."

"Like on purpose?"

"Now who would do something like that on purpose?" The woman looked at Elia as if she expected an answer.

"Well, who was in the wrong lane?" Elia asked.

"The other car. It come at them. And they tried to get clear, and they slammed into the trees."

"Did the other car stop?" Luis asked.

"Uh uh. Not at first. It kept going, then turned around and come back and slowed down, but then it just kept going, back the way it come from." The more she talked the more labored her breathing.

"I guess you told the police all of this," Elia said.

The woman nodded.

"What kind of car was it?" Luis asked.

The woman shook her head. "The police wanted to know that. I don't know cars."

Luis looked at her husband. "Do you?"

"Now woman, you told the police it were an army car."

"That's all I could say. It looked like one of them army cars."

"Like a Jeep?" Luis asked.

"If that's a army car, then, yes, like a Jeep."

"Accident?" Luis and Elia were driving back to Kiawah. Luis had both hands on the wheel; he watched the road as he spoke. "That was no accident."

Chapter 34

"I'm not waiting for Angel." They had returned to Vicente's house. "I'll leave my cell phone with you and if she calls me, tell her I'm at the spa."

"Want me to drive you?" Luis picked up the car keys.

"No, Honey." She looked around the living room and smiled mischievously. "You can keep packing." She gave him a quick kiss and left before he could comment.

She drove the short distance to the spa and checked in at the desk. "Is Bonnie Riser here yet?" Elia asked.

"Mrs. Riser telephoned and said she would be late, but for you to go ahead with your service."

"What about Angel Carter? Has she arrived yet?"

The receptionist checked the computer. "Her appointment was cancelled yesterday."

"She called and cancelled? She didn't tell me."

"I don't know who called, but we have you listed." The receptionist smiled and directed Elia to a sitting area in front of the stone fireplace. A flickering blaze added ambience.

That's odd, Elia thought. She dug in her bag for her cell phone to call Luis and let him know Angel may show up at the house to help pack. She came up empty handed.

She was called for her massage and followed a woman through heavy doors and down a hallway. One side opened onto individual dressing rooms.

She undressed and wrapped herself in a cozy robe. When she opened the door on the opposite side of the tiny dressing room, she found a pair of shower sandals and slipped them on.

An attendant led her to a wall of lockers. "Just leave your clothes in the dressing room, but you can put your valuables here."

Elia pulled a key out of one of the lockers and gasped. She retreated to the dressing room and searched in her pockets for another key. Her heart was beating rapidly. When she found what she was looking for, she willed herself to be calm. Her locker key and the key found in Vicente's banjo clock were identical.

"Are you okay, ma'am?"

Elia nodded and put Vicente's key back in her jacket pocket. She followed the attendant to another waiting area, the relaxation area, and listened half-heartedly as the woman pointed out the showers, steam room and sauna. But all Elia could think about was a key.

Chapter 35

While she waited for the massage therapist, Elia sat in an easy chair and looked out at the Kiawah River. She leaned back, put her feet up and tried to let her cares fall away. But they wouldn't.

"Ms. Christie? I'm ready for you."

She followed the therapist down another hallway lit with muted lamps. She vowed to relax, but once the session began, her mind raced.

An hour later she was back in the relaxation area and wrapped herself in a towel, left her robe on a hook outside the door, and stepped into the steam room. When she exited ten minutes later, an attendant was bringing in fresh towels.

"Has Mrs. Riser come yet?"

"I'm not sure; I'll check."

Elia headed for the sauna. Again she hung her robe on a hook and stepped inside. She didn't know how long she sat there. She felt herself drifting. It was very warm, but bearable. She had her eyes closed, but heard the swish of the door as it opened; then she heard the swish as it closed. She opened her eyes, but no one was there.

It got hot. Too hot. She felt dizzy, staggered to her feet and pushed on the door. It wouldn't budge. She tried again. Nothing. Again she tried. She felt herself panic in the enclosed room. She pushed hard on the door, as hard as she could. She pounded on the door, then carefully lowered herself onto the bench and tried to collect her thoughts.

"I've been in tight spots before." She spoke in a calm voice. So calm she almost didn't recognize herself. She wiped her forehead with her towel. She felt woozy, confused, lethargic. Her breathing was labored. She could feel herself losing control. She rose from the bench almost in a trance and pounded on the door. She screamed and the door swung open. She flew out, fell into the room and smacked into an attendant who was standing there with a robe in her hand. She stared at Elia.

"Are you all right?" The attendant grabbed a bottle of water out of an ice bucket on the side table. "You're so pink."

She guided Elia to a chair. "Drink this." She opened the bottle and stood there while Elia drank. Then she stepped into the shower and turned on the cold water. "A cold shower. You need a cold shower."

"I couldn't get out. The door was locked."

"The doors don't have locks."

"I'm telling you I couldn't get out."

"I picked up your robe from the floor in front of the door. Maybe that's why it was a little tight."

"How would my robe get on the floor? I hung it on the hook."

The attendant shook her head and shrugged. "I don't know, ma'am. Go on. Get into the shower. You'll feel better."

Elia was about to hang her robe on the hook outside the shower, but instead carried it inside with her. She let herself be led under the cold running water. The attendant pushed a stool under Elia and handed her another bottle of water. "Drink, please. You need this." She waited a minute, trying to avoid the water. "I'll wait outside."

Elia sat under the shower drinking bottled water. A few minutes later she stood and pushed the stool out of the way, threw her towel onto a bench inside the door, and let the rainfall-like shower of cool water wash over her. When she finally turned off the water, she felt better, but a frown creased her face.

She toweled off, wrapped herself in the robe, and gingerly pushed on the door. It opened immediately. She hadn't noticed that she was holding her breath as she tried the door, until she exhaled.

The attendant was waiting for her. She looked closely at Elia. "Feel better? You certainly aren't as pink."

"I'm fine. Thank you. You're very kind."

"Not at all. Now you rest for awhile." She picked up a basket of used towels and left the room.

Elia lowered herself into a chair, put her head back, her feet up, and closed her eyes. Am I paranoid? She left the spa without seeing Bonnie Riser. When she returned to Vicente's, Luis was standing on the front porch. He had a strange look on his face.

"What is it? What's the matter?"

"You didn't answer your phone; I tried to call you."

"You have my phone, Luis; I left it with you in case Angel called."

Luis met Elia as she was halfway up the front steps. "Luis. What's the matter? What happened?"

"The woman with Aaron Scharff. In the accident with Scharff…" Luis reached for Elia's hand. Elia, it was Angel."

Chapter 36

"Angel?" The two were sitting at the kitchen counter. Elia's hands were wrapped around a cup of hot tea. "Why was she with Scharff?"

Luis just shook his head.

"How did Angel know him? He lives in Connecticut."

"His wife said he had gone into Charleston on an errand. Maybe Angel was that errand."

"But how did they know each other? And where were they going together?" Elia asked.

"They have to have been coming here to the island. That road goes nowhere else."

"But Angel? Was she going to the party? Why didn't she say something yesterday when Bonnie was here?" She put her head in her hands. "Oh, Luis, I feel terrible. Here I was complaining about her, and she was in an accident."

Luis pushed back from the counter and stood. "Elia, let's pay our respects to Mrs. Scharff. She knew her husband was on an errand; let's see if she knew what that errand was."

Thirty minutes later, Elia and Luis were sitting in Mrs. Scharff's hotel room. Her suitcases were packed.

"I'm taking Aaron home today.

"We're so sorry," Elia said. She pulled out a card and wrote her cell number. "When you get home, and if you need to talk to someone, please call us. We both know the pain of losing someone in an accident. She placed the card in the grieving woman's hand and held her hand with both of hers for a few moments.

Luis leaned forward in his chair. "Could we ask you a couple of questions?" He waited a beat before he began. "You told us last night that your husband had an errand to run, that's why he was running late for the party. Did he tell you what the errand was?"

"He told me about the doctor who died in Bermuda. He read the paper he was going to present." She looked from Luis to Elia with red, puffy eyes. "He was concerned about the doctor's research."

"Meaning he didn't want the research to be made public?" Luis asked.

"No. I don't mean that at all. He was concerned about the drug. He's been doing a lot of research since he's been back from Bermuda.

"Do you know the problems associated with the drug?" Luis asked.

"No. Not at all. I just know Aaron was upset. So when we arrived here, he looked up the doctor's girlfriend. He called her yesterday afternoon. They had a long talk. I know, because I sat right here while Aaron was on the phone."

"It seems they were on their way to Kiawah when the accident happened." Elia said. "Yes. Aaron went to get her to bring her to Harry."

She nodded.

"Did Harry know where Aaron went? And why?"

Mrs. Scharff shook her head. "No. Aaron couldn't reach him when he left. They played golf earlier, then he talked with the young woman, and he left to see her soon after. He told me to go to the party and that he'd be along and bring the woman... her name's Angel, isn't it, with him. He wanted her to tell Harry what she had learned from her young doctor."

"And what was that?" Elia asked.

Again she shook her head. "I don't know. Aaron rushed out of here right after the phone call."

"The only thing he told me was to tell Harry that there is a problem with a drug and he was bringing someone to corroborate his story."

"Did you tell him?" Elia asked.

She brought a tissue to her face and wiped her runny nose. "I called him before the party and told him Aaron would be late."

"And you told him why?" Elia asked.

Dot Scharff nodded.

Chapter 37

"Have you had problems with Cyptolis?" Harry Millen asked. He was at the Jasmine Porch, a restaurant at The Sanctuary, with Jacob Riser. Before he could answer, Bonnie Riser joined them at the table.

"Don't let me interrupt you. I was stopping in for a cup of coffee and saw you two in the corner. Do you mind?"

Millen unenthusiastically half rose from his chair. "Not at all."

Bonnie pulled a chair out and sat down, folded her hands in front of her, and looked at the two men expectantly. "Really, don't let me interrupt you."

Riser glanced at his wife. She had dark circles under her eyes, and her smile looked forced. A slight frown crossed his face. He turned his attention to Millen and answered his earlier question. "Yes. A few."

"Any that I might not know about?"

"It seems that Cyptolis had been on the market thirty years ago. But the company took it off after complications were reported."

"That's impossible." Millen spit the words out. His face turned red. "Impossible." He took a breath and lowered his voice. "How would anyone know that? That's impossible."

"Is it?" Riser kept his eyes on Millen.

"Maybe the problems were ironed out." Both men turned to Bonnie. And both looked as if they had forgotten she was there.

"Excuse me, but your company did have thirty years to fix things; what's so impossible about that?"

"It's impossible because I would know if we had re-introduced a drug." Millen looked around the dining room, and again lowered his voice. "I run the damn company."

"Harry—" Bonnie began.

"Let me finish," Riser said. He looked at his wife and imperceptively shook his head, then again directed his attention to Millen. "How long have you been with Pavnor?"

"Eleven years."

"You weren't around thirty years ago."

"And you were?"

Riser shook his head. "I didn't have to be. I can read."

"What the hell are you talking about?" Millen said the words in a low voice. "What the hell...?"

"Cyptolis was taken off the market thirty years ago."

"No, you're wrong. I know what drugs we have; and I know what drugs we had in the past. Cyptolis is not one of them."

"I'm afraid it is. It was brought to my attention yesterday that it is. Thirty years ago the FDA investigated, and then the company—your company—pulled a drug off the market with the same components as Cyptolis because of hepatic side effects."

"Jacob." Bonnie Riser put her hand on her husband's arm. "That was a long time ago. Why are you getting upset? And who brought this to your attention?"

"Your wife is right. That was a long time ago."

"So you did know?" Riser asked.

"No. It is done—but not with the exact components. So I think you're wrong."

"I told you I can read; you do the research. Thirty years ago, young quadriplegic veterans from Vietnam were given a drug to lessen spasticity. There was a high incidence of liver disease —fatal liver disease." Riser stared at Millen. "I'm telling you, Harry, this is the same drug."

Millen leaned back in his chair and stared at Riser.

"The strange thing is the drug didn't have to be pulled; it needed only the required black box in the PDR and on the drug inserts to alert doctors of side effects."

"Pulling it proves that the company acted in good faith," Millen said.

"Then why, Harry, did it put the drug back on the market?" Riser almost whispered the words, as if he were tiring of a fight.

Millen said nothing for a minute; he just stared at Riser.

Riser returned the stare and waited for Millen to say more.

"You're the doctor, did you notice problems?"

"No." As soon as Riser blurted out the answer, he clamped his mouth shut and looked away from Millen's stare. He shook his head slowly, dejectedly. "That's not quite true. I didn't want to believe Cyptolis was causing problems, because, by god, it is a good drug."

"Then don't get upset, darling." Bonnie kept her hand on her husband's arm.

Riser looked at his wife, then shook his head again, this time as if trying to clear it. "Bonnie, please, I'd like to talk to Harry."

Bonnie's face seemed to harden. She breathed in deeply before she spoke. "I've got to run. I hope I'll see you before you leave, Harry."

Millen stood as she spoke. "Yes, I hope so." He said it absentmindedly and sat down as soon as she turned to leave.

Riser remained seated; he played with his fork. "Harry, why did you ask me if I had problems with Cyptolis?"

"Aaron. He told me the doctor who died in Bermuda had concerns and was prepared to present them at the meeting."

"How did he know what the paper contained?"

"I was under the impression that you told him."

Riser's face turned red. He blustered, "Only the gist. Only the gist."

"Yes, the gist. He talked to the doctor's girlfriend. Do you know her?"

"Angel."

"Angel. Aaron went into Charleston to bring her here to talk to me."

Riser pushed back from the table and stood. He looked down at Millen with derision. "It seems Pavnor Pharmaceuticals dodged a bullet."

Millen watched him leave. Through a clenched jaw, he muttered to himself, "Not for long. Not for long."

Chapter 38

"Yesterday was a bad day. I'm going to buy you a present." Luis parked the car at the General Store. "Wait here; I'll be right back."

When Luis returned to the car, he put a shopping bag and an empty bucket in the back seat and handed Elia a plastic tub. She pulled the lid off. "Yuck. What in heaven's name is this?"

"Squid. And don't insult my gift."

"I can't wait to see what I'll get on my birthday."

"That's in the back seat."

Elia turned to look at the cylindrical tubes lying on the back seat and a bucket and plastic shopping bag on the floor.

"Just wait. This is going to be a 'take our minds off all problems' type of gift."

They stopped at the hotel, asked the dining room to pack a lunch, and stopped in their suite to change into jeans.

"Ready? Let's go fishing." Luis held the door.

"One second." Elia grabbed her jacket. "Ready."

They drove until they found a pond with a dock bordering the water, one of many on Kiawah, and parked their car at the side of the road. A white pickup was parked nearby.

Luis reached for the hotel's cooler and the fishing rods, still unassembled in the tubes. Elia carried the bait, the bucket, and the shopping bag.

Another couple, wearing twin Boston Red Sox caps, were standing on the dock holding poles, their long lines flung far out in the water.

"Catch anything?" Luis asked as they set down their gear.

"Just bait." The fisherman motioned to a bucket of water with a few mullet swimming around. He stuck out his hand. "Earle. My wife, Janet. We're closing up shop; we'll leave the big catches to you." They reeled in empty lines and packed up. Before heading to their truck, the man pointed to the water. "Alligator nearby."

Luis put their poles together and threaded the lines. He pulled a large net out of the shopping bag and threw it over the water. It looked like a giant white flounder before it hit the water.

The net sank to the bottom. He lowered the bucket into the pond half filling it with water. Then he slowly pulled the net to the surface and dropped his catch into the bucket.

All this time Elia stood back and watched. "What about the squid?"

"The locals at the General Store said I should catch my own. Just in case I didn't, I bought the squid. But looks like the mullet are swimming. Let's see if something will bite them." Luis picked up a four-inch mullet and stuck the hook right through its eye and cast far out in the pond." He looked at Elia. "Want to take this and I'll bait your hook?"

"In your dreams. I'll bait my own hook." She skillfully thrust the hook through the mullet's eye and cast her line as far as Luis had.

Luis let out a low whistle.

"What'd you expect? My daddy didn't raise a sissy." She winked at Luis. "Contest?"

"I don't know. I have a feeling I'm going to lose."

"You're right."

While they were waiting for the first bite, a Lexus pulled up behind their car.

"This must be a popular spot," Elia said.

"And we know him."

Frank Hanssen got out of the car. "I thought that was you. Are they biting?"

"Yeah. Stealing our bait." Elia said. "What are you doing out here?"

Hanssen bent over the bait bucket and tapped the side of it. He seemed intent on watching the mullet bump into each other. He answered with his eyes on the bait. "I'm on my way to visit friends."

"Want to join us?" Luis handed Hanssen his pole.

"Maybe for a while. It's been a long time since I sat on a bank and fished." He took a breath, then said, "So much going on this week."

Luis nodded. "I'm sorry about Aaron. He was a friend of yours."

"He was." His shoulders slumped; he no longer looked like the Bermuda sailor.

"How did you get to know him so well?" Elia asked.

"Business."

"Business?"

"Business." Hanssen closed the door on the subject.

Elia kept her eyes on her line. "We talked with a couple who witnessed the accident. The wife said an army-type vehicle ran Aaron's car off the road. I guess that's a Jeep. She told the police, so at least they have that lead.

"Darn." She reeled in her empty hook. "Sneaky fish. Stole my bait." She rolled her eyes. "Again."

She baited her hook one more time and cast far out into the pond. "Frank, do you know why Aaron was bringing Angel Carter to the party?" She turned from the water and looked at Hanssen.

"What makes you think he was bringing her to the party?"

"Dot Scharff told us this morning."

"Is that right?" Hanssen stared out at the dark water and kept his eyes on his line. "Strange that she would want to come to a party after suffering her loss."

"She wasn't coming to party. Aaron was bringing her to see Harry Millen."

"Millen? Why?"

"We think she wanted to tell him about Vicente's findings on Cyptolis," Luis said. He was sitting on a bench untangling the casting net.

"But that has us wondering," Elia said.

"About findings?" Hanssen glanced at Elia, then at Luis, and finally turned his gaze to the water.

"Oh, we know the findings," Elia said. "But Millen? The CEO of the company, the one person who should know everything about every drug. It's why she would have to tell Millen; wouldn't he know already? That's what's strange. What else did she have to talk to him about."

She reeled in her line, saw her bait was gone, and jabbed another mullet through the eye with a hook.

Chapter 39

"Pavnor Pharmaceuticals is behind this." Hanssen had left, and Elia and Luis sat on benches on the dock waiting for a bite. "But I don't get it."

Luis looked at Elia. "Drugs are big business."

"I know, but murder?" She kept her eyes on her line. "Come on. One drug? How big a business is one drug?"

"A lot of money goes into one drug. Research and trials take years." He stood up to play a fish on his line. He slowly reeled in. Slowly, slowly. "*Caramba!*"

"So far we're tied. Here, try again. Elia reached in the bucket for another slimy mullet and tossed it to Luis. He baited his hook, cast his line, and sat beside Elia.

"But every drug has to go through that. What's so special about this one?" she asked. "It had already been approved, right?"

"Preliminary approval." He was silent for a minute. He stared at the water, his fishing pole seemingly forgotten. "A lot of money is spent just to get that approval."

"Are you talking research? Elia turned and look at Luis. Bribery? Are you saying the FDA can be bribed?" She looked astounded.

"No. Not at all. Just what I said before. Research and trials. That costs millions. But once it gets past that, perception and leaks can cause a drug to crash."

"Does that happen a lot?"

"It happens."

"But Luis, if every time a drug is recalled someone gets killed, there'd be a lot more dead bodies. Look at Vioxx. That was a big seller. Did you hear of anyone losing their lives over that recall?"

Luis only shrugged.

"So what is it about this drug that's so important that Pavnor would kill for?" Elia jumped up, her line taut. "I got something."

She kept her eyes on the water. Wait for it, wait for it, wait for it." Elia talked to herself, while she reeled in the first catch of the day. The fish fought her and when it reached the surface, it skimmed the water in an erratic dance. "Yeah! I caught dinner." She pulled the fish over the railing and plopped it on the dock, unhooked it, and dropped it into the bucket. It lay on its belly, its two eyes on one side of its head. "Flounder. We're having flounder for dinner."

Luis sat back and smiled as he watched Elia in her excitement. "I think my gift did the trick." He picked up the fish.

"What are you doing?"

"The fun part is fishing; let someone else have the same fun."

She grimaced. "Okay, throw it back. We'll stop at the market and buy a flounder." She baited her hook for another try. "We'll cook it at Vicente's." Elia got serious. "That's okay, don't you think?"

"I think Vicente would be happy for us to cook a meal in his home."

They sat quietly for a good part of the morning, but neither had another bite.

Luis began gathering up the fishing gear.

"I guess I won the bet." A grin spread across Elia's face.

"I let you."

Frank Hanssen pulled into a driveway and stopped in front of the closed garage door. He fingered the borrowed remote and pushed a button. The door slowly opened. He pulled into an empty spot beside a dark green Hummer. He killed the engine, pushed another button and the garage door closed. He sat there until he heard footsteps approach the door leading into the house. He looked at the Hummer, and whispered "Army-type." He visibly sighed, and waited for the door to open.

Chapter 40

Before heading back to Vicente's, Luis and Elia stopped at Freshfields and shopped at the market for flounder. "I'll be the chef," Luis said as they unloaded their groceries.

He opened a bottle of wine and handed Elia a glass of chilled pinot grigio. "Cooking with wine enhances any meal," he said with a grin. He rubbed his hands together. "Ready for my fish demonstration?"

Elia went up behind him and wrapped her arms around his waist.

"Are you planning on doing the Heimlich on me?"

"No. I'm planning on telling you how much I love you. I know you're trying to cheer me up." She gave him a squeeze. "You know what? It's working."

"You know what yourself? That's not all that's working. Go away."

"I'm gone. But come see me later." She stood on tiptoe and kissed the back of his neck.

"Elia, I'm working here."

"Right." She backed up and sat at the kitchen bar while he worked.

He put the fish on waxed paper and spread a light layer of mayonnaise on it then dredged it in bread crumbs flavored with garlic salt, paprika, and a handful of fresh chopped parsley. He placed the fish carefully on a pan sprayed with olive oil and put it in a hot oven. "Ten minutes."

"I'll do the coleslaw." Elia grated cabbage and mixed up homemade dressing—Nana's recipe. She had learned to cook American dishes from her dad and her dad's mother. She smiled as she thought of her grandmother. She could call Nana at any time and ask her how to prepare a dish and she'd always have the answer. A wave of sadness passed over her. So many loved ones gone. She stole a glance at Luis as he set the table on the deck. "Please, Jesus, keep him safe."

Elia checked her potatoes cooking on the stove, their skins popping open. "My part will be ready." She drained the potatoes and melted butter in the pan, added lemon, salt, and chopped parsley. She sliced a tomato as a side. "Some color for our meal."

They carried their meal to the deck. Luis refilled their wine glasses, and as they ate they watched the birds flying overhead. The egrets flew the same path every evening across the marsh to the nearby copse of trees bordering a pond. There the egrets pulled in their heads and clung to the trees like giant cotton balls. In the morning they would reverse the order and fly back over the marsh to begin a busy day of fishing.

"When do you think she's going to have the funeral?"

"Huh?" Luis looked confused.

"Dot Scharff. When do you think she'll have the funeral?"

Luis shrugged. "I don't know. She's carrying Aaron back to Connecticut now, so I imagine in a day or so." He lifted his wine glass halfway to his mouth, then set it back on the table. "What are you thinking?"

"Connecticut?"

Luis shook his head. "I should have seen this coming. Funeral?"

"No. I was just thinking that maybe we could talk to some people in Stamford about the drug. Some doctors?

"We are on our honeymoon." He enunciated each word clearly and reached across the table and put his hand over one of hers.

"Look, Luis, how can someone get away with putting a drug on the market that harms people—that kills people?"

"It's done all the time. Drugs do kill people. All the time. You give digoxin to someone who doesn't need it—or better yet —to someone who needs it, but give him a double or triple dose, and he can die."

"But—" Elia began.

Luis played with her fingers, then nodded. "But, this is different. There was no black box warning of the deadly side effect that damages the liver. And it was known by the makers. That is criminal."

"So? Do we go to Stamford? To Pavnor?"

"We don't have to go to Connecticut. I'd like to talk to some of Vicente's colleagues here in Charleston. I can't figure out what could get him killed. There must be more.

Chapter 41

"That's it." Luis put the tape on the last box. They had met with the owner the evening before and figured out what was Vicente's and what wasn't and had spent most of the day finishing the packing. "We'll drop these at the post office in Charleston."

Luis loaded the car while Elia did one last walk-through of the house. She nodded. "Yes, I think we're finished."

She got in the car, fastened her seat belt, and dug in her purse for her notebook and cell phone.

"Who're you calling?"

"Riser. To let him know we'll be staying awhile." She held up a finger, listened to a recording, and left a message.

Luis backed out of the driveway. "Before we go home I'd like to talk with Duke Middleton about some property."

"Who? And we're not leaving yet."

"No, we're not leaving." Luis drove slowly down the street and looked at the homes on the street, all painted subdued and varied tones of gray and taupe. "Middleton's the fellow who played a round of golf with Millen, Hanssen, and Aaron the day Aaron died. He's a realtor. I met him briefly and said I'd stop to see him before we left."

"Thinking of buying some property?"

"Not me. I heard Hanssen talking about it, though."

"And Riser?"

"He's got a house here already."

"Of course! How could I have been so stupid? Bonnie had a property owner's decal on her car. They come and go on the island as they please."

"So?" Luis reached the end of the island and turned onto Nancy Kerrison Parkway.

Elia ignored the question. "Don't you suppose that's who Hanssen was going to visit yesterday when he left us?"

"Riser?"

"Bonnie."

"I repeat. So?"

"Don't you think that's odd?"

"They're friends, Elia."

"No. They're more than that."

Luis glanced at his wife. "Meaning?"

"Collaborators."

"Collaborators?" Luis shook his head. "I think you have an overactive imagination."

Riser checked his messages then made a phone call.

Chapter 42

"Have you ever been to New England?" Elia glanced at Luis as they drove across the Maybank Bridge on their way into Charleston.

"We're not going to New England."

"I was just asking if you'd been there."

He shook his head. "I know you. No, I've never been to New England. It's always been important to me as a doctor, though.

"When I was in medical school in Lima my bible was *The New England Journal of Medicine*. I learned a lot from their case studies and discussions; it was like solving a puzzle. I'd get all the clues and have to find the solution—the diagnosis. Studying that journal opened up a new horizon for me to learn more.

"I can honestly say that was the stimulation to further my interest in medicine. The magazine comes out of Boston, and in Perú we referred to Boston as the brains of the United States; if you wanted to learn something in medicine, you went to Boston."

Luis looked over at Elia. "But this time, I think we'll learn as much in Charleston as we would in New England."

It was late afternoon when they parked their car in Charleston. The streets were busy. Pedestrians filled the walks; some meandered, others walked briskly. Elia and Luis held hands and paced themselves with the meanderers. Most of the tourists were dressed in shorts and tennis shoes. But Elia and Luis were on a date. She wore a soft-flowing turquoise sundress and had wrapped a matching light-weight shawl around her shoulders. Strappy sandals completed her outfit. Luis wore camel-colored linen slacks, and a black linen shirt open at the neck.

They peered in windows of restaurants they passed on their walk. On a side street they found an Italian restaurant.

They looked at each other and nodded at the same time.

"*Señora*, Italian it is."

"I've heard there are great Italian restaurants in Connecticut."

Chapter 43

Cramer was shouting at the camera. His shirt was wrinkled, his sleeves were rolled up, and he jabbed his finger at his unseen audience. "Don't do it! You'll be sorry.

"Okay. Let's hear it from Jeremy in our nation's capitol. What's on your mind, Jeremy?"

After the obligatory "boo-yah," the anonymous Jeremy posed a seemingly benign question, but it caused chest pains in more than one investor.

"I'm calling about pharmaceutical companies and—"

"Hold it, hold it, shouted Cramer. We're all friends here. Name it. Name it."

"This is a hypothetical question—"

"Don't do 'em. Gotta be something concrete." Jab, jab at the camera and in Jeremy's face. "But, okay, I'll answer a hypothetical question—a first for me. Go ahead, Jeremy from our nation's capitol."

"Suppose a drug passes almost all the steps required by the FDA to be eligible for the general public. The drug is on the market, still a few steps to go, though. But it is on the market. The company's profits rise with the news, right?"

Cramer interrupted. "In this hypothetical question, that's a rhetorical question, am I correct, Jeremy from our nation's capitol?"

"Well, the company's stock goes up. Here's my question."

"Hypothetical?"

"Yeah. What if there's a side effect?"

"Crash! Down the toilet. Sell, sell, sell." Cramer shouted at the camera.

"But the FDA doesn't know about the side effect."

"Hold it. Hold it right there, Jeremy from our nation's capitol." Cramer was shouting. "Two pieces of advice: Sell and," his voice went up half an octave, "Don't take the medicine."

"OK. That's enough of hypothetical questions. Let's hear it from Annie in Brighten Heights, Pennsylvania."

In Charleston, Kiawah, Stamford, Greenwich, TVs were switched off, and silence reined, roaring louder than Cramer. Then phones rang.

Frank Hanssen was on the train between New York and Stamford and missed the first airing of *Mad Money*. But he heard about it. The first call came from South Carolina.

"Why would someone ask that?"

"He gets all kinds of questions. What makes you think it's about our drug?" Hanssen wiped the sweat off his forehead with a swipe of his hand. "You said it was a hypothetical question."

"There are no hypothetical questions. Find the guy who called in." The line went dead.

The next call came from Connecticut. "Where are you?"

"On the train."

"Coming here?"

"Yes. Home."

"You missed *Mad Money*."

"I heard about it. So?"

"So lots of people are going to wonder if that's what's happening at Pavnor."

"It's not. Listen, I'll talk with you in the morning. I've got some calls to make." Hanssen snapped his phone shut and turned it off. A dead phone can't ring.

Millen set his phone down gently and picked up his Scotch and sipped it slowly. A sly smile graced his tired-looking face. His study overlooked a forested backyard in quiet Greenwich. It was a peaceful scene, but he turned serious and apprehensive about what was to come. What had to come. He paced about his study and stopped to look out the window. The sun's rays filtered through the trees as if a light from heaven was filtering down on the lawn. But Millen wasn't thinking of heaven—just the opposite. It was then he placed the call to Elia's cell phone.

Chapter 44

Luis turned on TV and caught the late–night replay of Mad Money. He was eating a bowl of strawberry ice-cream from room service and half listened to the caller's question about side effects. He perked up when he heard a reference to stock prices. He forgot the ice-cream and listened to the segment. He got to his feet and started pacing, a frown growing. He stood at the patio door and looked out at the ocean, not noticing its glistening under a full moon. A slight breeze carried a whiff of the sea's fish into the room.

"Side effects, stock prices." He said it softly. He stepped onto the patio and started circling the small area. "Side effects. Stock prices." He walked back into the room, and out again. In and out again.

"Luis? What are you doing? Aren't you coming to bed?"

"I think I know what's going on. And Vicente did too." He stood at the open patio door.

"We know that." Elia pushed past him and sat on one of the patio chairs. "Come here." She patted the seat beside her. "Why so excited?"

"It came to me when I was watching *Mad Money*."

"I heard the guy screaming. But what came to you?"

"There was a question about a drug and side effects. The question had to do with stock prices. Of course Pavnor would lose money if the news got out, but who else stands to lose?"

"I knew it!" Elia sounded triumphant. "Stock prices would plummet. Hanssen."

"Hanssen." Luis nodded slowly.

"So Vicente's report would have hurt Hanssen's pocket," Elia said. "But kill over it? I don't think so."

"But, Elia, it's not only his money. He's a stock broker. He makes money by enticing people to put their money in stocks that he considers a good bet."

"I hadn't thought of that. Can we find out what the stock's worth?"

"Sure. As soon as Wall Street opens in the morning."

The two of them sat looking out at the ocean; the only sound the crash of the surf.

"Something's not right." Elia turned to face Luis. "Why would Vicente keep something so serious to himself."

"He wouldn't. He planned on presenting his findings at the meeting."

"No, Luis. People were sick. Dying. Why would he wait for the meeting? Why not speak up earlier? Elia frowned. "What was he thinking?"

They were up early, but had to wait for the stock market to open before they could check prices. Luis had the TV on. The opening bell sounded and the race was on.

"I'm not surprised. The numbers look bad for Pavnor."

"What about other drug companies. Check them out."

"Falling." Luis shook his head. "One question and look at its effects."

"But the stock market has been in the cellar for a long time. What's so different now?

"Just have to look at the history. Pavnor has been holding steady. But since last night, it's down, way down. But so are other drug companies."

"I guess it makes sense. How would people know which company the caller was referring to? I'd sell, if I had a lot of money there."

"No you wouldn't, Elia. You're smarter than that. You wouldn't even put your money into a company that you didn't know everything about."

"Thanks for the vote of confidence, but how could I know something if even the FDA didn't know it? I think that one little tidbit in the guy's question is scaring a lot of people."

Luis stared at Elia. "That's it. You got it."

Chapter 45

Dot Scharff helped her kids load the car and kissed them goodbye. They had finished their college classes before the funeral, but she sent them back to school to clear out their dorm rooms for the summer. She closed the door and leaned against the cool wood and burst into tears. The house was quiet. Too quiet. She shook her head. She smelled fresh coffee and walked slowly into the kitchen. The table was cluttered with the breakfast mess.

"Life goes on." She was almost startled to hear her voice in the quiet house. She poured coffee, reached for an apron. Her kids called it her kangaroo apron because of the large front pocket. She loaded the dishwasher and worked slowly. Next, she went upstairs and stripped beds and gathered dirty towels. She dropped the laundry down the clothes chute. The cleaning she would leave for her housekeeper.

On her way downstairs, she grabbed a sweater and slipped it on over her apron. "Who cares," she said to the empty house.

She put a load of sheets in the washer, poured another cup of coffee and turned to Aaron's study. She stood looking into it from the middle of the hall.

"What is it, Aaron? What is it that killed you?"

She squared her shoulders, took a deep breath, and walked into the study. She smiled when she took in the chaos on her husband's desk. Books, papers, and sticky notes were scattered over his desk. His laptop was closed and sitting on top of the clutter, just where she put it when she brought it home from Kiawah. She shook her head. "Ah, Aaron. I'll miss you."

The book shelves were full, so packed that some books were in piles on the floor. She sat behind his desk and turned the computer on. She scrolled through the directory looking for something—she didn't know what. Slowly she read each entry. She had to go only to the Cs when she stopped. Cyptolis. She opened the file. "What?" She stared at a blank screen.

She turned to the desk and slowly started putting papers in neat piles. She looked closely at each paper she picked up. Underneath a stack of papers she found his flash drive. She slipped it into her apron pocket. She grabbed a tissue and wiped off the dust as she found clear spaces. She pushed back in the chair and picked up a tall stack of papers, placed them in her lap, and went through them.

She stopped suddenly when she reached the middle of the stack. She put her hand to her chest. A manila folder with Cyptolis—Problems was scribbled across the top. Thick black lines were scratched under the word problems. She opened the folder to find several typed sheets of paper and a stack of newspaper clippings.

Before she could read, a loud noise caught her attention. She ran into the laundry room, folder in hand, to see the washer dancing across the floor. She stuffed the folder into her kangaroo pocket and rearranged the wet sheets to balance the washer. Then she heard the doorbell. "What now?" She looked down at her apron, patted her hair and whispered, "So what," and went to the door.

"Dot." Lorraine Fegan was the CFO at Pavnor and looked the part. Her premature gray hair, the color of polished pewter, was set off by her black sheath and large silver jewelry.

She bent to hug Dot and stepped back to look at her. "I knew the children left for school today, so I thought you might need some company."

"I'm fine. I really am."

"Well you don't look fine."

"Of course I don't look fine. I'm wearing an old bathrobe, a dirty apron and my hair is curling in four different directions." She had her hands on her hips. "I really appreciate the compliment." She smiled, her first genuine smile in days.

Lorraine laughed and put her arms around Dot. "I love your spirit." Then she got serious. "Have you been out since Aaron died?"

"No."

"But you don't practice Shiva, do you?"

"Oh please. We'd really be in a pickle. No, we're reformed. None of that eight-day mourning period for me."

She slowly brought her hand to her mouth as if to silence herself. Her eyes filled with tears. "Who am I kidding? I'm mourning and will for a long time to come. I don't need Shiva to tell me how I should feel."

Lorraine nodded. "You're coming out with me. We'll drive up the coast and have a nice leisurely lunch. Go get ready."

Dot hesitated and looked around the house. "I have a mess to clean up."

"No you don't. Let your housekeeper do it. You get dressed, and I'll just sit right here and wait for you. I will not take no for an answer." She looked imperialistic and pointed up the stairs. "Go!"

Dot smiled. "OK, boss. I'll get ready." She pointed toward the living room. Go on in and make yourself comfortable." She turned to leave and then said, "Lorraine, we're right here in Greenwich; let's just go to the Avenue. There are so many nice places to eat there."

She hesitated at the foot of the stairs. "To be honest, Lorraine, you drive like you're in a race sometimes, and I just can't do that." Her voice shook.

"Of course. The Avenue is fine. I shouldn't have been so thoughtless what with Aaron's..." She let her sentence die. "And I promise I'll drive safely."

"I'm thoughtless too. I should have asked how you feel after your spill."

Lorraine rubbed her elbow and flexed her arm. "I was lucky all I broke was my elbow, but it's been months since my accident and it still bothers me."

"Don't say I never warned you. I won't let my kids..." She waved a hand in dismissal. "Oh never mind." She smiled again— her second smile.

Lorraine pointed up the stairs. "Enough about me. You go."

"It won't take me long." She hurried up the stairs. When Lorraine heard the shower running, she stole into the study and looked around. She shook her head when she saw the mess on the desk. But the laptop was what she was interested in. She was about to turn it on when she heard a whooshing noise coming from the kitchen area. She froze and listened. Then she walked silently into the kitchen and looked around. She heard it again. It was coming from the adjacent laundry room. She peeked around the open door just as some clothes shot down the laundry chute. Lorraine shook her head. "You're a crazy lady," she said to herself. Before she left the room she spied a window above a table covered with folded towels and clothes. She reached over the table, unlocked the window and made sure it opened easily.

Something struck Lorraine as odd. She cocked her head. It was too quiet. How long had it been since she heard the shower running upstairs?

Lorraine hurried from the laundry room and made her way to the living room. She pulled out her cell phone and sent a quick text message just as a hastily showered and dressed Dot Scharff descended the steps.

"I'll put my makeup on in the car."

Lorraine took a deep breath and didn't speak as they left the house.

"Maybe this is what I need," Dot said as she slid into Lorraine's silver BMW.

"I know it is."

Chapter 46

"A three-hour lunch. I feel like an executive."

"We don't usually window shop after our so-called executive lunches, but you needed some diversion, Dot. It's been a bad week." She patted her arm. "I'm so very sorry."

"I know you are. I appreciate your trying to cheer me up. But now I have to face life—and get on with it." She paused as if reflecting.

"What is it?"

"Aaron asked me to go along with him to Bermuda." She shook her head. "I should have gone."

Lorraine gave Dot's shoulder a reassuring squeeze. "We were busy most of the time while there, so don't have any regrets."

Dot nodded. She said good-bye to Lorraine in the driveway of her home and gave a small wave before she unlocked her front door. When she stepped inside she frowned and stood still, then turned slowly to her husband's study. She gasped and her hand flew to her mouth. His desk top was completely empty. She quickly scanned the room, then backed up to the front door and quietly let herself out of the house. Lorraine's car was nowhere in sight. She dug in her purse for her cell phone and called 911.

Lorraine Fegan had checked the time before she dropped Dot at her house. As she pulled away, she made a phone call. She liked what she heard. She snapped shut her phone and inhaled deeply. She would examine everything carefully and decide what to do later.

She had a lot at stake. Cyptolis had to succeed. Pavnor could not afford to lose favor in the industry—and especially on Wall Street. But most important to Lorraine Fegan was Lorraine Fegan. She had been trying to crash through the glass ceiling for years, and now that she could almost see daylight, she was not going to let anything—or anyone—get in her way. Harry is a patsy, she thought to herself. If he only knew half of what is going on with his precious pharmaceutical company.

Lorraine squinted her eyes when she said aloud, "Harry, it just might be time to enlighten you." She put on her blinker, got in the right lane, and exited off the Merritt Parkway to Stamford.

Chapter 47

Dot sat on the sofa in the living room while the two uniformed policemen went through her house opening closets and checking the attic and basement. It didn't take them long to finish up. This was routine for them. There have been burglaries in nearby neighborhoods, they told her.

"But don't worry. Robbers aren't usually armed. They're just looking for valuables; not people. But funny they didn't touch your TV or jewelry. Or the computer up in your son's room. Just your laptop."

As soon as they left, Dot locked the door and sat on the stairs and put her head in her hands and sobbed. She stood and walked into the study and frowned as she looked at the cleared desk. Her heart skipped a beat and she ran to the laundry room. She dug through the pile of dirty clothes under the chute until she found what she was looking for. She pulled her apron out from beneath wet towels and stuck her hand in the pocket and grabbed the folder. She turned the pocket inside out and found the flash drive. It lay in her open hand while she stared at it, her frown returning and then she ran upstairs to her son's room and turned on his computer.

Chapter 48

"Dr, Echevarria? This is Dot Scharff. Elia gave me this number."

"She's in the shower, but she can call you back. How are you, Dot?"

"Not good. Someone broke into my house."

"Oh, no! Are you all right?"

"I'm fine. I wasn't home."

"What did they take?"

Elia walked into the room almost buried in a plush Sanctuary Hotel robe. "Dot Scharff," Luis mouthed. "Dot, Elia's here." He handed the phone to Elia. "Someone broke into her house," Luis whispered.

"Dot, it's Elia. What happened? You had a break-in?"

"Yes, and they stole Aaron's computer and all his papers."

"Oh, Dot, I'm so sorry. Are you all right?"

"Shook up."

"Just his computer?"

"And papers."

"Do you know what was on the computer?

"I didn't at the time. I looked on his computer earlier. I was hoping to see something about the drug." She told Elia about seeing the empty Cyptolis file on the computer and about the flash drive and papers she found.

"They didn't take the flash drive or those papers?"

"They were in the dirty clothes pile."

"Excuse me?"

Dot explained how she had thrown her apron down the clothes chute with the papers and flash drive in the pocket. "Who would look there?" She gave a half-hearted laugh that seemed to get swallowed up.

"I'm so sorry to bother you." Her laugh was gone. "This is scary. I read Aaron's report, and there was more to the problem with the drug than anyone realized. I wonder if your young doctor friend in Bermuda even knew."

"What do you mean?"

"Aaron did a lot of research after Bermuda. He wrote his report while we were on Kiawah."

"What does it say?"

Dot was silent.

Elia spoke up. "Dot? What's the matter?"

"Elia, I don't think I should talk about this over the phone." She hesitated. "But there is one thing."

Elia listened then said, "We're coming. We'll be there tomorrow." Elia looked at Luis. She took a deep breath and waited for him to say something. He shook his head.

"Uh, Dot, I think we're coming. I'll call you later."

"We'll know more when we see her." She had ended the call and tried to stare her husband down. His dark eyes held hers.

Chapter 49

"I think it's related." She put her cell phone in her pocket. "So far as she can tell, all they took were some papers and Aaron's laptop."

"That's what people steal."

"Not papers. They didn't take the TV, jewelry, her son's computer, anything else. Just Aaron's computer—and his papers." Her voice went up a few notes with each word.

Luis sighed. "Why do you think it's related?" He opened a drawer and pulled out his gym shorts and rifled around until he found a pair of socks.

"Luis—stop." She patted the bed. "Please. Come here. Dot must think there's a connection; she called me."

Luis took a deep breath. "Why does she think that?"

"They took his papers."

"You said that." He seemed to ponder this. "What thief steals papers?"

"Didn't I just say that?" She turned on the edge of the bed and curled her feet under her robe. "But not all his papers." Elia repeated what Dot said about the papers and the flash drive down the clothes chute.

"What was on the flash drive?"

"She doesn't know; the computer's gone, remember?"

"The papers?"

"She read them. He started researching after he got home from Bermuda. He had a lot of notes. And newspaper clippings. I guess he started thinking." Elia shrugged. "A little late."

Luis and Elia looked at each other with puzzled looks on their faces. "Honey, I read Vicente's notes. There was a problem; he was planning on reporting it at the meeting." He stopped and looked puzzled. "Strange."

"Strange?"

"I had thought Vicente knew about the stock angle, but his notes don't mention that at all." He was silent.

"So maybe that's not in the equation?" Elia asked.

Luis looked confused. "He was going to report a problem."

"But he didn't, and no one else did either." Elia jumped up from the bed. "No one read his paper. That makes me so mad!"

Luis grabbed her hands and pulled her toward him. "I won't keep quiet. I promise."

She pulled her hands away. "Was he going to say anything about outsourcing the production to China?"

"China? No way." He shook his head. "Where does this come from?"

"Aaron. It was in his notes that Dot found."

Luis was still. "I'd like to see his notes. Better yet, I'd like to see what's on his thumb drive."

"Uh, good. I was hoping you'd say that." She stole a look at him.

"Meaning?"

"What I mean, we should go to Connecticut and see Dot." Before Luis could say anything, she added, "You could get the flash drive."

Now it was Luis's turn to jump up. He began pacing around the room, a determined look on his face. Elia followed him with her eyes. He stopped in front of her, took her hands, and pulled her to her feet. "Give me your phone."

She cocked her head and looked confused but dug it out of her pocket and handed it him. He scrolled until he found Dot's recent call and pressed the recall button.

"Who're you calling?"

"Dot," he then held up a hand and motioned her to wait. He shook his head. "No answer."

Again Luis held up his hand. "Voice Mail." Then, "Dot, this is Luis. When you get this message, if you can get to a computer, send me the contents of the flash drive as an attachment. We'll call after we read Aaron's report. Here's my e-mail address." He gave her the address and ended the call.

"So, we go to Connecticut."

"No."

Elia stiffened. "No?"

He ran his hands up her arms to her shoulders and let them rest there, his thumbs playing over her collar bone. "No, Honey." He said it softly and waited for an outburst. He put a finger under her chin to raise her head so he could look into her eyes. "No."

"Why not?" She kept eye contact. "Well, why not?" She lowered the pitch of her voice and squinted at him.

Luis almost laughed. She looked so determined.

"Luis. Why not?"

"Because in the ten days we've been married you almost drowned, we were chased by a maniac on a motor scooter, we were spied on while making out nude in a swimming pool, and you almost roasted to death at the spa."

"And you put all that on me?"

"I put it on me."

"I can take care of myself. That doesn't make sense."

"What makes sense is I love you. Stay safe. Please stay safe."

Chapter 50

Elia and Luis took one more run over to Vicente's house to assure themselves that they had taken care of everything. They locked the door and drove the short distance to Kiawah Island Real Estate Company. The expansive lobby was a salesman's first pitch. While the receptionist called Duke Middleton's office, they spent the short wait time looking at wall-sized colored photos of the flora and fauna that flourished throughout Kiawah. They turned when Duke Middleton came quickly out of his office with outstretched hand.

"Luis!" He said heartily. "Come in. And this must be Elia." He took her hand in both of his. "I am so happy to meet you, but so sorry about Dr. Pereda." He ushered them into his corner office. "Coffee?" He held up his cup. "It's fresh."

"I'll have a cup—black," Elia said.

"Luis?"

"I'll come with you, Duke. I doctor mine with a lot of milk and sugar."

When they left, Elia spent the time studying the office. She could see that Duke valued his family; pictures of what she assumed were of his wife and two children must have been taken years earlier, because other photos showed older children and youngsters—probably grandchildren. An award touting a hole-in-one on one of Kiawah's golf courses was on display, as well as a rock that served as a name plate, saying simply: Duke.

"Here you go." Duke and Luis sauntered in carrying steaming cups of coffee. "How long will you be on Kiawah?"

"We're not quite sure" Elia said, giving Luis a look that said she wasn't finished with the subject.

Duke leaned back in his chair. "Did Luis tell you Vicente and I played a round of golf not too long ago?" A smile spread across his face. He shook his head. "He wasn't a golfer."

Elia sat up straighter at this revelation. She set her coffee on the desk and started to dig in her purse. "Duke, look at this key. I think it's a locker key from somewhere here, since we found it at Vicente's. And it looks like one from the lockers at the spa where I had my massage. I assume it's from a men's locker room." She handed over the key. "Do you think he could have used a locker when he golfed with you?"

Duke took the key. "Sure. We played at Cassique. Let's go and see if this is one of their keys."

Ten minutes later Luis inserted the key into a locker. As he opened the door, he raised his eyebrows as if to say, "Here goes." He let out a soft whistle. A stack of papers was rolled up and stuffed inside. Without looking at them he left the locker room and met Duke and Elia in the pro shop. He tapped one hand with the roll of papers.

"Must be important to have them locked away like that," Duke said.

"I don't know if they're important, but his parents would probably like to have them," Luis said casually. He took a deep breath and let it out slowly. When they returned to the real estate office, Luis turned down an invitation for a second cup of freshly brewed coffee, thanked Middleton and made a hasty retreat.

They drove down Kiawah Island Parkway with Elia at the wheel. Luis devoured the papers.

Chapter 51

Late that afternoon, Lorraine Fegan was in her home office with a box of papers and a laptop sitting on her desk. She sat in her black leather desk chair with a small red pillow at her back. She was still wearing her black outfit; a Georgia Bulldog fan would have been happy with the color scheme. She hated football.

She poured herself a glass of Riesling and absent-mindedly rubbed her right elbow and flexed her arm as she looked at the box on her desk. She had started going through the papers as soon as she "found" them on her back patio when she arrived home. The laptop had been at the bottom of the box.

She picked up every sheet of paper in the box and quickly scanned each one looking for references to not only Cyptolis, but especially Pavnor. Aaron was involved in marketing, and most of his notes involved his ideas for getting Pavnor before the public. Scribbled in large letters across the top of a paper and underlined half a dozen times was the word outsourcing. In his distinctive backward lettering so like the lefty that he was he had written: China.

She looked at her phone and nibbled on her lower lip. "Crap. Bite the damn bullet." She picked up the phone and made a call. "Can you come over here? There's a problem." She listened a moment before she continued. "No." Her voice went up and octave. "It can't wait until tomorrow. And you won't want to talk about this at the office."

She listened and took a deep breath. "No." She tried to sound calmer, more understanding. "You don't want me dragging this into your house; you have enough going on over there." She held the phone tightly in her hand. "I'll wait for you." She cut the call before she got an answer.

Harry Millen laid the phone down as gently as he would a newborn babe. He stared out his study window hoping some of the tranquility outside would seep inside. He had left the office early to try to think. So much happening. He turned from the window and left his study and walked slowly up the stairs and entered his wife's room.

"Would you step outside for a moment, please?" His wife's private duty nurse nodded and quietly left the room.

Harry took his wife's thin hand, the skin as transparent as tissue paper. "Jeannie?"

She turned her head to look at him, her eyes glassy from morphine.

"I'm here." She gazed at him. "What is it, Harry?" Her voice was soft, too soft, but filled him with warmth.

He shook his head. "Work."

"Problem?"

"I'm afraid so." He took a deep breath. He looked away from his wife. "Everything's wrong."

"Harry, you've been spending too much time here with me." When he looked as though he would protest, she squeezed his hand and slowly shook her head. "No. And when you're not home, you're thinking about me."

He put his face to her hand and gently kissed the frail fingers.

She smiled. "You have a job to do—a responsibility to people like me. We have a plan. Take care of it. I'll be here when you get home." She caressed his face. "I promise."

He kissed her, reached into her bedside drawer for her lip balm, gently applied it to her dry lips, and kissed her again.

He smiled for the first time since he entered the room. "How do you do that?"

"Do what?"

"Put me on the straight and narrow?"

"A gift." She winked at him. "Now go and take care of business." She reached for him. "Harry?"

"Hmm?" He took her hand, which was so dry.

"Straight and narrow?" She closed her eyes. "We have to see this through." She opened her eyes and bore into him with her tired eyes. "You have to."

"I will." A shadow crossed his face. "I'm so sorry about your treatment. And so angry. I promise you, this will not happen again."

"No anger, Harry, please. Nothing gets done when you're angry. We talked about this. Go on now. Take care of your responsibilities. Take care of Pavnor."

He didn't hurry to his car. He walked like a man in a trance, then drove slowly down his winding driveway, the gently sloping stone wall his guide.

Chapter 52

Lorraine Fegan's fingers flew through the papers in the cardboard box once, twice, a third time. She absent-mindedly reached for a pencil from a cupful on her desk. She looked at the pencil, then at the cup with her college's insignia in gold on the maroon background. She stiffened. She learned a lot in college, but she sure as hell didn't learn this business. She gripped the pencil and thrust it back in the cup. She turned her attention to the box.

Before Millen arrived, she had calmed enough to peruse each sheet of paper. She still hadn't found what she was afraid she would. She had finished off a half bottle of Riesling by the time Millen pulled into her driveway. She stood at her window and watched him get out of his car.

He's aged, she thought. She had worked with him since he had taken over the reins of Pavnor. She considered him a colleague more than friend, but she wasn't heartless. She knew what he was going through with his wife. Jeannie was in the final stages of cancer that had racked her body for seven years.

"Damn you, Jeannie. If Harry had been paying attention to the company, this wouldn't have happened." As soon as she said this, she almost felt ashamed. But not quite.

She walked to the door and opened it before Harry knocked. "How's Jeannie?"

He shook his head. "The same." He looked past her to her study. "What's the emergency?"

"Harry, let me fix you a drink."

"I just had one. Let's get to work."

She pursed her lips disgustedly and led him to her study. He stood in the doorway and surveyed the mess.

"Please sit." She pointed to a chair. "I have a story to tell you."

He almost groaned. "Cyptolis?"

"What do you know?" She almost said, "What do you think you know?"

"I know this drug had been on the market under another name thirty years ago. I know it causes liver problems—the same problems it caused the first go round."

"I didn't know you knew even that.

"What do you mean 'even that'"?

She poured herself another glass of wine. Then she poured one for Millen. "Well, there's more."

Chapter 53

When Dot ended the call with Elia, she set her cell phone on her son's bed. She took the flash drive out of the computer and went back downstairs. Later, she wouldn't be able to hear her phone ringing as it lay in the upstairs bedroom.

She didn't miss the phone until early the next morning when she retraced her steps and found it upstairs. It was then she listened to Luis's message.

"Of course. Why didn't I think of that?" In two minutes she had her son's computer up and running and the Cyptolis file attached to an e-mail to Luis. Then she erased the file from the computer and shut it down. The flash drive was safely back in her pocket.

By the time Elia pulled in front of The Sanctuary and handed the keys to the valet, Luis had finished reading Vicente's papers. He hurried to the room, not speaking. He turned on his computer and immediately saw he had an e-mail attachment from Dot Scharff. He opened it and read Aaron's report. He took a breath and let it out slowly. "If you can stay out of trouble, how would you like to go to Connecticut?"

"What changed your mind?"

"Vicente. Scharff. China."

Chapter 54

Millen had spent a restless night after his talk with Lorraine. When his phone rang first thing in the morning he groaned.

"Harry, Luis Echevarria."

Millen sat up and swung his legs over the side of the bed. He answered in a low voice; Jeannie was sleeping in the adjoining room, her night nurse watching over her.

"We'll be in Greenwich later on today; do you think we can stop at your office?"

"Greenwich?" He frowned.

"We're coming up to see Dot Scharff. Her house was broken into yesterday."

"No! How is she?" He felt like saying, "Tell me something I don't know."

"She's okay, but Aaron's papers and laptop were taken."

"What else?"

"Nothing else, that she can see right now."

"That's strange."

"Right. That's why we want to see you. We think we know what was on the laptop."

"How could you?"

"Aaron's flash drive wasn't taken."

Millen wiped the sweat off his face. "And?"

"And Dot e-mailed the contents."

"I take it this has to do with Pavnor."

"It looks that way." Luis switched the phone to his left hand and picked up a pen. "What's a good time to run up to Stamford?"

"I don't have my schedule in front of me; call when you get up here." He ended the call and stared at the phone.

He peeked in at his sleeping wife and nodded to the nurse. After a quick shower, he dressed and went quietly downstairs.

"Life was better when I was in control," he mumbled to himself as he made the coffee. He felt like throwing the pot across the room, but he looked toward the ceiling and thought of his sleeping wife.

Jeannie's right, he thought. We have to see this through. See it through for her. He drank a cup of coffee and had another thought. He muttered aloud, "I may be losing control, but maybe it's better this way."

Chapter 55

"Elia, promise me you won't play cop." They had flown into White Plains and Luis was behind the wheel of a rental car.

"I don't play cop." There was an emphasis on "play."

"I mean it. No more. You get into too much trouble."

"I get into trouble?" She shifted in her seat to glare at him. "Plural pronoun, please."

Luis didn't answer. He kept his eyes on the road. "Check the Garmin. What exit do we get off?"

Elia glanced at their GPS. "Port Chester."

Luis nodded. His lips were pressed tight.

"I repeat. I get into trouble?"

Luis took an obvious deep breath. "Yes, you." He glanced at her and frowned. "Ever since Vicente died, you've—okay—we've had trouble." He recited the litany. "That's trouble."

"Do I have to hear this again? You keep going over every little mishap." She again turned in her seat to stare at him. "And you were involved in some of the mishaps."

"Mishaps?" He began in an accusatory tone, but ended on a conciliatory one. "How about this: Let's be careful."

Elia noticed the change of tone, and willed herself to calm down. She was raised by a Peruvian mother and knew how protective Peruvians could be. She couldn't understand it but came to accept it. Now married to a Peruvian, she asked herself if she had expected anything different. She had lived independently since her parents died; now she had to learn new ways. But, she thought, they both had to. Her musings were interrupted by the Garmin giving verbal directions to their exit. Once they were off the highway, Elia spoke up.

"Then what are we doing here if we're not going to play cop?"

"Uh huh! You admit it." Luis took his eyes off the road for a second and grinned at his wife. "We're here because I want to see what's going on with Vicente's drug."

"Fair enough. Let's talk. What do we know?"

"What I got from Vicente's paper. Six points. For starters, number one, Cyptolis causes liver damage." As Luis spoke, Elia ticked off points with her fingers. "Two, this drug has almost the same components of a drug that was prescribed widely in the seventies for countless numbers of paraplegic Vietnam veterans to treat spasticity. Three, the same side effects that they experienced then are being experienced today. Four, a good number of the patients today receiving the drug are Iraq War veterans."

"A connection."

"I don't think there's a conspiracy against veterans, if that's what you mean."

Elia shrugged. "So what is the connection?"

"There are a lot of soldiers coming home paralyzed." Luis was quiet for a moment. "A lot less than Vietnam. This war causes more head injuries and amputated limbs than paralysis, but we still have a lot of soldiers coming home paralyzed."

"Sounds like a conspiracy to me."

"Huh uh. The general public has been getting the drug, but the percentage of paraplegics in the service versus the general population is naturally much greater.

"But there's another problem that Vicente touched on that didn't show up during the Vietnam era of the drug."

Elia turned in her seat. "You hadn't mentioned another problem."

"I found it buried in his report. He couldn't figure it out and said he was going to investigate further."

He drove in silence.

"Well? I'm on number four. Are you going to share the fifth point?"

"Oh, sorry. Just thinking about it."

"Luis, what is it?"

"Number five, there seems to be a lot of bleeding."

"Bleeding? Where?"

"The liver. The liver damage associated with Cyptolis and the earlier drug mimics hepatitis, but what is showing up is hemorrhaging."

"The liver is hemorrhaging?"

"Yes, and other organs as well."

"Didn't anyone pick this up?" Elia sounded confused.

They were interrupted by the GPS giving directions to Greenwich. Luis made a couple of turns. "Vicente did."

Both were quiet. The only sound was the voice from the Garmin giving street-by-street directions to their destination.

Luis never got to number six.

Chapter 56

Dot Scharff met them at the door. "I'm so sorry to drag you up here." She looked tired. Her skin had a sallow cast to it, and her naturally curly hair was listless.

Elia put her arms around her and gave her a warm hug. "You didn't drag us. We wanted to come."

Luis bent down and kissed her cheek. "Let's see what's going on."

She led them into the kitchen. "Coffee first." She put some sweet rolls on the kitchen table and poured steaming coffee. "Please eat. There's so much food here. It's still coming in." Her voice cracked at the last words.

"Tell me about your children. They're both in college?" Elia sipped her coffee and nibbled on a roll. She nodded her head and looked interested while Dot talked about her kids.

Luis looked over at his wife and marveled at how easily she put Dot at ease. He finished his coffee and wanted to get at the business at hand. "Dot, tell us what happened."

Dot began the story. "Lorraine Fegan—so thoughtful of her to come over." She refilled the coffee cups and held the pot in hands, as if she needed its warmth. "She's been CFO at Pavnor for a couple of years, but has been with the company for a lot longer, for years.

"What about her?"

"Oh, she came over to take me out to lunch. That's when it happened."

"When it happened. The break-in." Luis said.

She nodded. "Come with me." She pushed back her chair and ran a hand through her hair. She shook her head. "I know I look terrible."

"You look fine." Elia stood and put her arm around Dot's shoulders. "Where to?"

"Aaron's study."

They followed her and waited beside her as she stood for a moment in the doorway of the study. She took a breath and let it out in a sigh.

"I'll miss seeing him sitting at his desk." She walked over and put her hand on the back of the desk chair. "I could see him whenever I walked through the hall."

"He worked at home a lot?" Luis asked.

"Not a whole lot. But he was in here every free minute since he returned from Bermuda." She moved her hand back and forth across the back of the chair in a soft caress.

Luis heard the wistfulness in her voice. He gave her a moment before he interrupted her thoughts. "Catching up? I know that's what I have to do when I've been away."

"No. He was upset about what happened in Bermuda. The doctor dying, of course. But then they buried his report."

"Who buried it?"

"I'm not sure." She pointed to some chairs. "Please." She frowned and looked confused. "I don't know." She looked from Luis to Elia. "Wouldn't you think it would have to be someone from Pavnor?"

"Most likely, but this wasn't Pavnor's meeting. It was a general scientific meeting." Luis moved some books off the chairs and he and Elia sat down. "It could have been the organizers of the meeting."

"You don't believe that, Luis. You know you don't. Why even say it?"

"Devil's advocate. But we'll try to find out."

"We'll be stopping at Pavnor while we're here, won't we Luis? So maybe someone can tell us."

Luis nodded. "I'd like to know." He turned his attention to the study. "His laptop and papers taken. Anything else?"

"Not a thing. That's why I think… No, that's why I know it has to do with Aaron's research on that Bermuda drug."

Chapter 57

The receptionist sat behind an L-shaped desk in the center of the small lobby. The walls were painted a hunter green but peach-colored valances on the windows brightened the room. Plants and lamps on tables lent warmth to the lobby. She called Millen's secretary, then directed them to the fourth floor. Millen waited for them at the elevator.

"Nice to see you again. I was surprised you had traveled this far. This is your honeymoon, isn't it?"

"Yes, but what a lovely part of the country for a honeymoon," Elia said.

"If you have time, drive along the coast. Quaint towns, great seafood, magnificent scenery."

"We plan to," Luis said, shaking Millen's hand. "One of these days. But, unfortunately, not this trip."

"Too bad." Millen ushered them down the hall to his office. "So the honeymoon's over?"

Luis chuckled. "I hope not."

"We're going back to Kiawah," Elia said.

"Well at least get over to the Avenue."

"The Avenue?"

"Greenwich's shopping area. Great place to people watch. And fabulous restaurants."

"We can do that at least. After we leave here we'll check it out." Luis looked at Elia and saw her nod in agreement.

"I'm curious. What brought you up here, if you're still vacationing?"

"Dot Scharff."

"Dot. Yes. When you called I was surprised. I wasn't aware that you knew her."

Elia looked confused. "We were there when she learned her husband had been killed, remember?"

Millen shook his head as if to clear it. "Terrible night." He shook his head again. "So you got to know her that night?"

"Actually, no. But we know her now."

"I just wondered." He paused a beat. "That's how you knew she was robbed."

"That's why we're here," Luis said. To see what was stolen."

"Well I could have told you that on the phone. Whoever it was didn't get much. I understand they only got to the study and then left. Probably scared off by something." Millen fidgeted as he spoke. He didn't make eye contact and instead shuffled papers on his desk.

"Harry," Luis got down to business. "There's something that's bothering me."

Millen raised his eyebrows. "Bothering you?"

"About Vicente's paper. At the meeting in Bermuda."

Millen stopped his fidgeting. "Ah, yes. Bermuda. I couldn't make that meeting; I sent some other people."

"His paper should have been presented," Luis said.

Millen didn't respond to Luis's statement, so Elia spoke. "Vicente was dead. Couldn't someone have read his paper?" She said it quietly.

"I understand how you feel, Elia."

"Was it something in the paper that you didn't want anyone to know about?"

"I told you I wasn't there. Someone else pulled that plug."

"You're the boss. The buck stops with you."

"You have no idea. If I had been there, that paper would have been presented."

"I don't know, Harry; I don't think it would have put Pavnor in a good light." Luis said.

"You're right. You don't know. I trust my subordinates to do the right thing." As he spoke, he moved to the door and stood with his hand on the doorknob.

"Well, Harry," Elia said with a trace of a syrupy southern accent, "maybe you should learn not to be so trusting."

She and Luis stayed put.

Millen looked from one to the other. "Is there something else?"

"No. We got what we came for." Luis said.

Millen returned to his desk and picked up the phone. "Madison, would you escort my guests out?"

"Oh, one more thing," Luis said. He turned back to Harry. "Are you planning to release Vicente's report now?"

"I'll have to review it."

"Good idea. Review it. And then look into why there is so much hemorrhaging." He turned to the door and took Elia's hand. "And check to see where Cyptolis is produced." They followed Madison out of the office.

Millen's face lost its color. He closed the door and dropped into his chair. "Damn you, Fegan. This could have been over." He picked up the phone and punched in her number.

He put his throbbing head in his hands. He dug in his pocket for his bottle of nitroglycerine and gave himself a short squirt of the red liquid. He sat still for fifteen minutes, not wanting to stand and fall on his face with the falling blood pressure from the medication. When he felt better, he left his office.

Chapter 58

"So what do we know now?" Elia and Luis strolled the Avenue in Greenwich and were now walking on neighboring streets.

"I think we know nothing." He shrugged.

"China. All Aaron said in his report was that he discovered that some drugs were being produced in China, and Cyptolis was one of them.

"That's not illegal is it? The China part?"

"No. It's not illegal."

"Then what's the problem with China?

"It's not smart." He paused. "Economical, but smart?"

"Luis, everything's made in China. Why not drugs? They're expensive. Economics count."

"*Si, pero...* "

Elia glanced at him. "You're thinking in Spanish, aren't you? I know something's percolating when you do that."

He shook his head. "I don't know. You're right. China produces a lot of everything, including drugs. He took a deep breath and blew it out forcefully. "This trip was fruitless."

"No it wasn't, Luis. We saw Dot." Elia waited for a rebuttal, but Luis had stopped and turned and was looking behind him toward the Avenue.

"What are you doing?"

"Did you hear that?"

Elia looked around. "What am I supposed to hear?"

Luis stood completely still. As he looked down the street, he saw the source of the noise. He held tight to Elia's hand.

"What?" Her voice went up a half octave. "You're scaring me."

"There's a guy on a motorcycle. Every time we turn down another street he's there."

Elia looked around. "Coincidence?"

"I hope." They walked quickly to their car, Luis glancing around like a member of Obama's Secret Service detail. "This was a crazy idea. I'll be glad to get back home."

"Home home? Or are we going to finish our honeymoon?"

Luis glanced down at his wife as he opened the car door. "Honey, we're never going to finish our honeymoon." He cocked his head as if in thought, then closed her door.

When he got behind the wheel, he turned to look at her. "Look, we've had a crazy couple of weeks. Let's forget about all of this for a few days and do some traveling while we're here."

"But—"

"No." He held up a hand. "Wait. Let me finish." He laid a hand on her arm. "A few days. A few days of no motorcycles chasing us, a few days of not looking over our shoulders." He moved his hand to her cheek and stroked it gently. "A few days." He said it softly and waited for her to speak.

She nodded. "What do you have in mind?"

"*Muchas cosas!* We can go into New York and see a play. We can take Millen's suggestion and drive up the coast. We can go all the way to Cape Cod. On the way we could stop in Newport. We could drive up to Boston." He looked at her with a questioning look on his face, his fingers twirling around in her hair.

She nodded again. "Sounds nice. Where shall we start?"

"Let's start in New York."

"Honey, I think the locals call it the City."

He started the car and pulled out of his parking place, glancing in the rearview mirror for company. Not seeing anyone, he winked at her. "The City. We'll go into the City."

He drove a couple of blocks passing St. Mary's Catholic Church and turned down a side street. "I know it's here somewhere."

"What?"

"The train station."

"We're going right now?"

"It's only a forty-minute train ride, I heard. Why not?" He drove another block and spotted the tracks. "At least let's check the schedule."

But he didn't pull into the train parking lot. Instead he drove past, turned another corner, then another, and yet another.

"Luis? What is it?"

"Nothing. I just want to make sure that goon on the cycle doesn't know what we're doing." He made a few more maneuvers then turned into the parking spot. "New York, here we come."

When they reached the platform several people were standing around. Luis checked the schedule, then his watch. He looked around and saw a machine, tapped the screen and waited for two tickets to spit out. Both he and Elia kept watching the others and looking over the railing at the parking lot below. When the train came around the bend and headed for the stop, Luis took one more fast look at the parking lot, and stiffened. He pulled Elia into an alcove and held her close until the train pulled out of the station.

"What? What, Luis?" Elia tried to peer over his shoulder. Did you see someone?"

"Someone thinks we're on that train."

"How do you know that?"

Without answering, Luis motioned her forward. They stood behind a pillar and looked down at their car.

The "goon" on the motorcycle had pulled beside their car.

"Oh my god!" Luis pulled his wife out of sight as soon as the words burst forth from her mouth.

Then he repeated her words, but softly, almost in a whisper.

An hour later, they had stopped at their hotel, packed, checked out, and were back on the road. This time they drove through Port Chester, New York, a village adjacent to Greenwich. The village was bustling with car and foot traffic. Restaurants, bakeries, hardware stores, were just a few of the businesses lining the main street.

One of the many restaurants geared to the large Latino population touted Peruvian food.

"Maybe we'll check out that one when we come back through here," Luis said with a nod toward the restaurant.

He headed toward the large building plastered with the huge red Lowe's theater sign. He entered a parking garage and didn't take the first parking spot he saw. He went up several levels, all the time checking his rear view mirror.

"Luis." Elia had her hand on his arm as he was about to get out of the car. "Stop."

Halfway out of the car with one foot on the pavement, he turned to look at her, his eyebrows raised in question.

"Let's drive up the coast and go into the City when we return. Someone's expecting us to be on the train. We don't want to have to wonder if someone's waiting for us at Grand Central Station."

He pondered her suggestion. "Pull out the map; let's see where we're going."

Elia's suggestion proved providential.

Chapter 59

"I thought you told me we had a sure thing here?" Frank Hanssen leaned against his car, his arms folded across his chest. His tie was loosened, but his sport coat was pressed to perfection. His gray slacks had a straight arrow crease down the legs and his tassel loafers looked spit-polished. The permanent crease at the bridge of his nose showed more of his personality than his put-together outfit.

He was in the parking garage of the Port Chester train station glaring at Lorraine Fegan.

"I am not the investment guru." She stood two arms lengths from Hanssen, feet apart and hands on hips. With her black leather pants and boots, she looked like a silver-haired Wonder Woman. "You are."

"Well I'm not the guru now. What the hell is going on?"

"You tell me. You called this meeting." She looked around the parking garage. "In your satellite office."

"The stock crashed."

"Frank, all stock has crashed. We're in a recession!" Her voice went up an octave. "What's that have to do with me?"

"Pharmaceuticals are not supposed to crash." He clearly enunciated each word through clenched teeth.

Lorraine stepped back. "What happened?"

"Where have you been?" He squinted at her. "Do you live in a cocoon?"

"What the hell are you talking about?"

Mad Money. He shook his head. "One lousy question and we're in the basement." He told her about the program and the question about a drug and the FDA being in the dark.

"You're crazy. One question." She didn't sound so sure.

"The point is our investors think it was our company, and they're pulling out."

"First of all, it's not your company." She was Wonder Woman again. "Second, if you think you've got problems now, just wait."

"What? What now?"

"Aaron Scharff is back from the grave."

Chapter 60

Millen let himself into the quiet house. He could smell something in the oven. Although Jeannie didn't eat much, the housekeeper cooked a full meal every evening. Jeannie insisted on it. She wanted Harry to eat. But he would have insisted on it anyway because he wanted his wife to eat. Or at least try to eat.

"Dinner's in the warming oven, Mr. Millen." The housekeeper had her pocketbook over arm. "I'll see you in the morning." As she opened the front door she turned. "I've got soup for Jeannie." Her eyes were sad.

Millen fixed himself a scotch and carried it into his study. He sat down on the sofa, the leather giving with his weight. "What the hell is going on?" He downed the drink.

He fixed a tray for Jeannie, added a plate for himself, and carried it upstairs to his wife's room. The nurse was giving her patient a glass of water. "There's some good food downstairs Peg; go and help yourself. I'll take care of Jeannie."

Jeannie smiled at her husband. "Clara made some soup, I see. Put it aside and tell me about your day."

"Nope. First we eat. Then we talk."

He helped his wife with the soup and wouldn't let her stop until it was half consumed.

"I'm finished." Jeannie Millen put her spoon on her tray. Her husband had covered it with a white linen napkin and had plucked a few dogwood petals from a backyard tree and fixed them in a tiny vase. She gestured at his tray. "And you haven't eaten a bite."

He shook his head.

"Harry, you have to eat." She had a twinkle in her eyes. "Do I have to feed you?"

He smiled, but there was no twinkle in his eyes, just tears.

"Harry, stop it. I'm feeling fine. I promise I'm not going to die tonight, so you can relax and eat your dinner."

He leaned over and kissed her forehead. "I'm going to miss you, Jeannie."

"I'm sorry about that, I really am, but I'm tired. So when I do go, please know I was tired—and ready." She reached for his hand. "Harry, you have to take care of the company. Then you can relax. Promise me."

"I'm trying, but Lorraine's working against us."

"Harry, take care of the company," she repeated. "Promise me."

"I promise."

She smiled. "Now eat!"

Later, with his wife sleeping peacefully upstairs after her morphine dessert, as she called it, he sat at his desk in his study and thought about their conversation.

He had told her about his meeting with Luis and Elia. "Bermuda was a fiasco—a mistake," he had told her. "Everything went wrong."

"It's my fault, Harry, not yours," she had said. "You would have been there but for me." She wouldn't listen to his protests.

Looking at her broke his heart. She wasn't shrinking away; steroids gave a false idea of weight; it was more a drifting away. Farther and farther every day. Soon she'd be beyond his reach.

He thought about their conversation.

"Talk to me, Harry," she had said. She had laid her hand, black and blue from numerous needle pricks, atop his. She sounded angry. "We've gone over this."

He smiled. "Things just aren't working out at Pavnor."

"Nothing is so bad that it can't be fixed." She smiled, but the smile never reached her eyes. "Is it?"

"I don't know. I've lost control." He took his wife's tray and set it on a table. "When Lorraine went behind my back with production, sending work to China…" He started pacing around the room. He clenched and unclenched his hands, a gentleman's anger control.

"That's done all the time. Why are you upset?"

"For one thing, she didn't clear it with me."

"Oh, Harry." She closed her eyes a moment. "Is this a pride thing?" She reached out for him. "You have enough problems without letting pride get to you."

Millen stopped walking and looked over at his wife. He walked slowly back to her bed, sat in the chair beside her, and put his head in his hands.

Jeannie put her hand on his head. "You've been preoccupied with me. She was just trying to take some pressure off you."

He raised his head and frowned. "By sending production to China? No. She did it to save money."

"And that's a bad thing?"

He shook his head. "I think she's into something else. And it's not to take pressure off me."

"Harry," she had said, "this is one more chink in Pavnor's armor. I think it'll work out after all."

"Ah, Jeannie, what am I going to do without you?"

He sipped a Scotch, placed it on his desk, and moved it in circles through the puddle it made on the mahogany.

Chapter 61

They followed the directions of the GPS to get onto I-95. The traffic was moving swiftly and Luis merged smoothly and stepped on the gas.

"We go through New Haven. Want to stop at Yale?"

Luis glanced at Elia. "Yale? Why?"

"Machu Picchu? Ring a bell?"

"*Por su puesto!* Of course! I had forgotten."

Yale University had a display of artifacts taken, or stolen, some say, from Machu Picchu in the early 1900s when Hiram Bingham from Yale discovered the ruins of Machu Picchu in Perú. Over the course of several years he carried crate after crate of gold and other artifacts out of the country. When the Peruvian government found out, it agreed to lend the treasures to Yale for a specified amount of time. The time has long since passed, and Yale has yet to return the treasures to Perú, the rightful owner.

"We don't have to stop; we've seen the real thing. Besides, I want to get to Cape Cod in time for a lobster dinner."

"Men. We haven't even had lunch yet, but you're already thinking of supper."

Elia opened the map. "Let me see what's in our future."

Luis heard the crinkle of the map, while Elia studied it. "Here's a place that sounds intriguing. Mystic Seaport." She tapped her finger on the spot.

"Just point the way, you're the navigator."

"Me and the GPS."

They rode in silence. Luis watched the traffic, which thinned once they were past New Haven, and constantly checked his rearview mirror.

"You're making me nervous."

"Can't help it. Better nervous than surprised."

Nervous and surprised would come later.

Chapter 62

They got off I-95 at the well-marked sign for Mystic Seaport and drove slowly past the welcome center through the picturesque town. Clapboard homes with picket fences lined the streets, flowering rhododendrons bloomed profusely. They drove past the seaport with small boats bobbing on the water. The site looked like it could have been a scene from *Jaws*.

"Hungry?"

Before Elia could reply, her cell phone rang. When she answered, she motioned to Luis that it was Harry Millen.

Luis mouthed, "Be nice."

She made a face and stuck her tongue out in response to his comment. As she spoke to Millen, Luis got the gist of the conversation. Millen wanted to see them.

"Harry, we decided to take your advice. We're driving up to Cape Cod. Martha's Vineyard? I don't know if we'll go; this is a quick trip."

"Wait a sec." She covered the phone. "He's got suggestions of what to do in Cape Cod."

"See what happens when you're nice?" Luis whispered.

"All right, Harry, we can meet again. Something new?" She shrugged at his answer. "We'll be back in your area in a day or two; want to set up something now?" She dug in her pocketbook for a pen and pad. "Shoot." She wrote down the date and time. "Lorraine Fegan. Got it. See you in her office."

She snapped her phone shut. "Yes, I'm hungry." She pointed to what looked like a shack with a crusty boat parked on the corner of the lot as a come-on for tourists, it seemed. "They say the shacks have the best food."

"Why did Millen call?"

"I'll tell you while we're eating."

"Who's thinking of food now, *señora*?"

They pulled into a shell-covered parking lot beside a yard-full of picnic tables. They stood, stretched, and then ambled to the take-out window to place their order. They could see through the windows that tables inside were occupied. They both turned around and looked at the picnic tables.

"Outside is fine with me," Elia said.

"Even better." Luis turned his attention to the menu. "Lobster roll. Yes."

"Make that two. And a bottle of water."

He looked at the selections and ordered a beer.

When their food was ready, they carried it to a table, took bites of their lobster rolls and sat for a minute savoring the delicacy.

"Millen?"

"He thought we were still in Greenwich and wanted to see us." She frowned. "Now that I think about it, he sounded kind of distressed, especially when I told him we weren't there."

"Distressed?" Luis was devouring his lunch while he talked. "Not too distressed that he could act as a tour guide."

"Maybe he's just being a gentleman."

"What did he tell you to see?" He held up a hand as he got up from the table. "Wait a second. I'm getting another lobster roll. Want one?"

She grinned at him, and shook her head. She ate while he was away from the table.

Luis returned with his seconds and sat down across from Elia. "What'd he say?"

"He thinks we should take the ferry to Martha's Vineyard, and he said to visit Mashpee in Cape Cod. He recommended a bed and breakfast there."

"Sounds like he's got our itinerary planned for us." He sounded sarcastic.

"You think that's strange?"

"I spent the last two hours looking in the rear-view mirror, and now someone is telling us where we should go." He pushed his beer bottle out of the way. "And you told someone where we were going. Maybe we should keep our plans to ourselves."

Elia looked at the rest of her lobster. Suddenly she was no longer hungry.

Chapter 63

Frank Hanssen had carried his files home on the train from the New York office. He now sat in his study at his computer and worked the numbers. He saw Pavnor stock sliding—and not in the direction he wanted. He had staked his reputation on this one company because of assurances he got from Fegan.

He pushed back from his desk. "Damn woman," he said through clenched teeth. He had lobbied his clients to put large chunks of their money into the business because he knew—yes, knew—that Pavnor would sail.

The new drug Cyptolis was touted as the best in its category of treating spasticity due to any number of illnesses and problems. With the military in Iraq and Afghanistan, and resultant spinal cord injuries, the drug was expected to hit the top of the charts. But something went wrong.

Hanssen wanted to strangle Jim Cramer. Ever since the *Mad Money* show with the hypothetical question about a pharmaceutical company, Pavnor's stock plummeted, investors were breathing down his neck, and his phone was burning up the wireless industry. It was tricky easing investors back into the fold after the beating Wall Street took in the past, but drug companies are usually a good bet. And this was a sure thing. He got it from the top. Or so he thought.

His home office was cluttered with folders strewn throughout the small room. He surveyed the mess. This room was no more cluttered than the rest of his condo. Ever since his divorce the year before, except for the way he dressed, he had been living like a slob. Mary Louise wouldn't put up with this, he knew. Even his study was in order when she was around. She'd enter his domain regularly and organize it.

He missed the order that she could make out of his chaos. But it was just that fact that got him in trouble. That got him caught. In one of her forays with the dust cloth she found his extra cell phone. She easily bypassed security and checked his messages. There were several. From women.

Hanssen thought of his stupidity, leaving the cell phone lying around. He had never once thought he had been stupid, let alone immoral, cheating on his wife. In fact, he had blamed her for snooping.

She showed she had a backbone, he realized, when she stood up to him. She took the kids and moved back to Virginia near her family. She kept her dignity. He now saw that.

And now he was having regrets. He missed the kids, even missed his wife. He was tired of playing around, and he no longer had an excuse when he wanted to dump a girlfriend. When his wife was still in the picture, he could tell the current girlfriend it was over because he and his wife were trying to work it out. Well that plan's DOA.

But he knew moving away was the best thing for the kids. He wouldn't want them seeing what their father had become, and he knew they'd be mortified if their friends found out about his cheating. "I screwed up."

He ran his hands through his hair then stared at the folders. He got up from his chair and began putting them in piles.

Pavnor. He thought back to when his troubles began. "Bermuda." He could have said rotting garbage and it wouldn't have sounded uglier. He slapped his desk with a file. One day he's sailing the Atlantic off Bermuda. Today he's shipwrecked.

It's not Cramer, he said to himself, who got me into this. Or the guy who called in to the show. How in the hell did that guy have an inkling about Cyptolis? Hanssen frowned at that thought, then shook his head. No. It was Pereda. He was now conveniently out of the picture; that turned out to be a stroke of luck. It seemed the gods were shining down on Hanssen just when he needed some shine.

But another frown crossed his brow when he thought of Pereda's death. He slowly brought his hand to his face and massaged his jaw. "Aaron?" He spoke aloud. "How do you figure in all this? Jake? What about you? What the hell is going on with that drug?"

He opened one of the files and fell heavily into his chair. Leaning back, he kept his frown.

He thought about Bermuda — and then Kiawah. One common denominator seemed to be Echevarria and his nosy wife. And he learned from Fegan they had come to Connecticut to see Aaron's wife and meet with Millen.

"What next?" He pressed his lips together in the universal look of disgust and conjured up a picture of Fegan. "You better fix this, bitch."

Chapter 64

The "bitch" had her own problems. Millen had called her after his talk with his wife and said he was going to meet with the Echevarrias and he wanted her there.

Lorraine Fegan held her phone so tight her knuckles turned white. "Who are these people that they think they have to save the world?" Fegan spit the words out. "And why do you think you owe them an explanation?"

"What's the matter with you? You should be concerned with the safety of our drugs. Those people are trying to get to the bottom of what's happening here. And what happened in Bermuda to their friend."

Fegan paced around her Pavnor office. Usually it felt like a haven for her. The walls were painted a soft taupe with off white trim that brought peace and quiet into her hectic and complicated life.

One wall held her diplomas that surrounded a large framed painting of the original building of her alma mater set in the mountainous town of Greensburg, Pennsylvania. She graduated from the same college as her mother and aunts. When she and they attended Seton Hill, it was a women's college; now it was coed.

She looked at the painting, done by one of her classmates, Ann Heckel, who had been an art student at Seton Hill.

A flash of guilt pulsed through her body thinking of what she had become. But quickly, and then the guilt was gone.

She was still on the phone with Millen. "I'm afraid I've been out of the loop," he said, then added in a regretful tone, "because of Jeannie. When they return we'll come by your office; you haven't met them, I don't believe."

All she heard was, "When they return." She stopped pacing. "Return? Where did they go?"

"Up the coast. To Cape Cod."

"Oh?"

"I gave them some suggestions, so they may be gone a couple of days."

"What kind of suggestions?"

"Just where to stay. A B&B in Mashpee. Why? You have a better idea?"

"No. Well, maybe. What B&B did you suggest? I might have a better idea."

"Paul Revere House. You know it?"

"No. I'm sure it's fine."

"You know, they have had a bad time of it. They were at their wedding and honeymoon when Pereda got sick and died."

"I'm not an ogre, Harry."

"I'll call you when they return. I want you to meet them."

"I'm looking forward to it."

Millen replaced the receiver. He looked confused. "Looking forward to it? I would hardly say that," he mused to the silent phone.

Chapter 65

"Elia, mind calling information and getting the number for that bed and breakfast Harry recommended?" They were back on the road but off the main drag. Their GPS was taking them on scenic, but slow, Highway 1.

"Do you think that's a good idea?" She had the map opened on her lap, her finger on their route. "You have me thinking. I don't think we should stay in Mashpee at all."

"How are we going to know who's threatening us? Or if someone is?" He reached over and ran his hand lightly over her cheek. "I can't stand this, Elia. I'm scared. Scared for you, and hell, scared for us." His voice cracked. "You keep saying either we're in, or we're out." He took his eyes off the road for a second to glance at her.

"And we're in now?" she asked.

"It's like we have to get on board the train, pay the fare, or jump off. From Bermuda to Kiawah to Connecticut." He slapped the steering wheel with his open hand. "We are on that damn train, and until we stop it, we can't get off."

"So we go to Mashpee and, well, to stick with your analogy, wait for the train wreck?"

"Sort of."

"All right. You're the conductor." She called information, then called the Mashpee Paul Revere B&B and made reservations for that night.

He pointed at the map in her lap. "Where to now?"

"Hmm, looks like we pass close to Newport. Want to stop?"

"Dinner?"

"Luis! We just had lunch." She laughed and felt the tension drain from her body.

"Ah, *mi amor*, it's good to see you laugh."

"Luis, it'll be okay. We'll be okay." She unfastened her seat-belt and leaned over and kissed his cheek. "I love you. We'll be okay."

"Safe. We'll be safe." He looked at her seatbelt. "Buckle up."

Chapter 66

Millen was hunched over a table in the small library at Pavnor going through the history of the company. He had Madison cancel appointments and hold calls. He was lost in his reading. His tie was off, shirt sleeves rolled up, and a bottle of water on the table; he forgot time.

He scratched his head with the sharpened pencil he held in his hand. He was so engrossed in his reading he didn't realize he had slipped back into the old habit he had developed while still in grade school. Jeannie had sat behind him in seventh grade and had been grossed whenever he was deep in thought and used his pencil as a head scratcher.

"It helps me think," he had told her then. When they began dating in college, she reminded him of his pencil head, as she called it. He assured her it was a thing of the past.

As he turned the page of a report and again put the pencil to his head, he stopped suddenly and looked at it. He smiled sheepishly and again looked around the room. He put the pencil down and continued reading.

He found the drug Abecour, and sat up straight in his chair. Indeed it had been given to quadriplegics during the Vietnam War to lessen spasticity. He read the indications and contraindications. Nothing was written about liver disease or deaths from liver failure.

After several hours of research, he found what he was looking for—a report coming out of the VA hospital in New Orleans.

Millen felt a tightening in his chest as he read. He closed his eyes and thought of the black granite wall in Washington.

"So many names and some are there because of a drug." When he realized he had spoken aloud, he quickly looked around the room to see if anyone heard him. He was alone.

Just as quickly, he began comparing Abecour's components with those of Cyptolis's. He nodded. They were the same—almost.

He checked his watch. Not yet five. He pulled out his Blackberry and found the number he was looking for.

"Pete? Harry Millen. I'm coming down. I have some questions." He paused. "Pete? See what you have in your files about Abecour."

Dr. Pete Archer had turned off his computer and was packing up his briefcase when he got his boss's call. Archer was a scientist who was on the team that evaluated data submitted by Pavnor's laboratory. He had heard the scuttlebutt about Cyptolis and wondered when his turn would come for questions, or blame. He took a breath and pushed it out of puffed up cheeks.

He went through the routine of booting up his computer. "So much for an early night," he said under his breath. He adjusted his black horn-rimmed glasses and did a little dance with his shoulders, an idiosyncratic thing he performed each and every time he turned on his computer. His co-workers talked behind his back, wondering what he would do if he were up at bat at a World Series game.

He pulled up Cyptolis data and reread what he had read a dozen times since trouble was brought to light. There had been a glitch in communication, he knew. Otherwise, the side effects would have been reported to him and his team. Reported before people died.

He found Abecour far quicker than Millen had. He scanned the data, studied the components and let out another deep breath.

Frowning, he kept reading and compared Abecour's side effects with those of Cyptolis. Components or radicals were identical except for a couple.

There is intense competition in the pharmaceutical industry. When one drug is doing a good job other companies jump on the bandwagon. They don't have to research from the beginning; that was done by the original producer. They need only look at side effects, for example, and add or change radicals to expunge or at least alleviate them.

Pavnor took Abecour and did change some radicals, but something went wrong. "How the hell did this slip past us?" In addition to the attack on the liver, there was another problem. Hemorrhaging.

He chewed on his lip and waited for Millen.

Chapter 67

They got off at the Newport, Rhode Island, exit and followed the signs to the center of town. The Welcome Center was adjacent to the Marriott. They parked and looked toward the harbor.

"*Vamos.*" Luis took Elia's hand. "I promise I won't stop to eat."

"Good, because we're going to Cape Cod, my love, today."

"Let's see what Newport looks like, first."

It was at least ten degrees cooler than Greenwich. Luis kept his arm around Elia to fend off the chill. And he continued his watchfulness, looking behind them every few minutes.

"Honey, no one knows we're here. Come on." She pulled him by the hand toward the wooden walkway that ran perpendicular to the water. The walk was lined with shops and restaurants, some not opened yet for the summer season.

An outdoor café, though, was open, and many of the tables were occupied with sweatshirt-wearing visitors.

They strolled to the end of the walkway looking into shop windows. At the end of the walk, at the railing overlooking the water, they looked across to the Hyatt sitting on a tiny island.

"I spotted something in one of the shops," Luis said, turning back the way they had come. "I'm buying my bride a present."

He guided her to the jewelry displayed on the front counter of a small store. "Do you like this?" He held up a necklace of white pearlized shells. "A remembrance of our ten minutes in Newport."

"Beautiful. But what can we get for you?"

"Dinner?"

"What?"

"Just kidding." He paid for her gift, helped her put it on, and hand-in-hand they headed back to their car, their sojourn in Newport over.

"You know what, honey?" Elia was now behind the wheel. "It's a nice feeling when no one knows where we are."

He reached over and massaged her neck. He didn't share her feeling.

Chapter 68

It took less than two hours to reach the Bourne Bridge crossing into Cape Cod. Native Cape Codders called the bridge the "most beautiful sight in the world," because it meant they were home.

Elia followed directions as the GPS ticked off turns. Circling two rotaries, something Bermudians called roundabouts, she was soon on the right track to Mashpee.

When they arrived in Mashpee Commons, they felt as though they were in old New England. This was a planned business venture after the citizens got tired and disgusted with the strip mall theory. Now the area was a walker's paradise. Shops, some with apartments above, restaurants, homes, all within walking distance. No more reliance on the automobile, for these forward-thinking people.

They easily found the Paul Revere and checked in. They walked with the clerk outside and around the corner of the building.

"You can go through the building, but this is your private entrance." He led the way up a flight of stairs, slipped a skeleton key in the lock. He opened the door to a peaceful-looking room furnished in eighteenth century furniture decorated in soft blues and creams. He handed Luis the key, with a red, white, and blue ribbon key chain, and held out his hand.

After he left, Elia had a confused look on her face. "I don't know why we're here after your concern that someone would know where we are."

"The train; remember?" He took her hand. "Come on; let's take a look around Mashpee; I hear it's a genuine Indian village."

"Our luggage. Shouldn't we unload the car?"

"It's early. We can do that later." Luis pulled the door shut and they started down the stairs. "Wait here, let me see if there're any brochures in the room."

When he returned, he had a determined look on his face. "Any?"

"Any what?"

"Brochures."

"Oh, uh, no."

Before they pulled away, this time with Luis behind the wheel, he opened the map. "Just in case we decide to go to Martha's Vineyard, let's check out Falmouth. Looks like..." He paused a moment, studying the map. "Here we go. If we decide to go to Martha's Vineyard, we'd catch the ferry out of Woods Hole." Again he was silent. "That's if we take the car over. No car, we'd catch it—here's the name—The Island Queen—at Falmouth Harbor."

"Are we even going to Martha's Vineyard? Which one of our so-called friends suggested that trip?"

Luis nodded. "Good point. Just in case. Falmouth. We stay on 28."

Twenty minutes later they drove slowly through the quintessential New England village. A statue of Falmouth native, Katherine Lee Bates, who wrote *America the Beautiful*, stands guard over children playing on the expansive library lawn in the middle of town, the freshly-mown grass giving off a scent of summer. Past the library, the shops throughout the village begin to awaken from their winter's nap.

"Let's stop here." Luis pulled into a parallel parking space between a pick-up truck and a VW. "Looks like a place we should visit."

Elia looked out the window at the shop. "Ice cream. I could go for that."

They ordered cones and sat at a sidewalk table. From their vantage point they checked out the shops lining the street and the tourists gazing in store windows.

"Hold on. Be right back." He disappeared into the ice cream shop. A few minutes later he returned with a few brochures in hand.

"Ever have dessert first, then your supper?" Luis took his seat at the table and spoke through a mouthful of ice cream.

"As a matter of fact I have. On our birthdays. Mom served us our cake and ice cream first. A special treat." She looked at her cone and sighed.

Luis reached for her hand. "In memory of your mother, let's pretend today is your birthday." He waved the brochures like a fan. "We are going to eat fabulous lobster, and then we'll get settled for the night."

Chapter 69

Pete Archer was taking notes when Millen walked into the office. He stopped writing and sat perfectly still while Millen took a seat. He had never seen him look so worn. Of course his wife was ill, but that's been an ongoing, off-and-on distraction for years. I guess the end is near, he mused. Distraction? I can't believe I called his wife's cancer a distraction.

Millen carried his jacket, hung it on the back of the chair in precise movements, and sat. "What's going on?"

"I'm looking, Harry." He tapped his notes. "About Abecour. The drug was good—except for the side effects. It was taken off the market thirty years ago. But now it seems Cyptolis is almost the same drug." He frowned as he was talking.

"I know all that. And it has the same side effects."

"It needs the black box. It does a terrific job. It's prescribed to alleviate spasticity associated with paralysis, and it does that."

"How did we put the same drug out there?"

"I can't answer that, but Harry, there's something else I can't answer." He held up his notes. "Yes, we had liver involvement, but..."

"But what?"

"But, I don't know why, if this is the same drug, why there is such a great incidence of hemorrhaging."

"I've been thinking about that. You said almost the same drug. I've been doing my own research. Some radicals were changed. Didn't seem to help the liver involvement. Do you think the change in radicals causes the hemorrhaging?"

"Could be. I'll have to go over all the components to rule that out."

"Something else, Pete. Could it be in the production process?"

"Could be." Pete sounded hopeful at this idea. It would certainly make him look better.

And it would certainly help Millen's cause.

Chapter 70

Luis and Elia pulled their plastic lobster emblazoned bibs off, opened the tiny packs of moistened wipes, and tried in vain to clean all remnants of their lobster dinners off their sticky fingers.

"A stroll before we go to bed?" Luis spoke as he held the door for his wife. Outside he took his thumb and wiped away a smudge on Elia's cheek. "I'd lick it off if we weren't in public."

They crossed the street to look into the window of Eight Cousins Children's Books and saw what looked like a family of five gathered around one of the clerks.

They continued down the street and stopped at another bookstore. Peeking in the window at the Inkwell they saw a table set up in the middle of the shop. "A book signing. Let's go in and get an autographed book." Elia tugged on Luis's hand. As they entered, she whispered. "There's no one in line; let's see what she's written."

Five minutes later, autographed book in hand, they spotted a cluster of people in the back of the shop. They joined the group as they listened to the speaker. Gerry Munroe was animatedly talking about her collection of vintage books and how she spent many happy hours scouring antique shops in search of books. "My rule: if published before 1899, I might be interested, after that—too new."

She held up several small books. "You'll see a lot this size in my collection. I do love my small books best. And to answer a question I get a lot; why are so many small. I always say, hmmmm, good question. I think they're small for several reasons—they could be carried in pockets, maybe they were cheaper to produce, and perhaps it was just the style of the time."

She pointed to a corner bookcase, just three-feet tall. "This is just one of the bookcases my husband, Bob, built to accommodate the small-sized books."

She was still answering questions when Elia and Luis slipped away. They drove to their bed and breakfast, got their luggage out of the car, and settled in for the night.

"My husband is full of surprises."

Chapter 71

Lorraine Fegan was in her car crossing over the Bourne Bridge onto Cape Cod, her headlights doing little to illuminate the dark road. She was on her cell calling Massachusetts information. When she got the number, she dialed the Paul Revere and asked for Dr. Echevarria. She was told he had checked in. She declined the offer to be put through to his room.

It was past midnight when she arrived at the Paul Revere. She tore out a sheet of paper from a notepad, folded it in half and wrote "Dr. Echevarria" on one of its halves. She combed her hair, put on fresh lipstick, stepped out of the car, and quietly closed the door. She held the note in her hand and walked into the B&B exuding confidence: spine straight, shoulders back, her height accentuated by her erect posture.

The clerk behind the counter had his head in his hands and looked as though he had been napping when Fegan tapped her fingernails on the polished wooden counter. He jumped. She smiled.

"Dr. Echevarria is expecting this note in the morning, would you please see that he gets it?"

"Sure. Do you want me to call his room?"

"Don't disturb him." She gestured to the cubbyhole behind the clerk. "Just put it in his box." She waited and watched where he put the note. "Thank you." With the room number now known, she looked like a canary-full cat.

When she returned to her car, she wondered how she would get past the clerk to get to the room. As she sat there, she saw a couple walk past the front door and go around to the side. She waited a few minutes, got quietly out of her car, and followed their path. There she saw private entrances. And looking up, she saw the Echevarrias' room. The light was off. She shook her head. "Honeymooners." She spat out the word.

She went to her car and carefully lifted a bag off the front seat. She returned to the side of the building.

Quietly, so quietly, she climbed the steps. From her bag she removed a roll of cotton. Working in complete silence, she unwound the roll and pulled off a long strip and set it aside. Then out came a pair of goggles and thick leather gloves. Donning them, she reached into her bag for one more item.

She gingerly pulled out a small lead-lined flask and carefully opened the lid exposing a long thin tube-like top with a plunger at the end. She took hold of the plunger and pulled it out of the flask. She now held a syringe. She inserted the needle under the door and pushed in the plunger and emptied the syringe into the room.

Swiftly, she took the cotton and stuffed it around the opening at the bottom of the door. Leaving her gloves and goggles on, she put the syringe back into the flask, and carefully laid it in the bottom of her bag. She put the roll of cotton on top, and quietly left the scene, only removing her gloves and goggles when she reached the bottom of the stairs.

When she got to the car, she saw the clerk walk down a hall. She hurried inside and quickly walked behind the counter, retrieved the note she had left earlier, and just as quickly made it to her car before the clerk returned.

She backed out of the parking lot with her lights off, turning them on a half block down the road. She started the long drive to Connecticut. She smiled. "One problem eliminated. Hah! Make that two."

She was entering the first rotary when she realized there hadn't been many cars in the parking lot at the Paul Revere.

She wondered where the Echevarrias had parked. Her smile disappeared.

Police, ambulances, fire trucks, and Hazmet gathered in front of the Paul Revere shortly after ten a.m. One ambulance had already left for the hospital and the guys in white had entered the room, their faces and heads covered with E.T.-like helmets, their hands in protective gloves. News trucks were out front reporting what they thought they knew: a possible terrorist attack in peaceful, picturesque Mashpee, Massachusetts.

Chapter 72

The Clairedge House B&B on Cape Codder Road sat at the edge of Buzzard's Bay. Ten steps down from the rose-bordered manicured lawn, the rocky beach was lapped by icy water.

They sat on the patio looking at seemingly endless water. Not far was a white-flecked rock extending four feet out of the water, a perch for cormorants as they fly over the Bay. They turned when Claire brought out a fresh pot of coffee and French toast made with locally-baked Portuguese sweet bread.

"We Portuguese are plentiful in Falmouth, so this bread is definitely authentic." She gestured toward the house where her husband could be seen talking with another couple. "I didn't bake it. We have George to thank for picking it up this morning at the bakery." She opened the screen door and was about to step into the house when she said, "The water's cold, but you have to put a toe in, at least."

Elia and Luis sat side-by-side gazing at the water while they ate their breakfast. "This place is a jewel, honey. I'm glad we decided not to stay in Mashpee after all." She had a thought. "You did cancel that room, didn't you?"

"Uh, no. Guess I paid for two rooms."

She shook her head. "Crazy guy." She looked back at the house. "But it's worth it. Cape Cod personified—weathered wood, emerald green grass, fragrant flowers." She held up her coffee cup and motioned toward the water. "The view."

Luis finished his French toast and eyed Elia's half-finished breakfast. She laughed and pushed her plate over to him.

He mopped up the remaining bread with syrup, took a swig of coffee, and wiped his mouth with a cloth napkin. "That was good. Now let's listen to Claire and put our toes in the water."

They picked up thick towels from a pile on a chair and disappeared from view as they descended onto the rocky beach. They gingerly walked over the slippery stones to the water's edge and spread out the towels. They settled themselves, took off their shoes, and obeyed Claire.

"OK. Enough for me." Elia pulled her legs up and put her arms around them.

"A half minute. I guess that counts." Luis followed her lead. "I've spent a lot of time in the Pacific in Perú, and right now I'd say this is as cold."

Later, they were about to pack their car and say goodbye, when Claire suggested they stop at a local spot for lunch.

"Eat. Then come back and pack."

Again they obeyed Claire. They followed her directions and found themselves at The Clam Shack at Falmouth Harbor.

They sat on aged picnic tables on the dock and ate fried clam rolls and drank root beers. Beside them, close enough to touch, was the Island Queen—"the Queen"—to the natives.

"That's the ferry we'd take if we were going to Martha's Vineyard," Elia said.

"Maybe someday we'll come back and visit there."

"And Nantucket," Elia added.

"Let's pick up our luggage and get moving," Luis said as he climbed off the bench.

Chapter 73

Claire and George sat at the kitchen table watching CNN. Claire's hands were clasped tightly in front of her. "Come in, come in." She motioned to Elia and Luis. "Oh this is horrible! There's been a terrorist attack."

"Oh no! Where?" Elia looked at the TV.

"Here. Cape Cod. Mashpee."

Elia lowered herself into a chair. "Mashpee?" It came jagged.

Luis stood behind Elia; she felt his fingers tighten on her shoulders. Her breathing was shallow. "Where in Mashpee?" She asked as though she were afraid of the answer.

Claire turned to look at her. At a B&B. The Paul Revere."

They listened to CNN coverage. A housekeeper, who had already cleaned one room, had gone up the outside steps to a second floor room. From what the police could ascertain from the semi-conscious woman, she had knocked on the door and announced "housekeeping." When she didn't get a response, she tried to open the door, but it was stuck. She saw a wad of cotton under the door and removed it, opened the door, and immediately became disoriented. She stumbled backward and fell down the stairs. She lay there unconscious until a passing guest found her and called 911. By the time help arrived she had regained some consciousness. She was taken to the hospital with what appeared to be a broken arm. "She's being evaluated for other injuries," the reporter said.

The cameras showed the Hazmat team. CNN reported that a gas had been dispensed into the room. "Authorities say it's fortunate the maid fell backward instead of forward into the house.

The gas would have killed her." The reporter closed with, "Terrorism has not been ruled out."

"We know those people," Claire said quietly. "The owners. They're good people, for washashores."

Elia reached for Claire's hand. "I'm so sorry about your friends. Claire, what do you mean by washashore?"

"Canal-jumper," George answered. "A local."

"Oh, George, be clear." Claire turned to Elia. We're natives; there are only about eleven percent of us left. Locals are permanent residents not born here, certainly not natives. We call them washashores or canal-jumpers."

She pointed to the TV. "Those are good people."

Lorraine Fegan sipped coffee and mindlessly watched TV. Magazines had been kicked to the floor by her bare feet perched on the coffee table. She sat up straight when the screen flashed scenes from Mashpee.

She spilled her coffee on her white silk pajamas when she heard, "A maid entered an empty room and was overcome by fumes in what authorities say was a premeditated plan to poison."

"What the hell!" She jumped up, ignoring the hot coffee that splashed on her hand. She turned up the TV.

"Where the hell's the rest of the story?"

Chapter 74

"Millen." Luis was driving south on I-95. "He's the only one who knew where we were going."

"Not only that, he sent us to that B&B. He wants to see us when we return. Did he really think we'd be returning?" She fanned herself with her hand and leaned over to adjust the AC. "Is it me, or are you hot too?"

"I'm sweating. Our adrenaline has kicked in. If we had any doubts someone's been trying to kill us, we can relax and know we're right."

"Real funny." She wasn't smiling. "If he knew he was going to kill us, why did he want the meeting?"

"To throw us off?" Luis shrugged.

"Well, let's throw him off. We'll keep that appointment."

"He tried to kill us; think that's a smart idea?"

"Well he didn't suggest meeting him in a dark alley; we'll be in the Pavnor building." She fiddled with the AC. "Feisty adrenaline." She picked up the map to fan herself. "And we aren't even going to be meeting in his office. We're meeting in Lorraine Fegan's office."

"Dot Scharff's friend." He nodded. "Didn't Dot say she's second in command?"

"Exactly. Maybe we can enlist her to help us uncover what's going on."

"Maybe. If this thing doesn't end, we'll be forever looking over our shoulders. Do you have Pavnor's number?"

She dug in her pocketbook for her notebook and leafed through it. "Uh huh. Who do you want to call?"

"Lorraine Fegan."

"Don't have her number, but I'll call Pavnor. Want to make an appointment with her?"

"I think so. We're meeting with her and Millen day after tomorrow."

"Got it. You want to tell her what we're thinking without Millen around."

"She might have the same thought." Luis kept his eyes on the road. "Let's go into New York tomorrow and meet beforehand."

She pulled out her cell phone. "Any chance you remember the train schedule?"

"Vaguely. If we catch one about eleven, and no later than noon, we'll make a two o'clock show."

"I'll try to set something up about 10." She started punching in the number for Pavnor. "It'll be a relief to get someone else involved."

Chapter 75

Lorraine Fegan showered, chose a linen pewter-gray outfit, one shade darker than her hair that she pulled back into a 1970s chignon. Fatigue and the out-of-style hairdo added ten years to her face. She looked in the mirror and noticed the tense pucker of her mouth. With the palm of her hand, she tried to smooth her face. "Relax," she told the face that stared back at her.

She took three deep breaths, and patted on makeup. "Damn. How did things get this far?"

She arrived at the office late afternoon, stopped at her secretary's desk and picked up her messages. "Anything urgent?" she asked, as she leafed through the pile of pink slips.

"Yes. I marked them. Two. One from Mr. Millen and the other from Elia Christie."

"Elia Christie?" She wrinkled her brow. "Elia?"

She rifled through the messages. "Millie, I know of only one Elia, but her name is Spanish."

"She didn't sound Spanish. She and her husband," she stopped in mid-sentence. "That's her, Lorraine. Her husband has a Spanish name. Sorry, but I didn't write it down. A long name."

"Well?" She tapped her fingernails on the pile of messages.

"Oh, sorry. She and her husband want to come in to see you in the morning. They said they have an appointment with Mr. Millen and you day after tomorrow, but they have to see you before."

Fegan's fingers stopped. She thrust the messages at Millie. "Find it."

Millie pulled it out of the stack and Fegan grabbed it. She turned and bolted into her office and slammed the door.

Millie looked at the rest of the messages, took a deep breath, and opened Fegan's door.

"Your other messages," she said as she quickly walked to the desk and laid them in front of Fegan.

Fegan stared at Elia's message. "What?" she barked.

Millie had her hand on the doorknob, ready to escape. "Your messages." She pulled the door shut behind her and muttered, "Your Royal Highness."

Lorraine put her hand over her fast-beating heart. "What's going on?" she said aloud.

Chapter 76

Elia and Luis were back in Greenwich when Lorraine returned the call.

"We haven't met, Ms. Fegan, but we're friends of Dot Scharff's."

"Lorraine. Please. Yes, Harry Millen has mentioned you, so I feel I know you."

"Actually, he's the reason we're calling. We're meeting with him and, I understand, with you day after tomorrow."

Lorraine looked wary. "Yes? Is there a problem with the time?"

"No, no, it's fine."

"Yes?" She tapped her fingers on the messages Millie had dropped on her desk. She didn't try to hide her impatience.

It wasn't hard to miss the tone in Fegan's voice. "Angry," Elia mouthed to Luis while pointing to the phone.

"Lorraine, we need to talk before the meeting."

"It can't wait until our scheduled meeting? I'm very busy."

Elia rolled her eyes at Luis and grimaced. "I don't think so. Listen, something's going on at Pavnor and we think you might be able to shed some light on things."

"Me? How do you think I can help?" Lorraine felt perspiration running down her back and chest, the linen wrinkling at a fast pace.

"Maybe we shouldn't talk on the phone. May we come in?"

"Now?" Fegan looked at her watch.

"No. Tomorrow."

Fegan opened her appointment book. "Would four work for you?"

"Could we make it early morning? Luis and I are going into New York for the afternoon. And we think you'd want to hear this as early as possible."

Lorraine pulled her blouse away from her chest and used it as a fan. "Let me think." She was silent for half a minute. "If you're taking the train, will you leave from Port Chester?"

"I guess. Why do you ask?"

"I live in Rye, right near there. There's a coffee shop close by; I can meet you there. It'll save you a trip all the way over here."

"That sounds good. Is ten okay?"

Lorraine made a note in her appointment book. "That's fine. Look for Johnny Cakes. See you in the morning."

"Oh, wait. One more thing. Please don't tell Harry Millen about our meeting, or that I said we'd be going into the City."

"You can be assured I won't say a word." Fegan ended the connection. She picked up her messages, held them in her hand, then turned to her waste can and dropped them in. "I don't need any more problems."

Chapter 77

They parked and walked around the corner to Johnny Cakes. "How are we going to know Lorraine when she gets here?"

"Luis, look around. Do you see anyone dressed for business? These people have on jeans and shorts."

They ordered coffee and watched the door. They weren't the only ones watching that door. A half block away, Lorraine Fegan sat in her car with a clear view of the coffee shop. Her fingers tapped the steering wheel. She turned on the engine, drove closer, and circled the block before she found a parking space to suit her. "What is their game?" Her tapping fingers played the finale. She opened the car door. She opened another door and stepped into the coffee shop.

"That's gotta be her." Elia was about to wave when Lorraine signaled to them. "How did she pick us out?" Elia looked down at her clothes. "I'm not dressed up."

Luis shrugged and stood to greet Fegan. "Thanks for meeting us." He introduced Elia and himself and offered her coffee.

She declined and sat opposite them. "What seems to be your problem?" She spoke with a distinctive Boston accent. Elia expected to hear "Haavud" any minute, if Harvard would happen to factor into the conversation.

Luis took over. "It's not our problem, Ms. Fegan; it's yours." He sounded annoyed.

Lorraine's face hardened. "Mine?" The perspiration trickled down her back.

"Pavnor's."

"I'm aware of Cyptolis, if that's what you're referring to."
She ran her tongue over her lips and shifted slightly on her chair.
"We're on it."

"But there's more, and I think it's high up."

Lorraine stopped fidgeting. "How high?" She could feel the
beating of her heart.

"Millen."

"Harry?" She laughed. "Harry?" She visibly relaxed.

"You're surprised; so are we." Elia leaned forward on the
table almost knocking over her coffee. "But look, he heads the
company and it's his job to make a profit."

"You think he deliberately put the drug back on the market?" She sat back in her chair. "Hmmm, interesting."

"We don't know," Luis said, "but once it came out, we think
he's been trying to cover up the fact that it had been out years
ago—and pulled."

"And he certainly doesn't like us poking around," Elia said.
"We think he's trying to scare us off. Or worse."

"What are you saying?"

"Someone's trying to silence us," Elia said.

"Silence how?"

"Kill us."

The words hung in the air like the aroma from their coffee.
Finally Fegan spoke. "Why are you telling me this?"

"Because we're meeting with Millen tomorrow, in your office, I believe, and we need your help to find proof," Elia said.

"Have you talked to the police?"

"Here, no." Elia looked at Luis. "We will."

"No!" Lorraine blurted out the word. "I mean, you should
definitely have proof before you talk to the police. Harry is an
important person in this area."

Elia nodded. "That's why we're talking with you."

"I don't know what I can do."

"Can you go back into your records and find the history of Abecour?" Luis asked. "I can find only so much; but you can delve into Pavnor history."

She held up her hands to stop him. "Abecour? What's that?"

"Cyptolis," Luis said. "I thought you said you knew about the problems Cyptolis was having."

"What is the connection with Abecour?"

"Same drug."

Lorraine ran her tongue over her lips again. "I knew this, but I wondered what you knew." She looked at her watch. "I have a meeting this morning." She pushed back her chair.

Elia took hold of her arm. "Don't you want to hear how many times Millen tried to kill us? And how many people he did kill?"

"Tell me."

Chapter 78

Luis and Elia climbed the stone stairs to the Port Chester train station.

He inserted his American Express card into the machine and bought two round-trip tickets to Grand Central Station. As they waited for the train, Luis kept glancing down at the parking lot.

"Now what?"

"*Nada*. Just habit." He turned his attention to the oncoming train. When they got on, Luis took the window seat. He grinned at his wife. "I didn't forget; you like the aisle."

And he liked the window seat. He leaned close to the window and stared out at the few embarking passengers. He glanced right and left, not really knowing who he should be concerned about.

Most getting on the train were Hispanics; some were young mothers pushing baby carriages and holding toddlers by the hand, others were tattoo-sporting teens taking one more drag on unfiltered cigarettes before throwing the butt on the ground. It wasn't until the train pulled away that Luis relaxed. He closed his eyes for the rest of the trip.

New York City's Grand Central Station was teeming with rushing people. "Everybody's in a hurry." Luis held Elia's hand and followed the signs to a street exit. "What's their urgency?"

"You, my darling husband, have been in the South too long."

"Guess you're right. I'm from the deep South, really deep; born and reared."

"And I'm from Pittsburgh; I'm used to folks moving fast."

"The pace is slower in Augusta, but even there it's much faster than what I imagined for the South."

"No wonder. Augusta has a lot of Yankees."

"I noticed that. Wonder why."

"Lots of reasons." To tick off her points, her fingers pressed Luis's hand that was wrapped firmly around her own. One, the Medical College of Georgia has physicians on staff and in training from all parts of the country and the world."

She pulled on his hand. "Speaking of pace, let's pick up ours." They followed the crowd across a street. "Two, ditto for Fort Gordon. Soldiers from every state in the union, our territories, and like the medical college, all over the world, have been, and are, stationed there. And Fort Gordon is home to the Signal Corps, bringing more diversification to the city.

"Three, Savannah River Plant is right across the Savannah River in South Carolina."

"I can see the medical college and the army base, but the nuclear plant? How does that figure in?"

"Big time. Pittsburgh is a big part of the story."

Luis looked down at his wife as they walked toward the theater district. "You're enjoying this, aren't you?"

"Do you want to hear Pittsburgh's connection or not?"

"I'm listening."

"The bomb plant—that's what Georgians and South Carolinians called it for years—was constructed in 1950 at the direction of the government and the Atomic Energy Commission."

"To make bombs."

"Officially to manufacture materials for national defense."

"And Pittsburgh's connection?"

"That was later. DuPont, a company from out west built the plant, which goes along with the diversified population of Augusta. But Pittsburgh. About 1989, Westinghouse took over the management."

"I'm waiting."

"For what?"

"Pittsburgh."

"Westinghouse is based in Pittsburgh." She sounded exasperated. "I think our next trip will be to my home town. Let you see Pittsburgh for yourself.

"But I digress. When Westinghouse took over, they sent their people to run the plant. And who were these people? Pittsburghers." She smiled triumphantly. "They settled in Augusta and Aiken, across the river in South Carolina."

"Took you a while to get to the bottom line." Luis stopped suddenly. Speaking of bottom. My stomach has bottomed out."

"There you go again—thinking of food. Are we going to catch a show?"

"*Si, señora*. But lunch?

She pointed down the block to a cart on a corner. "Hot dogs?"

"When in Rome." They hurried down the block for an elegant lunch on the streets of New York.

Ten minutes later, munching hot dogs and drinking ice cold bottles of water, they stood in line for tickets to the matinee of *Waiting for Godot*, with Nathan Lane.

With minutes to spare, they settled into their seats and watched the curtain rise.

Chapter 79

When the curtain fell after the final bow, they were herded from the theater onto the street.

"Next time I pick the show. It'll be a musical," Elia said.

He smiled at her as they turned to walk toward Park Avenue. "What's next?"

"St. Patrick's Cathedral." She pointed in front of her. We can go to Mass and then—I know you're going to like this one—have dinner."

They were guided by pealing bells to the New York landmark. They slipped inside and mingled with the tourists before walking up the aisle and entering a pew.

The 150-year-old cathedral, reminiscent of a European church is the largest gothic-style church in the United States.

Luis compared it to his gold-laden boyhood church in Perú. He could describe both as grand and cold. Then he thought of the warm atmosphere of St. Mary on the Hill, their parish church in Augusta.

Although the tourists were behind ropes and far from the sanctuary, there was still a low overtone of voices from those not participating in the Mass. Traffic sounds filtered in to add to the cacophony that should never be present at Mass.

"Beautiful church, but not home," Elia said when they were out on the street.

"I was thinking the same thing." He looked back at the cathedral. "But I felt safe there."

"Here I feel safe. So many people, and not one is Harry Millen."

"I'll drink to that." He pointed to a restaurant down the street. "Giambelli 50. Care for Italian tonight?"

"*Perfecto*."

As soon as they entered they were greeted by a small woman with a welcoming smile. On the wall behind her was a large framed photo of Pope John Paul II shaking hands with her husband, Franscesco Giambelli, during a visit to New York.

Elia stood looking at the photo. "The Pope ate here?" She crossed her hands on her chest, as if John Paul II were going to give her his personal blessing.

Mrs. Giambelli led them to their table and explained that the Pope did indeed have his meals at their restaurant.

"Please, can you sit down and tell us what it was like?" Elia's eager face showed her interest. "What did you serve him?"

Mrs. Giambelli had no trouble remembering. "Italian antipasto, angoletti risotto, filet of sole with porcini mushrooms and fruit salad." She practically sang the menu. She added, "He must have liked it, because he asked for the same when he returned for dinner." She excused herself and went to greet other diners with the same warmth she had shown to Luis and Elia.

"New York is busy, busy, busy, but this place is an oasis." Elia sipped wine while Luis studied the menu. "And the Pope was here!"

"Spoken like a good Catholic girl." He put the menu down, held up his wine in toast: "To my beautiful wife, who today got the thrill of her very young life."

They touched glasses. "To my husband the poet; could anyone know it?"

As they approached the door after dinner, Mrs. Giambelli was there to say good night. She hugged Elia and pulled a long-stem red rose out of an arrangement and presented it to her. To Luis she gave a laminated photo of the Pope taken in the restaurant. "A memory for you," she said.

Even though the sun had long since gone down, the streets were crowded, giving them a sense of security. They strolled toward Grand Central Station and arrived in plenty of time to catch the train. They settled in for a forty-five-minute ride.

The train slowly emptied as it headed toward Connecticut. When it reached Port Chester, the last stop in New York, they were among the few people getting off. There was a lone light illuminating the stairs leading to the near-empty parking lot. They held hands and hurried to their car, constantly looking around.

Elia shivered. "Toto, we're not in Kansas anymore."

Chapter 80

They jogged through Old Greenwich, enjoying the cool summer morning. Traffic sounds were muted on the tree-lined residential streets.

"What good do you think Lorraine will be?" Elia had slowed to a walk. "She didn't seem too—what's the word I want—I don't know—warm? Willing?"

Luis slowed to match her pace. "We caught her by surprise. She looked shocked when we told her about Millen."

"I noticed," Elia said. "You work with someone every day and then find out he's crooked and a murderer."

"It'll take her time to get her mind wrapped around that idea."

Elia frowned. "I've been thinking. If Harry Millen is responsible, Luis, how could he have caused Aaron Scharff's death? He was at his own party when it happened."

Luis stopped in his tracks.

"What?" Elia stopped a few steps ahead and looked back.

"Vicente. Millen wasn't in Bermuda." He caught up with her. "And he wasn't at the dive site."

They walked back to the hotel in silence.

Chapter 81

They were ushered to Fegan's corner office by her secretary. Lorraine came around her desk to shake their hands. "Harry is on his way down with one of our scientists." She motioned to two chairs facing her desk. "Please sit down."

She pulled two more chairs toward her desk. "I've been thinking about what you said yesterday." She settled behind her desk.

"But..." Luis put his hand on Elia's knee before she could finish.

Fegan continued. "And I think the only two conclusions I can come up with are first, it's impossible for Harry to be involved in anything detrimental to Pavnor." She paused and glanced at the door.

"Two?" Elia prodded.

Fegan gave her an impatient look. "Two, he wouldn't want anything detrimental to happen to Pavnor, so maybe he would do something, well, illegal."

"But have you looked into it?" Now it was Elia who looked impatient.

"No, I haven't." Again she looked at the door. "Let's see what Harry has to say." She nodded toward the door.

Harry Millen barged in with Pete Archer close behind. "Sorry I'm late." He shook Elia's hand, then Luis's. "This is Doctor Archer; he's been researching the Cyptolis problem."

"The problem I see is that the drug is on the market under a different name than thirty years ago," Luis said.

"Yes, and we address that," Millen said. "I want to keep you abreast, Doctor," he said to Luis, and you, Ms. Christie, because I know how distressed you are about Dr. Pereda's death and the fact that his research paper wasn't presented at the conference. I understand you want Dr. Pereda's findings made public. And one of his findings is that the drug is almost identical to another that had been pulled from our line years ago.

"Lorraine, would you like to explain how the drug got on the market. How it had FDA approval?"

Lorraine sat behind her desk with her hands clasped on her blotter. "All right. First, we definitely had approval. Let's go back thirty years. Abecour had been prescribed for spasticity in cases of paralysis. When the liver function problems became known, Pavnor recalled the drug. With Cyptolis, the liver function side effect was thought to be eliminated." She looked at Dr. Archer. "Pete, you can explain better than I. Can you help me out?"

Pete Archer cleared his throat, rotated his head from one side to the other, and swallowed visibly. He nodded.

"It's the same drug—and it isn't. Some of the radicals were changed, and that was thought to have taken care of the liver problems. Cyptolis had gone through the trials." He looked at Elia for emphasis. "There are several stages. And Cyptolis is poised for universal release by the FDA."

"How can it be given to patients if it's merely poised, to use your word, for release?" Elia asked.

Archer cleared his throat and stopped the head spiral in mid twist. "That's the last trial. This is a long process, and Pavnor was on the last step. That's what the final trial is."

"So it was ethical to prescribe Cyptolis without final FDA approval?" Elia asked.

"Yes, of course," Lorraine answered. "It's done all the time."

"But what about the liver problems Vicente found?" Elia asked.

"I think I can answer that," Luis said. "I've gone over his report. He reported on an indiscriminate number of patients with hemorrhaging in the liver. This is a different problem with the liver than with the original drug."

Elia looked from Luis to Archer.

Archer took a deep breath and seemed to make an effort to answer without clearing his throat. No head twisting this time. "We investigated after seeing his report."

"So the FDA will rescind the approval?" Elia asked no one in particular.

"Not necessarily." Lorraine said. We can place a black box around it." She looked at Elia.

"I know what that is. What happens if the FDA won't accept the black box designation?"

"Then Pavnor recalls the drug, and all bets are off," Millen said.

Luis spoke up. "Do you know why there is hemorrhaging?" He looked at Archer. "If the drug is the same, or at least very similar except for a few radicals, why is there hemorrhaging?"

"This is a new development. When we find out we'll be able to eliminate the problem."

"Who reports the new findings to the FDA?" Elia asked.

"I'll take care of that," Fegan said.

Millen looked at Fegan and shook his head. "No, I will." He motioned with his head to the door. "Ready, Pete?" He turned his attention to Luis. "Call me if you have any questions." With that he and Archer left.

When Luis and Elia turned to leave, Elia looked up and saw a water-color painting in fall foliage shades with mountains lavish with orange and red-leafed trees in the background. In front of the mountains was a nineteenth century turreted building. The artist blurred the building and put the emphasis on the mountains.

"What a beautiful scene," Elia said. "Is it an actual place?"

Lorraine seemed distracted but looked over at the painting. "My alma mater, Seton Hill." Then in an offhand way, as if she were accustomed to the next words, said, "It's near where the plane crashed on 9-11." With that she ushered them out the door and closed it quickly as they walked away.

They didn't speak as they walked to the parking lot. "Did you hear what Lorraine said?"

"I heard what everybody said but I don't think we heard anything new." He sounded angry. "What was this meeting about?"

She waved her hand in dismissal. "No, not that. About the painting."

He frowned in confusion. "The painting?"

"I heard that from someone else lately, but I can't remember who, or why."

"Heard what?"

"That's near where the plane crashed on 9-11."

Chapter 82

Luis gathered up his razor, shaving cream and toothbrush and stashed them in his kit. Elia leaned on the doorframe watching. "If I didn't know better I'd say you're in a hurry."

"I should have followed my instincts." He shook his head. "Time to talk to the police. Should have done that earlier." He started pacing around the room.

Elia chased him down and stood in front of him. She put her hands on his shoulders. "Honey, calm down. The police are involved up here.

"They're investigating the break-in at Dot's. Charleston and Kiawah police are looking for the people who broke into Vicente's. They're looking for whoever caused the accident that killed Aaron, and may I remind you the Bermuda police are investigating Vicente's murder.

"We came; there's nothing that's going to change that, so quit beating yourself up."

Luis took a deep breath. He pulled Elia into his arms and put his face in her hair. Then he held her at arms' length. "Something is going on at Pavnor."

"Ya think?"

"Not funny, Elia. Millen chases us to Cape Cod, for what. He tries to kill us, then calls us to Pavnor to explain things." He shook his head. "He didn't tell us anything new. And did you notice, no one said anything about the drug being produced in China?"

"Why was that?" Elia sat on the edge of the bed watching Luis pace in the small space. "Does he think we'd never find that out? And why should it matter anyway?"

Luis pulled his clothes from the closet. He turned to look at her. "That's what makes me think that fact is important. Important enough to hide it from us, or at least not share that piece of information."

"But China. I don't know, Luis. Everything's produced in China. We talked about this."

"That's what I mean. Makes me think he's hiding something else."

"Then let's stay and find out what that something is."

"Nice try, *chica*." He picked up her empty makeup bag and handed it to her. "Let's go back to Kiawah. I want a little less anxiety in my life. Something's going on, and it's here." He turned her toward her empty suitcase. "So I don't want to be here."

"Luis?" Elia was bent over her suitcase and slowly stood. "Why would Harry arrange a meeting if he thought we'd be dead?"

Chapter 83

Hanssen couldn't get Bermuda out of his head. It started with Vicente. Certain people didn't want him to present his paper. It was fortuitous that he had gotten sick before the meeting. Who could have predicted that he would die? And then the police and the questions. So far they haven't asked the right ones. Things were fine until that business on *Mad Money*. Who the hell was that jerk? And was he talking about Pavnor? That's problem two. What a damn mess.

Hanssen sat at his desk and chewed on his thumbnail and stared into space. People weren't supposed to die. Now besides Pereda, Aaron was dead, and Pereda's girlfriend was dying.

He thought about Luis and Elia. "Clueless." He said it with a shake of his head. "They're involved in this, and they're clueless."

"Damn." He pushed back in his chair so fast and forcefully that he hit the back wall. "I may get into a lot of trouble, but it's just money. They've been in the wrong place at the wrong time since Bermuda." He didn't realize he was speaking aloud. He picked up the picture of his wife and kids and stared at it for a full minute.

"Maybe for once I should do the right thing," he said softly as his thumb brushed over the faces of his family, now gone from his life. "Even if I don't know what that is."

He pulled out his Blackberry, scrolled down, found the number he was looking for, and punched it in.

After the preliminary greeting he said, "Luis, we have to talk." Hanssen made the date. "Kiawah. Okay. I'll see both of you there." He ended the call and said aloud to the empty room, "Dr. Echevarria, I have a surprise for you."

He turned to his computer, checked airline flights to Charleston, then pulled up a blank document and began typing.

Hanssen attached his document to three e-mails then left for the airport. "Might as well let them know what's about to hit them."

Chapter 84

Luis and Elia arrived in Charleston as the sun was setting. They checked into The Sanctuary and had dinner at the Jasmine Porch before settling into their suite. Elia had ordered a light dinner of shrimp and grits. She pushed her food around her plate.

"What are you thinking?"

"I don't want to spoil anything, Luis, I really don't."

"But?"

"But why are we back here?" She held up a hand. "Don't misunderstand. It's beautiful here." She gestured toward the ocean barely visible in the waning light. "But aren't you ready to go home? To start our life in Augusta?"

"I'm ready. I should have asked you what you wanted to do before I made plans."

"Ah ha! A good lesson to learn early."

"But I wanted us to have a peacefully normal honeymoon before we start back to work." He reached across the table and took her hand. "We'll go home. First, let's have a few relaxing days here without looking over our shoulders. We can feel comfortable here."

"Comfortable?" She looked around the restaurant. "I'd say more than comfortable."

"Safe." He glanced at Elia. "I mean safe." He nodded and looked determined. "Let's relax." He squeezed Elia's hand. "I want to give my undivided attention to my wife."

"So we're really giving up?" She said it with regret. "After all we've been through?"

"What else can we do? You said yourself, the police are investigating."

"I did, but it wouldn't hurt to do our own little thing on the side."

"Are you *una loca*? Every time we do, something scary happens."

"We can do it from afar."

The waiter came and picked up the bottle of Pinot Grigio from the ice bucket, wiped the dampness off the bottle, and refreshed their wine glasses.

When they were alone, Luis remained silent. Finally he spoke. "I do want to do more research." His hands were flat on the table and he raised them just inches, keeping his wrists firmly planted in front of him. "Wait. I want to do more research, but quietly."

"Quietly. I can be quiet." Then she said: "Quietly?"

"I'll do my research and not share my findings with anyone from Pavnor. If things begin to look too murky, I'll turn everything over to the police and let them finish the digging."

"Oh that'll go far." She wore her most cynical expression to go along with her statement.

Chapter 85

Elia woke with a start and reached over to touch Luis. Like a blind person, she moved her hand up and down where his body should have been. He wasn't there. She squinted at the bedside clock. The time stared her in the face: 3:10 a.m. She climbed out of bed and padded into the living room. Luis was hunched over his laptop, the computer's glow the only light in the room. He must have been engrossed in what he was reading because she startled him when she touched his shoulder.

"Honey, don't sneak up on people like that."

"Now who do you think it could have been?" She leaned over and kissed his cheek. "What are you doing here in the middle of the night?"

"I couldn't sleep. Had to get to it."

"It?"

"Research. You're right. We can't stop."

"I'm so glad to hear you say that."

"Do you have the feeling no one cares?"

"I do."

He turned from the computer to better see her. "We don't know how the investigation is going with Vicente; we don't know what's going on with Aaron's accident investigation." He turned toward the computer. "But I can sit here and do some of my own research."

"What are you reading there?" Elia nodded toward the screen.

"Drug production in China. There's a mountain of articles about problems in the Chinese plants." He tapped the screen. "I'm reading about contamination in this article." He turned back to Elia. "I'd like to know who at Pavnor gave the okay to go to China."

"And why we weren't told about China at the meeting with Millen and Archer."

Luis nodded. "Who wanted to keep it quiet?"

"And why?" Elia added.

Elia left Luis at the computer and crawled back into bed. Three hours later she stretched and felt Luis beside her. She slipped quietly out of bed and walked silently into the bathroom. She washed her face, brushed her teeth, and dressed in running clothes. Luis had not stirred as she stole out of the suite.

The hotel lobby was quiet as she pushed open the heavy door to head for a run on the beach. The sun was still below the horizon. She reached the beach and decided to run east to better see the imminent sunrise. The farther she ran, the less developed the island. In the distance was the Ocean Course and clubhouse, but she couldn't see them yet in dawn's light.

She loved early morning runs. But she slowly slackened her pace to a walk. Then she stood completely still.

Breaking through the silence of the morning was a motor. She cocked her head. Then she saw it.

Coming from the direction of the Ocean Course was a vehicle, a truck maybe. Its headlights were out, but she could make out its shape. The rising sun shone in her eyes as she tried to see more.

An eerie feeling came over her as she looked to the ocean and then to her left toward the dunes. There were no homes in this area. She was completely alone—except for the truck. It wasn't traveling fast.

Elia willed herself to calm down. The truck sped up. The driver turned on the headlights and high beams and raced in

Elia's direction. She moved closer to the water to give the truck plenty of room on the hard sand.

The truck headed straight at Elia. She ran into shallow water and scattered the sandpipers scrounging for food. They flew off as the truck roared past within inches of Elia. Its left back tire spit out wet sand as it screamed away.

Elia put her hand to her heart and took some deep breaths. She heard a sound behind her and saw the truck making a u-turn.

"Oh my god!" She looked at the ocean, then at the dunes. She made her decision. She raced across the wide beach and scrambled up the dunes just as the truck came barreling toward her. It looked as though it were going to try to cross the dunes. It nosed into the soft sand and stopped. It backed out and raced east. By now the sun was up and the truck was more visible. But Elia was racing away through the brush and did not see that it wasn't a truck after all.

She ran down a path away from the dunes and then stopped gasping for breath. She stepped off the path into the woods and bent from the waist and gagged with dry heaves. She spotted a fallen tree trunk and sat down to catch her breath. She hadn't thought about hiding, but when she heard a car coming down the road from the east, she tried to make herself invisible. She pulled up her shoulders as if she were a turtle. As it was, the thick foliage camouflaged her.

The car was going slowly. The fact that it was just a car relieved her anxiety. She was about to stand and continue on her way back to the hotel when she caught a glimpse of the driver as it turned in the direction of The Sanctuary.

She stayed hidden for at least twenty minutes, hoping Jacob Riser was no longer prowling the island.

Chapter 86

Lorraine Fegan was getting tired. "Why me? Why does everything happen to me?" She was in her bedroom with a suitcase thrown open on the bed. She folded her clothes with the precision of a drill sergeant and packed them neatly guaranteeing no wrinkles when she reached her destination.

"Why the hell do I have to take care of everything?" Her teeth were clenched as she reached for her Riesling and drained the glass. She raised her arm and was about to throw her empty wine glass against the wall. She stopped herself in mid throw, looked at the $300 cut glass in her hand, and lowered her arm. She filled her glass from the bottle on her bedside table and took a large swallow.

She laid black pants and a long sleeved white silk blouse on her bed and carefully placed tissue paper between the folds.

She opened a drawer in her bedside table and felt to the back and retrieved a key on a tiny chain. In her closet on the far wall hidden by hanging clothes was a small door, the size of a medicine cabinet. She pushed clothes aside and unlocked the cabinet. Inside were drugs arranged in alphabetical order. She drummed her fingers lightly on the door as she perused the selection, as though she were deciding on which outfit to wear. Her hand landed on the D section. She palmed a small bottle and quietly closed and locked the cabinet. She tucked the bottle into her carry-on bag.

"Why the hell do I have to take care of everything?" She would repeat that phrase many times as she went about taking care of Pavnor business—and her own.

Chapter 87

Elia made her way back to the hotel keeping to paths and away from the road. She entered The Sanctuary through a side entrance and walked down the long corridor past high-end shops, not yet open for the day. Before stepping into the lobby, she peeked around the corner looking for Riser. She hurried across the lobby, ducked under the wide staircase, and reached the elevator. She watched numbers light up as the elevator raced to the first floor. The car stopped on two. For a moment Elia didn't think of a consequence, but when it started descending again her heart dropped as fast as the car. Color drained from her face. She was looking around for a corner to hide in when the doors opened.

Two people dressed for a run stepped off the elevator, nodded to her, and walked toward the door leading to the beach.

She patted her heart, stepped into the elevator and rode up to her floor. She tried to slow her breathing.

"What the hell were you thinking?" He burst onto the deck and roared at his wife. His face was red and his veins looked ready to burst. She whirled away from the view of the ocean, her eyes wide with surprise and fear at the anger in her husband's voice. He reached her in seconds and grabbed her arms. "What the hell were you doing on the beach?"

She cowered thinking he would hit her. But then she stiffened. She freed herself from his grasp rubbing her arms where his hands had been. She leaned away from him, her back hitting the railing, and crossed her arms in front of her chest. "How dare you speak to me that way." She spoke in low tones, a contrast to his roar. She looked at her husband with contempt. "You're a loser."

Jacob Riser went slack, like a deflated balloon. "Bonnie, what's going on?" He almost whispered the question.

She looked past him into the house and swept her arm toward the house and then out toward the ocean. "Do you think we could afford this house and the place in town on what you bring home?" She paused but a second. "Our trips? Our cars? My jewelry?"

He frowned in confusion.

"Sure, frown. I'm the one who pays the bills, so I'm the one who knows how much money we have—or don't have. I'm the one who knows when we need more money. I'm the one who invests our money. I'm the one who makes the money. Not you."

"I know about our investments." He sounded like a kid protesting.

"You know about your investments; but you don't know about mine."

"Why don't you tell me?" He lowered himself into a chair; she remained standing with her back to the ocean. "And why don't you tell me why you were trying to run down that woman on the beach?"

She sneered at him with hate-filled eyes. "Someone has to do something."

Her comments seemed to deflate him even more. "What's going on, Bonnie?"

She turned from him and looked out toward the beach. "You saw me out there?" She said it quietly. Her anger, too, had dissipated.

"I did." Riser followed her gaze. "Why?" He stood and leaned on the railing beside his wife and looked at her.

"You don't know what's going on? You don't care?" She sounded incredulous. "Jake, wake up." She said it through clenched teeth. "You don't want to know." She shook her head in dismissal.

"Know what?"

"The damn drug, you moron." She clenched the railing. "You're a damn moron."

"And you're a shrew. Now tell me what's so damn important that you have to run down that woman."

She shrugged. "All right." She sang it in that annoying way. "Maybe you should know. But you're not going to like it."

Chapter 88

Luis was still sleeping when Elia let herself into the suite. She stole into the bathroom and took a long hot shower. Wearing nothing but a towel wrapped around her wet head, she got into bed and snuggled up to Luis as if he were her security blanket.

As she lay there listening to Luis's even breathing, she felt herself getting angry. First she was angry with the people who were trying to frighten her, then she became angrier at herself for letting those people succeed. A guilty wave passed over her as she thought about Vicente and Angel and Aaron.

She lay there getting herself more upset as she thought of the past two weeks. My wedding. What memories. Still snuggled up to Luis, she kissed him softly on his shoulder. She smiled. When he sleeps, he sleeps. Well I can't. She slipped out of bed, dressed, and tiptoed into the sitting room and out onto the balcony. She looked toward the east and thought about the truck. How did Riser get rid of the truck so fast and into the car? She wondered where their house was in relation to The Sanctuary and made a mental note to find out.

"What the hell were you thinking?" He had his hands on his wife's shoulders and stared into her eyes. "*Madre Mia*! You could have been killed." He pulled her to his chest. "Jesus! Elia you're *una loca!*"

Elia ignored his outburst and continued with her story. "He got rid of his truck and came looking for me on the road." She frowned. "I can't figure out how he did that so fast."

"Why didn't you wake me up when you got home?"

He reached out and caught her hand. "Come here." His dark eyes bored into her emerald greens. "No more early morning runs alone." He wrapped her in his arms. "No more."

Chapter 89

"Here's part of the problem." Luis and Elia were sipping their coffee on the patio of the Jasmine Porch. Their waitress had just filled their cups, put the carafe on the table, and departed quietly.

"Bleeding." He said it and stopped. He was looking out at the ocean.

Elia put her hand on his arm. "Luis? Bleeding? We know there's bleeding."

"Yes, but why now? If this is the same drug from before, and bleeding wasn't the problem then, why now?"

"Maybe it's not the same drug after all. Maybe we're all wet."

Luis bit into a pineapple-filled pastry then looked at it as if he were surprised he had even picked it up.

"Luis? Are you here?" Elia dipped her head to get him to look at her.

"Look at this pastry. I bet they bake them right here in their kitchen. But even if they didn't." He picked up a strawberry-filled one and took a bite. "I don't taste any pineapple in this one."

Elia looked at both pastries, both now with teeth marks. She held out her hands and wore a "What are you talking about?" expression.

"And do you know why?"

"Why you don't taste any pineapple? Luis! What are you talking about?"

"I don't taste any pineapple in the strawberry pastry because the kitchens here have strict guidelines." He took another bite.

"Remember the peanut scare traced to the plant in Georgia?" He didn't wait for an answer. "Unsafe practices made a lot of people sick all over the country and even killed some."

"Are you saying the drug was made in unsanitary conditions?" She frowned. "Pavnor? Unsanitary?"

"Maybe."

"Just maybe?" Elia looked impatient. "Luis, quit talking in riddles. What are you saying?"

"Yes, Pavnor is responsible, but the drug isn't processed there, remember. It's made in China."

"Of course." Elia snapped her fingers. "They don't have the same standards we have here in the States." She looked at both teeth-marked pastries. "But what's new here? We already knew about China."

Luis ran his finger over the rim of his coffee cup. "That's what I was looking for last night." He pushed his cup out of his way, laid his hands on the table, and drummed his fingers.

"And?" Elia leaned across the table and put her hands over the drummer's.

His fingers stopped drumming. "And I wondered why patients were hemorrhaging."

"And Vicente?"

"No. We know why he hemorrhaged; he was given a lethal dose of heparin." He retrieved his hands and played a few beats. "But Vicente's death put me on this track. Heparin."

"Patients are given heparin along with Cyptolis?"

"Think of these pastries. Strawberry is strawberry; pineapple is pineapple."

"Yes?" She drew out the word and waited for an explanation.

"Strict standards here." But Cyptolis is produced in China." He reached for the carafe and poured himself hot coffee. "Want some?" She shook her head. He picked up the pineapple pastry and took another bite." He held it out for her to taste.

"You're enjoying this, aren't you?" She leaned back in her chair and stared at him.

"Think Georgia peanuts. Think contamination. Think bleeding. Think heparin."

"Ah. Cyptolis and heparin are made in the same facility. Of course. I remember reading about contamination in a Chinese company that produced heparin." She frowned. "And Vicente knew why the patients were hemorrhaging, and he planned to expose Pavnor."

"No, that's not why Vicente was killed."

"But I thought that's what you meant." Elia looked across the table at Luis and shook her head. "What do you mean?"

"There was nothing in Vicente's report about China. I don't think he knew. And if he did, like you've already pointed out, it's almost what isn't made in China."

"But why was Vicente murdered? And Aaron?"

"I don't know why people had to die." He was still holding the pastry. He looked at it as if he couldn't figure out how it got in his hand. "We're missing something here. What is it?"

Lorraine Fegan caught a plane out of White Plains for Charleston. When she arrived late afternoon it was raining. As she deplaned, the look on her face was as dark as the day. "Why the hell do I have to do everything?" Her mantra was still intact and she recited it as she got behind the wheel of her rental car.

"I'm here." She was on highway 526 when she made her call. She listened to a tirade, then said quietly through clenched teeth. "Because it's obvious you screw everything up, that's why." She hit the off button and took some deep breaths to calm herself.

"Damn blood pressure." She put her hand to her neck hoping to relieve a choking feeling. "Why do I have to do everything?" She hit the steering wheel with both hands. "I feel like a damn closer."

Chapter 90

"We're going home." Luis was standing on the balcony looking out to sea.

Elia turned and leaned against the railing and looked at Luis. "I thought you wanted to see this to the end. Why change your mind?" She tried to keep criticism from her tone and struggled not to say, "again."

"You." He glanced down at his wife.

"Me?" Her voice rose a few notes.

"Yes, you." Before he could say more, Elia pounced.

"You're the one who wanted to come back to Kiawah."

"This is too much," he said.

"Luis, what's the matter with you. One minute you want to get to the bottom of this, the next minute you want to close the book and go home. I want to know what's going on, I want to know the end of this story."

"It's dangerous." Luis kept his voice low.

"Luis, don't quit because of me. Maybe it's the reporter in me, or maybe—just maybe—it's because my childhood friend was murdered on our wedding day."

She shook her head. "Luis," she continued, "we can't stop until we get to the bottom of this."

He shook his head as if in amazement.

"What?"

"You're a tiger." He pointed to himself. "But me? I'm frightened. You have no idea how frightened I am."

She saw the tears in his eyes. "It's me. You're frightened for me." She wiped his tears away. "I'm scared. But I'm not dead yet, so don't picture me so vulnerable."

He wrapped his arms around her. "It's too hot here. Things are too hot here."

Elia released herself from his embrace. "Honey, we've been going back and forth ever since Vicente died. Either we're in—or we're out." She put her hands on his arms. We've been in since the beginning. Let's finish this." She said it quietly, calmly.

Luis shook his head. "*Mierda.*" He again shook his head, planted a quick kiss on Elia's lips, and again swore softly.

Chapter 91

Elia was on the balcony, her feet on the bottom rung of the railing, Luis's laptop slanted on her thighs.

Luis came out carrying two iced teas and looked over her shoulder. "Googling. What're you looking for?"

Her fingers flew across the keyboard. "Huh? Oh." She shook her head as if to shake herself out of the zone, that far off land that the mind drifts to when thoughts are flying around inside the head. "Just curious."

"About?"

"Seton Hill." She frowned. "Something's bothering me. 'Where the plane crashed on 9-11.' Why did I hear that exact same phrase somewhere?" She punched some more keys. "Okay. I'm in."

Luis pulled up a chair and sat beside her. "That happens to me."

Elia turned to look at him with a question in her eyes.

"You know. I can't put my finger on something. It'll come."

"Luis, how old do you think Lorraine is?"

"I don't know. Forty-five? Forty-two? Forty-seven? She looks fit; I don't think the gray hair can help us. And it's obvious she's not a smoker; her skin is good."

"Let's say she was twenty-one when she graduated." The keyboard clicked. She shook her head. "Not that year." She kept typing. "She's single, right?"

"How would I know?"

"She's single, or at least she's still using her maiden name." She put her face closer to the computer. "Look. Here she is." She turned the computer so Luis could see. "She was already gray in college."

He took a quick look before Elia claimed the laptop again. She cozied up to the screen to look at Fegan's classmates.

They were all women. It wasn't until several years later that the all women's college became coed, and several more before it became a university.

Elia perused the online yearbook and quickly scanned the graduation photos. "What?" She sat back in her chair and brought her hand to her face and played with her lower lip. Then she looked at the screen again and thought back to Bermuda and the boat and the dive.

"Bonnie Senzo." She looked at Luis. "Bonnie Riser." She pushed the computer at Luis. "And she didn't have that golden hair in college."

"Important?"

"Not the hair." She took the computer back. "They knew each other twenty-some years ago." She looked off into space.

"Majors. Let's see." Her fingers played the keyboard. "Lorraine majored in chemistry and pharmacology. Makes sense, I guess."

She scrolled down to S and Senzo. "Another double major." She frowned.

"Well?" Luis was staring at her. "What's it say for Bonnie?"

"Forensic science and pharmacology." She turned to Luis. "Bermuda. She knows pharmacology—and all that CSI stuff. Bonnie? Vicente? Bonnie and Harry?"

Luis held up his hands in a stop signal. "*Parate.*" Number one, Harry didn't murder Vicente; he wasn't in Bermuda. Number two, what the hell are we doing?"

"Here you go again. You're having second thoughts." She started ticking off points on her fingers. "Let's start with number two. What we are doing is helping the police." Now it was she who held up her stop sign. "Wait. The police. What are they doing? Have we had any information from them about the break-in at Vicente's house? No."

Luis got to his feet and opened his mouth to speak.

"I'm not finished. The police. What about the police in Bermuda? I talked with Vicente's parents the other day, and they've heard nothing." She swiveled in her chair to watch Luis who was now pacing back and forth on the balcony. "So to re-iterate, *señor doctor,* we're helping the police."

Luis stopped pacing to look at her. "It looks like we're do-ing their work."

"Somebody has to do it." She turned back to her comput-er and looked at the Seton Hill page again and nodded. Number one. Harry wasn't in Bermuda, but Bonnie and Jacob Riser were. Riser tried to run me down on the beach and then tried to hunt me down on the road. He's a doctor, knows about drug interactions." She pointed to the computer screen. "And look what Bonnie majored in. She's the perfect person to help mur-der Vicente."

Luis leaned against the railing, his arms folded in front of him, and looked down at his wife, the computer cradled in her lap.

"Well?"

He turned to the sea and hit the railing with an open hand. Staring out at the ocean, he said in a low voice, "Riser. He dove with us. Your air hose. Sliced."

Chapter 92

Riser staggered from the house. The woman he married had no mea culpas. She had looked at him with eyes as hard as steel and full of hatred and contempt.

He drove off the island and pulled off the parkway at Freshfields Village and stopped, motor running. Relaxed-looking tourists sauntered throughout the open-air village in and out of the upscale shops. He rested his head on the steering wheel, his hands forming a cushion.

He had seen that look of contempt before. Many times. But enough. She tried to kill that woman. "No." He shouted inside his closed car. A family of four walking past jumped at the noise. They looked, then hurried on. He hit the steering wheel with the palms of his hands. "Damn it. No!" He maneuvered back out on the parkway and turned toward Kiawah. "Not this time, Bonnie, not this time."

He dug in his pocket and pulled out his cell phone. He found Luis's number and made the call.

"First Frank, and now Jake. Sounds like a summit," Elia said when Luis ended the call.

"Sounds like a train wreck."

Chapter 93

"Honey, I called Angel's parents; she's awake now. Let's go see her." They had finished breakfast and had strolled down the boardwalk to watch the tide come in.

"You called her parents?" Luis asked. "That's kind of intrusive, don't you think?"

She ignored that question. "I knew the hospital wouldn't tell me anything. And before you say another word, I asked if we could visit."

"And?"

"And they said that would be nice."

Luis bent down and kissed his wife on the cheek. "You <u>are</u> nice." He looked at his watch. "When?"

"Now?"

They arrived before lunch and found Angel sitting up in bed. Her face was swollen, and black and blue was turning a mustard yellow. Her head was bandaged, and an IV was running into her arm. She looked better than the last time they saw her. She looked confused when she saw them.

"I'm Elia Christie, and this is my husband Luis Echevarria. We're friends of Vicente's. Do you remember us?"

As if a dark cloud dissipated, a look of recognition settled on her face. She nodded and smiled tenuously. "We were going to meet." She frowned. "Did we meet?"

Elia stood at Angel's bed and covered her hand with her own. "We met for a few minutes, but you had the accident before we saw each other again."

The dark cloud reappeared. "My mom told me Mr. Scharff died."

Luis pulled chairs up to the bed. They sat quietly for a few moments. "Do you remember why Mr. Scharff was bringing you to Kiawah?" Luis spoke soothingly.

She frowned and shook her head. "I remember he picked me up." She sounded frustrated. "Why? I'm trying to remember."

"About Vicente?" Elia asked.

"I guess." Again she shook her head.

"Your head injury," Luis said. "You still have some swelling; you'll remember."

She nodded and closed her eyes. "I hope so," she said sleepily.

Luis's own eyes flew wide open. "Damn!" he whispered.

Elia looked alarmed and turned quickly to Angel.

"What is it?"

"Angel? Can I ask you a question?" Luis said softly, bending close. "Angel?" He touched her shoulder.

"She all right?"

"She's sleeping. Damn," he repeated. "Let's go. We'll come back."

"What was that all about?" Elia asked. They were on Bees Ferry Road going toward Kiawah.

"Where is my head?"

"What are you talking about, Luis?"

"Vicente's papers."

"Okay…"

"The ones I found in the locker at Cassique. I know what he was so upset about, and why he felt he couldn't tell anybody."

"China, bleeding," Elia began ticking off the reasons.

"Old news." He pointed behind him in the direction they had just traveled. "I want to talk to Angel."

"Are you going to share?

He slapped the steering wheel. "Ethics." He slapped the wheel again. "What was I thinking? There's someone in Charleston I want to talk with."

Chapter 94

Luis looked up the number, made the call and an appointment. He snapped his phone shut. "Okay, let's go see Vicente's chief." Luis held the door and waited until Elia gathered her purse and notebook. He picked up the papers he found at Cassique. "Got a paper clip in that portable office?" he asked with a nod toward her purse.

She rummaged a minute and came up with one. He clipped the papers together and rolled them in his hand. "Let's go."

She motioned to the papers. "Is this number six?" she asked as they waited for the elevator.

"Number six?" Luis pushed the down button and looked lost at her question.

"We were ticking off the problems and never got to six. Is this it?"

His face cleared. "As a matter of fact, it just might be; I'm thinking."

They arrived at the hospital and were directed to the third floor office of Dr. Paul Kittrick.

"You left the papers in the car."

"Not the time for them."

Kittrick's door was open. He sat behind a pristine desk. Sharpened pencils stood like sentries in a pewter cup. His blotter was spotless and centered perfectly on the desk. One sheet of paper was in the center of that perfect blotter. Three books were in a perfect little stack on a corner of the pristine desk.

His laptop was open and sat three inches to the left of the sheet of paper.

When his secretary tapped on the door and opened it for Luis and Elia, he closed the laptop, straightened the already perfectly placed sheet of paper, then stood.

He shook their hands and motioned for them to sit. He sat, opened a drawer and pulled out a bottle of hand sanitizer, gave himself a couple of squirts, rubbed his hands together, put the sanitizer away, then looked at Luis and Elia as if that dance had never been performed.

"Vicente. You want to talk about Vicente." The paper on his desk must have moved, because he had to rearrange it.

"We do." Luis and Elia had discussed ahead of time that they would keep each other cool. So far so good with the first seconds. "Before Vicente died, he told us about some problem he was having at work."

"Problem?" The books must have moved; he set them straighter.

"We weren't sure what the problem was at the time; he died before he could tell us."

Kittrick moved the computer a fraction of an inch, rearranged his pencils, and centered his chair at his desk. Elia stared at him as he did his calisthenics. To her credit, she didn't sneak a peek at Luis.

She cleared her throat and put herself back in the game. "But we think we have a good idea what was bothering him." She kept with the "be cool" plan and kept her tone emotionless. The same tone she used when interviewing people for stories. She had found that if people detected that she had her own opinions on a subject, they would be reluctant to give their own. Some wouldn't even talk with her.

Kittrick put his folded hands on the desk on top of the perfectly placed sheet of paper. He stretched them back and forth, cracking his knuckles. "He did have some trouble here, I can attest to that," he said with a nod. More cracking.

Luis took a breath, as if he were about to jump off a high dive. "Vicente seemed frightened when we saw him in Bermuda."

"I imagine he was. He was sick."

"It was more than that. He didn't want to go to the hospital; he was scared." Luis kept his eyes on Kittrick's face. "Why do you think?"

Kittrick straightened the three books. "Hospitals are scary places."

Elia changed the subject. "Vicente could be outspoken, we know. Is that why you didn't choose him to be chief resident?" She asked it so innocently.

He nodded and permitted himself a satisfied smile. "He was that, for sure. Couldn't have someone like that as chief." He must have seen the disgusted looks on Luis and Elia's faces. "The chief is an ambassador."

"I thought the chief was your best resident," Elia said, her patience evaporating.

"He argued. About the resident program. If he thought the residents weren't getting the training and guidance he thought they should, he'd bring it up at meetings. He argued—or should I say—questioned treatment plans. Now I ask you, does that sound like someone who should be chief? Is that a good doctor?"

"That's an excellent doctor," Luis said. "And sounds like an excellent chief. Since we know he was outspoken, and we know he was worried about side effects of Cyptolis, did he talk to you about it?" He leaned forward in his chair, looking anxious, as if the answer would solve the riddle.

Calisthenics with the books. Kittrick sighed. He gave a great imitation of a harried mother after twenty questions from a four-year-old. Then his demeanor changed. He sat up taller in his chair, reached for his pencils and stopped midair. He refolded his hands and cracked knuckles.

"He did argue. He wanted to stop the Cyptolis. I wouldn't let him."

"But the liver involvement." Luis raised his voice. Elia reached over and touched his leg.

"It relieves spasticity. It's the best drug on the market."

Luis sat back in his chair and breathed deeply. "Pavnor should have black boxed it."

"Luis. The bleeding. Don't forget the bleeding," Elia said.

"Did you notice hepatic bleeding in your patients?" Luis asked.

"Some. Nothing out of the ordinary."

"But it was out of the ordinary. Hemorrorhaging." Luis took a deep breath and didn't wait for a reply. "Look Dr. Kittrick, we don't want to get you into trouble. We just want to find out why Vicente was murdered. And to do that, we think we have to find out more about what was going on in his life."

Kittrick started to interrupt. Luis held up his hands to stop him.

"What was important to him. And that was Cyptolis. But why was it? We think we're getting close, but we aren't there yet. Please help us."

"Why is it so important to you?" Now it was Kittrick who held up the stop sign. "Don't get me wrong. We all want to know who killed Vicente." He carefully rearranged the perfectly aligned books. "But what's your fascination with Cyptolis?

"What don't you get? It's because of that drug that Vicente died. What we don't know is what is so damn important that people had to die. Because we don't doubt for a minute that Aaron Scharff died for the same reason." Luis pushed back in his chair and stood. "Let's go, Elia, we'll find our answers somewhere else."

As a parting shot, Elia nudged the pile of books out of alignment.

At the door Luis turned to Kittrick and seemed about to say something. Elia grabbed his hand. They left without another word.

Kittrick pulled a Chap Stick out of a drawer, smeared some on his dry lips, stood it on its end in the center of a paper. He studied it, moved it a smidgen, studied it. Then he whacked it across the room.

He quickly retrieved it, wiped it off, and returned it to the center of the paper. Moved it a smidgen, studied it, moved it.

Elia spoke first once they were outside. "What do you make of him?"

"I think he's OCD who can't stand a glitch anywhere. I think he didn't want any waves in his neat little ship, so he ignored Vicente's concerns. As he said, Vicente spoke up about a lot of things. And he didn't give any credence to any of it. This was just one more rant from his least favorite resident. He ignored it."

"So he's not a bad guy."

"Oh, he's a bad guy, just not our bad guy."

Chapter 95

"Who do we see first?" Elia asked, as they drove back to Kiawah.

"Why not meet them together?"

"When and where?"

"Today. Want to call them?"

She didn't answer, just scrolled through her numbers. "Frank called us first; I'll start with him." She made the call and Hanssen set a tentative time and place until she could talk to Riser.

"He suggested Bohicket Marina. He said to keep right at the roundabout and head toward Seabrook. The marina'll be on our right." She looked at Luis. It's daylight and there'll be people around, so I guess we can go through with this."

"Let's see what's going on."

She tapped in Riser's number. She got his Voice Mail and left the message as to where and when they'd meet. She added that Frank Hanssen would be at the meeting as well.

Bonnie Riser listened to the message, then passed it on to her husband.

As they neared the marina, Elia said, "I'm telling you right now, I'm not getting on a boat with those two."

Riser looked up the number for management at Bohicket Marina and placed a call. Then he talked with Hanssen. "I booked one of those second floor spaces the marina rents out so we can talk privately. If you don't see us when you get there, I got Suite 202 above the boat rentals."

He snapped his phone shut than looked startled. "I didn't see you. What are you doing here?"

"I live here." Bonnie had her handbag over her shoulder. "I'm going out."

"Where?"

"Out." She left the house without another word.

Chapter 96

Bonnie Riser arrived at Bohicket Marina twenty minutes later. Lorraine Fegan was right behind her. They parked their cars at the far end of the parking lot and walked together to the patio area in front of shops that faced the water and the myriad of neatly docked boats. Fegan had a large shopping bag.

"What's in the bag? What are we going to do?"

"I know exactly what we're going to do." Before she said another word, she stopped and looked closely at Bonnie, then at the shopping bag. "Go back to the car and watch for them to arrive." She held up her cell phone. "Call me when you see any one of them." She started to walk away, then turned back. "And don't let them see you." Fegan walked in the direction of Suite 202.

When Elia and Luis arrived, Riser and Hanssen were sitting on a concrete bench facing the water engaged in deep conversation. They both stood. Riser pointed to a seat set at a ninety-degree angle to the bench he and Hanssen occupied. There was an awkward silence as they sat. Finally Riser broke it. "We have to talk."

Luis nodded. Since they hadn't called this meeting, he and Elia had decided to let Hanssen and Riser run it—for awhile.

"First of all, you have to know I didn't know anything about this." Riser paused. "Until lately." He looked at Hanssen, then looked around the marina. "Look, we have a lot to talk about, but not here."

Elia looked at the boats and felt her heart skip a beat. Riser followed her gaze. He pointed behind him. "I rented office space so we can talk in private."

"We can talk out here," Luis said.

"Please." Hanssen spoke for the first time. "This is long and involved. I had no idea things would get this bad. It started with your friend."

Luis started to object.

Hanssen held up his hands. "No. Pereda didn't do anything wrong; he was trying to help." He shook his head. "It got him killed."

"You know who killed him?" Elia asked, anxiously leaning forward.

"I know why. I'm not sure who." Hanssen said.

"I think I do," came from Riser.

Luis and Elia stared at Riser. "Are you going to tell us?" Luis said.

Riser stood. He pointed to the second floor of a wall of windows behind him. "Please. Let's get out of here."

Luis looked at the two men. Both looked guileless, lost, sad. He shifted his gaze to Elia. She gave him an imperceptible nod.

They followed Hanssen and Riser to the side of the building and started up the stairs that hugged the outside of the building.

"I'll be there in a minute," Elia said. She motioned toward the ladies room. Luis glanced at her then followed the others upstairs.

Lorraine Fegan joined Bonnie Riser in the parking lot. "I saw them go upstairs." She looked at her watch. "Go on; I'll meet you at your house."

"You never told me what we're going to do."

Fegan looked at her for a moment without answering, her lips pressed together in disgust as if she were sucking on a lemon. "Do you really want to know? Go home."

"Lorraine, maybe we should slow down for awhile."

"Later. Go home."

Bonnie shrugged, a twenty-first century Pontius Pilate hand washing, and got into her car.

Fegan watched her drive away, then pulled out a small black box. She tapped the button on the detonator as calmly as if she were tapping in a number on her cell phone.

Elia was about to climb the stairs when the door to 202 blew out and debris flew over the patio. She looked confused, then ran upstairs, screaming. "Luis! No!" Fire slammed out of the room. She didn't hear the sirens already sounding, the running feet, the screams.

She pushed herself to the door. "Luis!" she screamed.

Someone grabbed her from behind and pulled her away from the heat. She struggled to break free. "Leave me alone." She was sobbing, and swallowed gulps of hot air. "My husband's in there." She pushed away and leaned against the wall sobbing. "Luis," she said softly.

More running feet. Someone grabbed her again and pulled her away from the searing wall. Arms wrapped around her.

"No!" She fought the hold and thrashed to escape her captor. She turned to face the person who denied her her grief. Before she could scream, her head lolled back and all went black. She was caught before she hit the floor.

Fegan stood among the thrill seekers watching the drama play out in quiet Bohicket Marina. When she saw Elia being half carried out, half walked out, she swore. The people watching the scene looked at her and, almost as though it were planned, frowned in unison. She was even more profane when she saw who was walking with Elia.

Chapter 97

"Madison, get me Lorraine Fegan," Millen told his secretary on the way to his office. "I want to see her now." He emphasized now.

His secretary entered his office two minutes later with a stack of messages and one of her own. "Lorraine's out of town for a day or two." She set the messages on his desk in a neat pile. "I asked." She smiled at him. "I knew what you were going to say."

"Well?" He wasn't in any mood to play games.

"Her secretary made reservations for Charleston. She said she'll have Lorraine stop by when she returns."

He pushed back from his desk and turned to look out his window. The parking lot below wasn't particularly soothing, but the tree-filled field beyond could normally relax him. Not today. "Get me to Charleston ASAP." He ignored his messages and brushed past Madison on the way out. "I'm on my way to the airport. Have the company plane waiting for me."

She leaned against Luis as he lowered her onto a bench; the smell, heat, and chaotic activity adding to her anxiety. "I thought you were in there," she said.

"I thought you were." His voice was raspy, his face drawn.

"How could you do that to me? I saw you!" She broke down; tears flowed. She wiped them away with the back of a hand. "I saw you go up the stairs when I went into the ladies room. Where were you?"

"I went back to the car to get Vicente's papers." He put his arms around his wife. "It's okay, it's okay." He took a breath and released it slowly.

They sat quietly amidst the madness unfolding in front of them. Elia broke the silence. "That wasn't to scare us; that was to kill us."

Luis only nodded.

"But Jake and and Frank?" She looked over at the blown out window, the fire still smoldering. "We were supposed to be in there; they were going to step out, and then bang? The bomb—or whatever that was—went off too early?" She chewed on a nail as she considered her words.

"Or maybe we had it all wrong. Hanssen and Riser had nothing to do with any of this?" Luis stared at the boats in the marina, a frown creasing his face. "But the dive. Your hose cut. If we eliminate Scharff, Hanssen, and Riser, we're left with Bonnie Riser."

"But, Luis, her husband. She killed her husband."

"She was in Bermuda, here when Scharff's car was run off the road, here when you ran on the beach."

"It was Jake I saw on the road that morning on the beach."

"I can't figure that out. And Millen? I don't get it," Luis said.

"Our trip through New England. He knew about it."

"Who did he tell?"

She frowned. "Lorraine Fegan?"

Luis drew himself back and looked at Elia. "How do you know he told her?"

"I don't. But he could have. Look over there at that mess. Explosives. Fegan majored in chemistry."

"Slow down, *chica*. We've spent the last two weeks suspecting three men who are now dead.He stood and took her by the hand. "You able to walk to the car?"

"I'm fine." She held tightly to his hand.

"We've been so wrong about this. Let's go home."

She nodded her assent. "Home."

○

"Jake? You killed Jake? And Frank?" Bonnie's shock showed through in her breathless question. Her eyes were glass, her face twisted in anguish. "Jake?"

"Oh knock it off. You didn't care about Jake when you were screwing Frank. Or anyone else."

"What do you mean?"

"Are you serious? You're a tramp. You've screwed more guys than a New York street walker."

A slow cynical smile spread across Bonnie's face. "Jealous. You are jealous. I had the guys in college—and even now—and you had your job. And Frank." She smirked. Not biblically, of course.

She continued, "It was Frank who helped us make a pile of money with his astute investing. Sure, you gave him the drug information so he could manipulate the market in our favor, but you stupid woman. You killed our golden goose."

Chapter 98

B efore they reached the hotel, Elia's cell phone rang. She fished it out of her pocket and looked at the display. "Raf? Is everything okay? Where are you?"

"Everything and everyone is fine, Elia. I'm in Pittsburgh. I've been meeting with my spiritual director and talked with the bishop."

"And?"

"And I'm on leave for two months."

"Until you decide?"

"Something like that." He waited a beat. "I just need time to think and pray."

"Will you return to Colombia?" Now it was her turn to take a beat. "I mean if you decide to continue in the priesthood."

"I made my vows. I'll always be a priest, but, well, Sis, let's talk about this later. What about you? Are you all right? You sound kind of, I don't know, down. Are you okay?"

"I'm fine. A lot has happened. Long story."

"Where are you? With cell phones, I never know where I'm calling."

"Kiawah." She looked over at Luis, who was turning down the road to The Sanctuary. "Since we left Bermuda, our troubles have continued." She proceeded with the litany of their adventures and ended with the explosion at Bohicket Marina.

"Today? Put Luis on."

She handed Luis her phone. Luis had a short conversation. He snapped the phone shut and handed it back to Elia. "Raf's coming. I'm booking a room for him."

◻

"Raf gets in about ten." Luis looked at his watch. He sat beside Elia, his arm around her, her head resting on his chest.

She stretched and yawned. "Okay. Give me a minute."

"Honey, you're tired. Stay here. I'll pick him up and bring him here after he checks into his room."

"You don't mind?"

He kissed her on the nose and hugged her tightly. "I'd do anything for you. Even make an airport run for your brother."

"Tell you what. Call me when you get close, and I'll meet you in the lobby." She reached for her phone that was plugged into the charger. "I'll be ready; and so will my phone."

He stood and looked around for his keys, spied them, and stashed them in a pocket. He pulled Elia to her feet and wrapped his arms around her. "Quite a day." He buried his face in her hair.

She looked up and met his eyes. "I love you, Luis." She disentangled herself. "Go on, *guapo*, my handsome husband. I'll meet you in the lobby." She gave him a quick kiss and shooed him out the door.

When he left she filled the tub and lowered herself into the hot water. She turned on the jets and let herself drift off as the jets massaged her tense body.

What happened today? She asked herself. Were Frank and Jake setting up an ambush for us when we stepped in the room? Did they mess up and set off the explosion too early?

But what excuse would they have used to leave us in that room while they conveniently left? She shook her head. I don't get it. What is so important that people are being murdered?

She dressed and put on a touch of lipstick. As she swiveled the tube to close it, she stopped midway. "But why?" She set the lipstick on the bathroom counter and looked in the mirror and talked to her reflection. "Motive. What's the motive?"

She was startled by the ring of her cell phone. She checked caller ID. "You got the package?"

"Yep. Raf is all wrapped up nice and neat."

"Where are you?"

"Just getting off 526. We'll be there in thirty minutes."

"Good. I'll order some sandwiches and meet you in the lobby in thirty. I have a theory."

"Oh?"

"I think Jake and Frank botched the job. Thirty minutes. We'll talk about it then."

She put her cell phone in her pocket and left the suite. But her theory would soon be shot to hell.

Chapter 99

Harry Millen sat at the bar and commiserated with Phil the barman. He had flown out of White Plains on the company's private jet and arrived late afternoon. The trip south afforded him several hours of undisturbed thinking. He still didn't know what he was going to do, but he knew he had to do something. He promised Jeannie. They owed Pavnor.

"Trust, Phil. We should be able to trust that what we put in our bodies is safe." He rambled on. "And effective."

Phil wiped the hardwood of the counter with a clean cloth. He had been on the receiving end of many one-way conversations, so he just nodded and said nothing.

"We think every pill we swallow has been reviewed and approved by the FDA. False sense of security, that's what we get for our stupidity. For our laziness." He took a long pull on his Scotch, set the glass on the bar and swiveled his finger over it and pointed to the melting ice at the bottom. He pointed to Phil, then to his empty glass.

Phil set another drink, Millen's third, in front of him and took the empty glass away. The drinks on the plane had fortified him even more for what lay ahead. He wasn't sure what that was yet.

"Do you know that unapproved drugs can be sold here? In the good ol' U.S.A?" Another pull on his drink. "Oh, sure, the FDA says that's only two percent of all prescriptions filled by pharmacies." He glared at the barman. He raised his voice. "That's close to 72 million unapproved meds a year!"

He took a deep breath. Then another. He took hold of Phil's arm. The barman skillfully broke the hold. "Do you think I have a beef with the FDA? Well, I don't." He stared down at his drink and now spoke in a soft voice. "No I don't. My beef lies elsewhere." He looked at his watch. "What time does *Mad Money* come on down here? I want to make a call. Another one."

Chapter 100

Elia took the elevator to the first floor and stopped at the Jasmine Porch to order sandwiches and hot chocolate to be ready in a half hour. Then she walked past the spiral staircase toward the lobby.

There were several seating arrangements throughout the generous room. Even with the eighteenth century furniture, the room seemed cozy. A fire crackled in the huge stone fireplace, and even though it was a warm evening, it didn't throw off enough heat to warm such a large room.

At the opposite end of the room from the fireplace, and at the entrance to the bar, a pianist played soft music. Elia sat near the fireplace and could see that a few people sat at the bar, and several tables were occupied as well. She didn't even look at them; she was so engrossed in her thoughts. But she was noticed.

Her attention was drawn to the fireplace, the fire so tame compared to the fire and explosion she witnessed that afternoon.

The music across the room was melancholy, or maybe it was her mood.

She walked to the wall of windows and stood next to the door and peered through the glass. Lights shone on the carefully manicured lawn. She pushed on the heavy door and stepped out onto the patio that faced the lawn and the ocean beyond. She ambled across the lawn to the boardwalk.

Her phone vibrated. "Luis?"

"It's Raf. I hear you have some food for us. I'm famished."

"Why am I not surprised? It'll be ready when you get here. I'll meet you in the lobby."

"I hear the ocean."

I'm outside walking on the boardwalk. It's lovely here, Raf. I'm so glad you're coming."

"Hold on; Luis wants the phone.

"Where are you?"

"I'm right here at The Sanctuary. On the boardwalk."

"Go back inside. Get off the beach. Please." It wasn't a request.

"I'm not on the beach." She looked back toward the hotel. "And I'm not alone; there are two women out here walking this way."

"Please." Now he pleaded.

"I'm on my way. See you in the lobby in about half hour?" She shook her head. *Peruanos*, she thought. Just like Mom. I should be used to them.

"Half an hour."

They clicked off and Elia walked toward the lights of the hotel. Because the lights shone in her eyes, it was difficult to see the women who were almost upon her.

"Hello, Elia."

Luis slammed on the brakes. Raf shot toward the windshield, his seatbelt holding him back. The car behind him swerved and squealed.

"*Mierda!*" He let up on the brake and sped toward Kiawah. "Call her back," he ordered his brother-in-law.

Raf stared at Luis.

"See if she's okay."

Raf punched in the number. "She was fine a minute ago. What's the problem?"

Luis raced through a yellow light at Maybank Highway, and slowed behind a dawdling pick-up truck. He waited for his chance, swung into the left lane, and bolted forward around the truck.

"What? Is it ringing?" Luis asked.

Raf stared at the phone with a puzzled look on his face. "For a minute, then it stopped, like she answered then disconnected. I'll try again." He hit the redial button and listened. He shook his head. "Went to her Voice Mail." He looked at Luis who was trying his best to barrel down the road behind law-abiding drivers. "What's the matter?"

"Two women."

Lorraine Fegan reached out and snatched the cell phone from Elia's hand. When it rang, she flipped it open, slammed it shut, and threw it into the dunes.

Harry Millen stood at a window in the bar watching.

Chapter 101

Elia watched her phone fly through the air; her lifeline snapped in two.

Fegan's expression was as evil as a Halloween mask. Bonnie looked from Elia to Fegan; Fegan took the lead.

"Move." She motioned toward the beach with her head.

Elia looked back at the hotel and thought about running. Fegan blocked her way.

"Nope. Not going to work." She had her hand in her pocket.

"What's going on?" Elia tried to keep her tone calm. She jerked her head toward the dunes when she heard her cell phone ring.

Fegan looked in the direction of the ringing phone. "That won't help you." She poked Elia in the side with her pocketed hand.

Elia hadn't seen a weapon, but after the explosion, she couldn't be sure of anything. "Luis knows. He's on his way."

"Good."

They walked down the stairs onto the hard sand and had gone no more than thirty steps when Elia dropped to the ground.

Luis squealed to a stop at the security gate, raced down Kiawah Island parkway to The Sanctuary, jumped out of the car and yelled to the valet as he ran through the hotel door, "Call the police. Send them to the beach."

"Get the hell up and walk."

"No." Elia extended her neck to see the face of the woman looming over her like a vulture. "You're going to kill me."

Fegan said nothing.

"I want to get ready."

"Ready?" It was a sneer.

"Right. You know. Get ready to die. Pray. Isn't that what you learned at Seton Hill?" She didn't wait for an answer. "Isn't that what you learned in a Catholic school? To pray? To ask for forgiveness? To ask Jesus to carry you home?" She tried to keep talking; she knew Luis was on his way. And she hoped she sounded unafraid. In reality, she knew she was rambling. Anything but dying. *Sorry, Jesus, but I really don't want to go home yet.*

"Shut the hell up!" She kicked Elia in the leg. "Move."

"No. Why'd you kill Vicente? Why Aaron?" She looked at Bonnie. "Why Jake and Frank?"

Bonnie turned to Lorraine. She threw her shoulders back and stared at Lorraine. "Jake? Frank?" Her voice rose on the scale. "Frank was part of this. Jake's my husband! Why?"

"Shut up."

"For money." She looked at Elia. "For money."

"Shut up."

"God, what did we do?"

Elis was getting a stiff neck looking up from the sand watching the scene like a tennis match. The ball was in Lorraine's court, if that was a gun in her pocket.

"If you're going to kill her, let her know why." Bonnie sounded weary.

Fegan glared at Bonnie. "Me? If I'm going to kill her? Puhleeze, how many times did you try? Right here."

Elia's mouth fell open. "I thought it was Jake."

"Jake wouldn't have the guts," Lorraine said as she jerked Elia to her feet.

Elia faced the women and tried to look relaxed. An Academy Award performance. Her heart was racing, as fast as she hoped Luis was driving.

"Walk." Lorraine pulled her gun from her pocket.

Bonnie started talking. "It was Lorraine. She wanted to save money for the company, so she sent Cyptolis to China for production. But the conditions there are shitty. It got contaminated by the heparin that is produced there." She spit out the words.

"And heparin is an anticoagulant. So, bleeding," Elia said.

"You wanted to save Pavnor money, so you had the China thing going. But what is so important about Pavnor that you couldn't just take the drug off the market? So the company loses some money. It happens. Lots of problems in drug companies. Look at Pfizer. It's still here." She sounded incredulous.

Lorraine shook her head as if Elia were in left field. "Did you happen to check their stock report?" Lorraine said, as if she were talking to a slacking high school student.

"Whose stock report? Pfizer's? Pavnor's?" Elia asked.

"Walk." She pushed Elia in front of her.

"That's where Frank came in," Bonnie said. "Lorraine kept the problems quiet."

"Why? You don't own Pavnor. It's not your baby. Why care so much?"

"Investors. Frank talked up the new drug, had clients clamoring to get on board."

"And you were investors." Again Elia stopped walking. "Vicente. Who killed him?" She looked from Bonnie to Lorraine.

"Doesn't matter. I was able to get my hands on something that would help him along. He was sick anyway." Lorraine was flippant.

"But why? His report from the meeting didn't even mention China."

Lorraine shook her head in dismissal. "China is just one piece."

"Harry Millen?" Elia looked from one to the other.

"Millen?" Lorraine forced a laugh. "I don't know when he discovered problems."

"He's an investor." Elia could have called him a pedophile and it wouldn't have sounded nastier.

"Hardly." She frowned. "I don't know where his head is."

"Lorraine, his wife is dying," Bonnie said.

Lorraine shook her head and again frowned. "Something is strange. He should want this kept quiet, but he's been asking people a lot of questions." Her frown deepened. She waved a hand as if shooing a fly. "I'll think about it later."

Elia had enough of their musings. "So it's about the same drug from years ago having the same side effects. You put it back on the market with another name. You knew patients would have liver involvement. People died. Why?"

"Cyptolis is a good drug for spasticity."

"Lorraine," Elia said, her voice rising, "Didn't you hear me? People died! And a lot of them are our soldiers."

Elia turned her attention to Bonnie. "Jake was a doctor. How could he be involved?"

"He wasn't. He didn't know anything until just lately."

"But Bermuda. The boat. My hose was slashed; I know it was. And the motorcycle chasing us, and the night we were in the pool." She looked from Bonnie and Lorraine. "And at the spa."

Lorraine pointed at Bonnie.

"I just wanted to scare you with the hose and the spa. That was Frank at the pool."

"And the beach?"

They were walking. Bonnie was silent.

"You were going to kill me?"

"I really don't know."

"And the motorcycle?"

Bonnie looked at Lorraine.

"You? In Bermuda? In Connecticut, too? Elia frowned as if disbelieving. Then her eyes opened wide. Cape Cod?"

"What does it matter? Move!" Lorraine poked her with the gun.

"I'm not moving." Elia tried to dig her feet into the hard sand. "What about Aaron and Angel?"

"I liked them," Bonnie said. "But Aaron asked a lot of questions. Angel didn't know much; she just knew Vicente had questions. She didn't have to die. That part was an accident."

"Well good news, Bonnie. She's recovering. But why kill Jake and Frank?"

Bonnie again looked at Lorraine.

"Frank sent me an e-mail saying he was getting out, and he was going to talk with Jake. And both of them were going to talk to you," she waved the gun at Elia, "and your husband."

"Lorraine, it's over. Put the gun away; let's go back." Bonnie put her hand out. "Give it to me," she demanded.

"Hell, no!" Her face contorted into an insane–looking mask. "It's done when this one is gone."

"No. There are others," Bonnie yelled. Lorraine, her husband! It's over."

"It's over after him."

"No! Now! It's over now!

"You can rot in the ocean with this one, but I'm finishing this."

She raised her gun and pointed it at Elia, then at Bonnie, then back at Elia. She waved the gun from one to the other, back and forth, back and forth. She pulled the trigger.

Millen pushed open the door and walked quickly toward the women. He descended the steps and looked down the beach. Clouds blocked the moon, but he heard the shot and the scream. He ran toward the sound, his gun in his hand.

The gunshot and scream competed with the sounds of the ocean. Both Elia and Bonnie dropped to the ground. Bonnie clutched her belly.

Fegan fixed on Elia. Elia rolled and swiped her legs at Fegan's feet, intent on knocking her down. Fegan dodged and again took aim.

Elia curled into a fetal position, holding her head with her arms. She heard the shot and waited for the impact.

She peeked out from under her arms and saw a man racing toward them. She glanced at her body, confused, then looked at Lorraine. She was on the ground. Still, very still.

She crawled to Bonnie and pressed her hand on her belly trying to stop spurting blood. She whispered her name.

Bonnie looked at her, her breathing coming fast. "I'm sorry."

"Help is coming." Blood pulsed through her fingers. She put her lips to Bonnie's ear and whispered her mother's long ago message: "You're not alone; you're never alone." Then she prayed the Lord's Prayer.

Harry Millen reached them with his gun drawn. He stood over Fegan's body.

"No!" came as a huge roar from a man flying though the air. Millen was hurtled to the ground, tackled by a man in black—tackled by a priest.

Luis rushed to Elia. He put his hands on her cheeks and stared into her eyes and scanned her body; he saw the blood on her hands and clothes. "Where are you hurt?"

"It's not mine." She looked over at Bonnie.

Luis pivoted and leaned over Bonnie. He ripped off his shirt and tried to stem the bleeding.

"Raf, she needs you," Elia said.

Raf handed Millen's gun to Elia. "Watch him."

She pointed the gun to the ground. "You have it wrong." She motioned to Bonnie. "Raf, her name's Bonnie.

He nodded and knelt in the sand beside his brother-in-law; Luis's eyes said it all.

"I'm a priest," he said gently. With one hand he stroked her face, with the other he blessed her and gave her absolution.

She looked up into his eyes and moved her lips. "Thank you, Father." She died lying on the wet sand of the most beautiful beach in the world.

Chapter 102

Elia sipped hot tea at a table in The Sanctuary bar. Luis and Raf were with her. The police were still milling around, doing what crime fighters do. She had told her story to the police, starting from the beginning in Bermuda.

When she got to the final pages, to the final moments of Bonnie and Lorraine's lives, the fog over the past weeks lifted.

"What's going to happen to Harry Millen?" Elia asked the investigator taking her statement. Millen was across the room, talking with another cop. "We thought he was the one behind all the deaths, but he saved my life."

"Can we talk to him?" Luis asked.

"We have his statement, go on."

"Sis, I'll be outside. I already told him I was sorry for tackling him." He kissed Elia on the cheek and patted Luis on the shoulder. "I'll see you later."

Luis and Elia approached Millen. He had his head in his hands and looked nothing like the high-powered executive from Pavnor Pharmaceuticals. When they sat across the table from him, he raised his head. His eyes were red-rimmed, his skin gray.

"Why are you here, Harry? Why come back to Kiawah?" Luis asked gently.

"So many things didn't fit, but then they started falling into place." He looked from one to the other. He fell silent.

"But why are you here? Elia repeated Luis's question.

"I found out Lorraine was on her way here; I knew you were here. I knew about all the close calls you had." He shrugged.

"Harry, you knew about Cyptolis. You knew it had been on the market before."

"The problems started on my watch, so I had to fix them."

"You saved my wife's life, and for that I'll be eternally grateful." Luis paused. "I know your wife is ill. I'm sorry."

Millen nodded. "Thanks." He pushed back from the table. "It's any time now." He took a deep breath and let it out in a puff of air.

"Are you going home now?" Elia asked. She looked at her watch. "I mean soon. No flights tonight. Or do the police still have questions?"

"I think they're finished with me for the time being. I could go tonight; I flew in on a company plane." He shook his head. "Long day. I'll leave tomorrow."

He left them sitting at the table.

Elia had her chin in her hands and pondered Millen's words.

Raf walked down the steps onto the sand. He turned his back on the bright lights the police had set up to gather evidence. They were still working the site, working against the clock, against the tide, trying to finish up before the ocean cleansed the area.

Environmentalists had hurried to the beach worried about the loggerhead turtle population confused by the lights. If it had been later in the season, it would have been disastrous for newly-hatched turtles who head to the ocean following the light of the moon over the water, but when they detect light from elsewhere, they move toward it; toward the opposite direction. But this early, they hadn't hatched yet.

During the summer season, residents facing the ocean are asked to close curtains or turn off ocean-facing lights, so as not to confuse and entice the hatchlings into running into the dunes and into the clutches of predators like raccoons, instead of running into the ocean. Loggerheads can live to be a hundred, but first the babies have to get to the water. Already so many loggerheads have died in the Gulf of Mexico due to the oil spill.

No way do environmentalists want to lose even one of their babies.

Raf walked slowly. He kept his eyes on the water, seemingly mesmerized by the undulating waves. He walked for at least thirty minutes. When he turned to go back, he could no longer see the lights from the investigators.

He saw no one else on the beach. Clouds drifted over the moon and the beach turned black—black and empty. But he didn't feel alone.

He felt his mother and father's presence. He could hear his father saying he was proud of him. But more, he felt his heavenly Father beside him. He felt a warmth enfold him, a warmth he was familiar with.

He dropped to his knees and then, just as he had done on his ordination day, he prostrated himself before God. He rested his head on his arms. He thought of sitting with Bonnie Riser minutes before her death giving her absolution and the look of gratitude in her eyes—not just gratitude—but peace. He had helped her die with a peaceful heart.

He knew with all his being in those last minutes of that woman's life that he was in the right place, doing what he should be doing.

He thought of Lorraine Fegan, whom he had blessed in death and prayed that God would forgive her.

Words from the *Letter to the Hebrews* entered his thoughts. "You are a priest forever, according to the order of Melchizedek."

With his head on his arms, and stretched out on his stomach on the beach, he let the tears flow.

Chapter 103

Elia had a hard time sleeping and was out of bed early. Luis rolled over and stretched out his arm. He rose on an elbow to look at Elia's side of the bed when he didn't feel her beside him. He found her in the sitting room.

She was pacing around the room, a frown wrinkling her forehead. "Luis, if I were dying of cancer, and the time was—well—'any time now,' would you leave me and fly away to make sure an acquaintance wouldn't be hurt by someone?"

He sat down on the sofa and watched her pace. "What are you thinking?"

"It's Millen. Why would he do that?" She stopped in front of him. "I mean, if he suspected Lorraine, why didn't he do something about it."

"I'd say he did."

"I mean earlier. I don't mean now." She raised her hands in question. "Why wouldn't he just call the police?"

"Maybe the same reason we didn't. Do you think they'd listen to him?"

"What do you mean?" Her voice went up a pitch. "Two men had just died in an explosion. He had his suspicions. Don't you think if he had told the police, they would have looked into it?"

Luis nodded slowly.

"Why did he come here? His wife is dying. And why didn't he go home last night? He has a private plane, for crying out loud!"

Luis stood and put his arms around her. *"Calmete."*

She took some deep breaths, forcing herself to listen to her husband, forcing herself to calm down. She looked up into his dark eyes. "He didn't come here to protect us. He came here to kill Lorraine."

Chapter 104

Harry Millen ate breakfast at the Jasmine Porch and considered what to do. He and Jeannie had planned this so well, but they hadn't planned for so many innocent people to be hurt, to be killed.

They just wanted Pavnor Pharmaceuticals to perish. It was Pavnor's fault that Jeannie was perishing.

Jeannie had lived with cancer for seven years. The first six were okay years, if living with cancer can be called okay. Between chemo and radiation treatments, they lived a normal enough life. Jeannie played tennis twice a week, they golfed together, and they traveled. But a year ago, when cancer popped up again, Pavnor had a new drug in the final stages of trials. It looked good, sounded good, hell, it sounded like a miracle drug. Jeannie signed up for the trials, and she got in. But a strange thing happened. Instead of slowing the cancer—they knew the cancer would never go away—she got worse. Her life was hell; his life was hell. Ulcers all over her body, excruciating joint pains, a hacking cough that left her exhausted, nausea and vomiting, diarrhea.

He checked; other patients in the trial experienced the same side effects, which are really no surprise for any type of chemotherapy. But their cancers, like Jeannie's, grew. Grew fast. Grew wildly.

Everybody had signed waivers exonerating the drug company and oncologists from any wrongdoing. These patients just wanted a chance at living. Instead they died too soon.

Jeannie became obsessed with the failure of the drug and the fact that it was manufactured by Pavnor. She wanted to destroy Pavnor. Harry felt so guilty that his company had manufactured the drug that little by little, he decided Jeannie was right.

He had been in the dark about the problems with Cyptolis, and only found out after Vicente's death when he started researching the drug. If Vicente hadn't died, the problems with Cyptolis would have been exposed. Pavnor would have fallen. Jeannie would have died in peace. And he could have stayed in the background. But Lorraine tried to keep the lid on. She almost ruined everything. She almost ruined Jeannie's peace.

Jeannie was adamant. Pavnor had destroyed her chance of living. Granted, it had been a lucrative job for her husband, but now it had to die; she would kill it. Like it was killing her.

Jeannie surprised Millen with her zeal, her determination. When he thought of his wife's fervor, he borrowed an adage to his purpose: "Behind every diabolical plan there's a woman." His job was to carry out her plan.

Millen finished his breakfast, called for a car to the airport, checked out of the hotel, and rode away from The Sanctuary with just two more items on his list.

He placed a call to Jack Alexander at *The New York Times*, as he sat on the plane waiting to take off.

"I'm ready, Jack." He told his story and left nothing out, except his wife's hand in the matter, and the ending. Jack would add that later on his own.

Luis called Raf's room. "We're going down to the Jasmine Porch for breakfast, can you join us?"

"You look good, brother," Elia said when Raf sat down at the table. "After that flying leap through the air and the landing in the sand, I thought you'd never get cleaned up."

He smiled sheepishly. "You don't know the half of it." He looked down at his black suit and gave a satisfied nod. "The hotel cleaned it for me."

Elia told Raf about the conclusion she had come to. "But as to why, I guess we'll have to ask Millen."

"If he'll tell us," Luis said. He looked at Raf. "You do look good, Raf. Rested, or something."

"I am. Rested, or something." He looked from one to the other. "I'm staying."

"Here?" Elia asked, her brow wrinkling in confusion.

He reached across the table and took her hand. He smiled. With his other hand he touched his Roman collar. "Here. I am a priest. Forever."

Elia's eyes filled with tears. "I knew it." She nodded. "I knew it. You just had to know it for yourself." She squeezed his hand. "Where will you go? Back to Colombia?"

"I'll see my bishop in Pittsburgh and go where I'm sent." He leaned back in his chair with a pleased smile on his face. "A good feeling."

"Do you want to tell us what…?" She let her question fade.

"Someday." He put his hands flat on the table and tapped it twice in finality.

Luis and Elia said goodbye to Raf at the Charleston airport and continued on to Augusta. Home.

Chapter 105

Harry Millen tiptoed into his wife's room. She opened her eyes and raised her eyebrows in question. He nodded.

"Why don't you take the afternoon off?" he said to the nurse. "I'll stay right here with Jeannie."

"I was just about to give her some morphine."

"I'll do it." He took the bottle and stood at the window until he saw her car travel down the driveway.

He emptied the morphine into his hand, went to his closet and pulled out his own stash. He smashed the pills and mixed a large dose with apple juice, and an even larger dose with Scotch.

He sat on the edge of Jeannie's bed and helped her drink her juice. He gulped down his drink. He told her about the beach scene.

She smiled.

He went to the bathroom and filled a basin of warm water and came back to his wife's bedside. He gently washed her face, then removed her nightgown and helped her into a fresh one, a soft rose-colored cotton with long sleeves and ruffles at the neckline and wrists. He combed her hair and touched her lips with a pale lipstick.

"You're beautiful; know that Jeannie?"

She smiled and shook her head. Even that was an effort.

He returned to the bathroom, washed up, and put on clean sweats.

He lay down beside his wife and put his arms around her. "Pavnor will be finished tomorrow when the paper comes out." There were no more items on his list.

Again she smiled. Her eyes closed.

Harry let his mind wander. He thought of the "plan" and the people who were harmed by it. When he had discovered that Abecour and Cyptolis were the same drug with the same side effects, he and Jeannie waited for Pavnor's star to fall. But Fegan got involved, stopping Pereda from reporting his findings.

He frowned. What was your motivation, Lorraine? What were you after? What did you want? My job? What?

All he and Jeannie wanted was Pavnor to be ruined for producing the drug she took for her cancer. He had no idea that another drug was causing problems, not until Vicente came to him about Cyptolis and Abecour. He encouraged Vicente to write his paper. The meeting in Bermuda would have exposed the problem—exposed Pavnor.

He put his head in his hands. Am I responsible for Pereda's death? All this trouble? God, what did I do?

He kissed his wife. She seemed to be barely breathing. The interval between each breath grew longer. It wasn't only the violently growing brain tumor that affected her lung function, but the massive dose of morphine he had administered. For fleeting moments during the past weeks he had thought how easy it would be to cover her face with her pillow and help her along. Help her rest. End her suffering. Now it was time. She had suffered enough. He shook his head and smiled ruefully as he thought of the trite expression: her work here is finished. Our work here is finished. Well, it was finished.

As he lay beside Jeannie, he prayed he would be forgiven for his silence. And he prayed that Jeannie, too, would be forgiven for her zeal, her... He shook his head; he didn't want to have such thoughts of Jeannie, especially now at the end. But the thoughts lingered. So he prayed that she would be forgiven for the hate she had for anyone involved with Pavnor.

He was gentle with her in his arms. His eyes grew heavy, his own breathing depressed. "You did well, my love," he whispered. "We did well."

Acknowledgements

Dear readers, thanks for coming back.

So many people have encouraged me since I first began writing. Of course, family in the States and in Perú come first, but strangers who read my first book are the ones who pushed me to write this one. People I met at book signings and through e-mail kept after me. So to all of you out there, whom I no longer consider strangers, but friends, I say thank you.

To those who read sections of the book, or the whole enchilada, I say thank you. Gerry Munroe taught me the ways of native Cape Codders, my daughter Suzy took me to the Avenue in Greenwich, Connecticut, the coffee shop in Port Chester, New York, and rode the train with me to New York City. The rest of the kids, Ted, Maria, and Carlos, read drafts and gave me suggestions. My sisters Ann Heckel (who also appeared in my story) and Helen Collins, and my mother Margaret Polonus read drafts. To Don Rutledge, my good friend and realtor extraordinaire on Kiawah Island, thanks for lending me your nickname and Kiawah expertise.

To my friends who appear in this book, I hope you like yourselves. If not, hey, this is fiction.

Seton Hill in Greensburg, Pennsylvania, my alma mater and that of four of my six sisters, is important to me, as that is where I learned my craft, so naturally, it has a "cameo" in the book.

Colleen Ryan, my editor, friend, cohort, read this story after each draft. She made my book better with her astute criticism. And to all the people at Mason Dixon House: Gosh, I love you guys!

My husband, Edgardo, kept throwing ideas at me; in fact, this story was his idea. His experience treating Vietnam veterans during the late 1960s and early 1970s in New Orleans and Pittsburgh is the impetus for this book. As I wrote this story, I had our men and women in uniform in my thoughts and prayers. To them I say thank you, be safe, and God bless you.

And thank you, Jesus.

spm